CALISTA

LAURA RAHME

CALISTA

ISBN-13: 9798728861942

11 Boulevard Lelasseur, 44000 Nantes

Cover by Ross Robinson
www.rossrobinson.com.au

Original artwork
Hendrick de Fromantiou
A still life with flowers, c.1633

This is a work of fiction. The names, characters, locations and incidents portrayed in it are the work of the author's imagination, or have been used fictitiously. Any resemblance to actual persons living or dead, locations or events is entirely coincidental.

For all the forgotten children.

Chapter 1

Miss Vera Nightingale

SHE had never warmed to the Greek village girl. She found her peculiar in the manner she wore those coral beads round her neck, the way she barely spoke, and made few efforts to adjust to her new life in England.

Halfway down Alexandra Hall's grand staircase, Vera paused and raised her eyes to the towering oil portrait. The young woman in the painting had been an illiterate peasant once, yet here she was, in all her glory, decked out like nobility in a blue crinoline dress. She sat on a chair of dark velvet, beside a stained-glass window, the red glow of a lit candlestick in the background. Vera ran her gaze across the canvas in disbelief.

Aaron had once boasted about commissioning this portrait but Vera hadn't believed him. He'd acted upon just another one of his whims. Her deluded brother had called upon an artist to remake his wife's nature, despite all evidence it was pure foolishness.

Vera scrutinised the portrait, taking in what she called the affected grace of the peasant girl. She felt a familiar wave of contempt as she stared at the subject in the painting. Beneath the layers of silk and despite the netted braids on her raven head, there was not a trace of English blood in that woman. The sitter of the portrait was an imposter. Vera shuddered, feeling suddenly uneasy. She looked down the stairs, expecting to see a shadow lurking there.

When she had first met Calista, the Greek girl was only twenty-two, spoke not a word of English. What had planted the idea in Aaron's head? There had been many women in his life, including the middle-aged Russian countess who doted on him in his twenties, but Vera had waved off his philandering. She saw his rampant thirst for discovery as the passing fancy of a young man.

Surely at forty-five, which he was, upon returning from the Mediterranean, he knew better. He had not. She remembered their ultimate discussion at their parents' home.

"Brother, you will stop this nonsense before we all regret it, won't you, now?" The snow had begun to fall and icy crystals burst on her lips as she spoke.

He had turned to her, a maverick in a fur coat. The swarthy outline of his face seemed harsher after months in the islands.

"Vera, has it ever occurred to you that I set out on this journey to find a wife? And find a wife, I did."

"You'll shame us."

"Well, you'll have to learn to live with it because I shall marry that girl and that's my final word."

Upon delivering this unexpected rebuke, he had deserted her. She'd felt like a frozen statue in their family's snow-swept garden. She had watched as he hurried off to his carriage in large strides. She'd even wondered if he wore such a thick coat to better conceal his soul's secrets. She'd never felt so estranged from her beloved Aaron.

Vera recalled her wounded pride, and how days afterwards, she'd taken friends into her confidence over cakes and Darjeeling tea.

"My dear brother has expressed his wishes to marry a Greek peasant girl."

She'd sat in mortified silence as her two close friends exchanged glances and carefully absorbed the news.

"What shall you do, my dear?"

At those words, deadly thoughts had crossed Vera's mind. She'd sunk her butterscotch fingers deep into the tea.

"I suppose I shall have to make my peace. After all, I am only a woman," she had muttered beneath her breath. "If only our parents were still alive. My father could have put sense into Aaron's head."

Her friends had shaken their heads but Vera sensed that their sympathy had in it something that smelled like relief. They were eternally grateful to not belong to such an incongruous family.

"Fancy that, wandering off to the United States of the Ionian Islands. And whatever for?" had sighed her childhood friend.

Vera had pondered over this, losing herself in the never ending stirring of her tea.

"You should see her eyes," she had replied. "She's seen things."

Her friend then had the presence of mind to remember the Greek War of Independence. "Didn't Lord Byron set off to Greece and die there?" she'd asked, hoping to change the subject with some vague political statement.

Vera had not answered. Her thoughts had drifted.

"Do you think she endured much hardship during the war?" insisted her friend.

Vera had startled.

"The war? Well, I… perhaps. I don't know. But she's a queer one. The look in her eyes... I think she's half-mad. Yes, that's what I think."

"Well if you ask me, Vera dear, your brother is as strange as they get."

"Yes, of course. But this girl…"

On the staircase, Vera bit her lips, recalling this conversation. She had suspected it, hadn't she? Still staring at the portrait, it seemed to her that a hint of menace shone out of the sitter's eyes. They came alive. Vera quickly averted her gaze. Her trembling hand clutching at the balustrade, she stepped down to the entrance hall.

As Vera reached the landing, a coldness clung to her spine; a fear that the woman in the portrait had followed her. She rubbed the back of her neck where the hair had risen. Alexandra Hall's desolate silence tormented her. She fought her mounting dread by assembling pieces of the past.

Before his marriage, Aaron had built Alexandra Hall, god knows why— a Georgian masterpiece in the middle of the Berkshire countryside. After marrying Calista, he had changed.

Her brother had adopted the life of a recluse. Vera remembered how she'd confided to her friend:

"It's her, you know. She won't have anything to do with us. No pity for his family." No room for the sister who loved him more than anyone.

"Just dreadful," had replied her friend.

"She has him trapped, and nowadays, he barely leaves his cursed mansion."

As her memories flooded back, Vera lingered in the entrance hall, her own voice echoing in her mind. *His cursed mansion.*

Odd, how she had sensed it all along.

Her silk shawl slipped off her shoulder. She reached with her hand to wrap it back over her thin frame. She picked up the lamp by the window sill and walked with it towards the parlour. Her full skirts traced a giant black shadow on the wall.

The entire parlour was shrouded in darkness save for its far wall. There, within a marble fireplace, embers glowed.

Vera advanced through the room, holding up the lamp, feeling her way past the sofa, the Empire armchairs. As she passed the main table, her heart raced. Two dozen pairs of eyes looked down upon her from the walls; a host of faces from afar, immortalised in oil paintings set in gilded frames.

Portraits took up most of the height on each wall, rivalling with one another for space: here, a wealthy Dutch merchant and his pet monkey; there, a Polish hunter hiking in a thick forest with his dog; nearby, a fierce warrior in a golden armour rode a royal elephant from Siam; above, a spoilt Spanish princess sported a mean grin while cradling her puppy; and across, a lion was tamed by his Egyptian master…

Over the last fortnight, Vera had stared at those paintings for hours. She knew them all. Her brother's tastes sent a chill down her spine.

A distant noise echoed in the entrance hall. Somewhere in the house, a door had slammed shut. Vera calmed herself. It was likely one of the maids.

She reached the low-back chair near the chimney. She would rest here, by the fire, well away from the malevolent presence that had watched her for days. It could surface in every room if it wished. It liked to play games. But here, by the warmth of the flames, she felt safe. It did not like the fire. She leaned over, and threw a log into the hearth. A pleasant crackling sound filled the parlour which glowed a bright red.

Vera glanced apprehensively at the dozens of portraits. They were no longer just paintings. A hundred eyes held her gaze and watched her. This room was the heart of Aaron's questionable home, the heart of Alexandra Hall.

With a name as grand as Alexandra Hall, one could sum up her brother's delusions of grandeur. It was an understatement to say that Aaron Nightingale relished adventure and drama in his life. No sooner returned from an expedition with his amateur archaeologist friend based in Egypt, he had built Alexandra Hall two years before his marriage. Right here, on the land of their grandparents.

He had the old Berkshire cottage demolished and in its stead, he'd laid foundations for a Georgian mansion. If it had seen visitors, for Aaron preferred to dispense with visitors, this house would no doubt have been the talk of London.

It possessed all the graceful airs of a wealthy country estate. Its heavy entrance doors had come at a pricey sum, with each upper glass pane engraved with a majestic A, entwined with an N — Aaron's initials. In the years following her brother's marriage, the upper pane on the right door sported the new initials, C and N, in honour of his wife.

Gentle shade was a welcome balm in the summer when one strolled the veranda along the colonnades. As far as the eye could see, the lawns stretched for acres and were well-tended. At least for a while, thought Vera, cynically.

English pleasures abounded in this oasis of peace and one had only to venture past the rose garden with its mosaic fountain, and there, one would find a small creek shaded by willows.

This magnificent house made of large brick, boasted two storeys with high ceilings, an enormous entrance hall with a grand curved staircase, and three dozen rooms of which the parlour was the largest. Or was it? Vera recalled that there existed another room somewhere in the house. She had seen it in the construction plans, but it was years ago.

She entertained the idea that if Aaron had ever amassed a treasure then it would be kept in that room, wherever it was. But so far, she had found nothing. Instead, a terror had welcomed her.

Vera had only visited Alexandra Hall on three occasions upon its completion. There had been the awkward welcome when the peasant girl, Calista, had arrived in England. The wedding had followed a couple of months afterward, and it had been the only time when Aaron had suffered guests. Friends from as far as France had attended, together with past medical colleagues, scientists, and Aaron's questionable business partners. Even their younger brother, John, had stayed over.

John was an engineer. He actually did something for a living, unlike Aaron whose profession Vera had never defined. To think that all those years when he attended lectures in Paris had amounted to nothing.

The third occasion came a few years later. Vera had travelled to Berkshire upon receiving Calista's letter. That awful letter… It had not changed her mind about the Greek girl. Nothing pleased her about Calista.

And even then, in that month spent near Aaron, Vera had sensed there was something not quite right about this house. How could she explain it? It was a feeling that the entire structure existed as a shell for something other than a home.

For within its walls were thousands of curious objects. There were rooms filled with oddities from decades of travel. They showcased the gifts Aaron had been granted by friends, figures of import in fields as varied as archaeology, museum curation, and natural science.

Her brother had stocked these treasures, and now they were neglected, arranged only for display purposes, and on the face of it, Alexandra Hall dazzled with elegance while serving as a coffer for the spoils – however strange these were — of an intrepid life. But Vera was no fool.

Aaron once boasted of the fortunes he made as a private moneylender and his knack for investments. She'd heard him say that he would never strive to earn an income. And after he wed the peasant girl, Vera had imagined Aaron would cease to roam. He would sire children and fill this new home with their laughter.

Mrs. Cleary, the housekeeper would serve tea and cakes to rosy cheeks, as all of them sat by the colonnades, and Aaron would open Alexandra Hall to his family and friends. Later in the afternoon, Auntie Vera would read books to the children by the willow trees, her forgiving gaze falling upon her half-breed nephew, or maybe a niece who had the decency to resemble Aaron; both children dressed in starched white clothing.

Alas, the last time Vera had imagined this scene was during her last visit, while Calista lay ill in her bed. Vera had been reduced to tears, her thoughts overrun by the endless sound of that garden fountain. She recalled how she had clamped her hands over her ears and wished for that noise to die.

Had the water's rush reminded her of the inevitable passing of time? Perhaps like the ticking minutes she had lived? Or did its torrent evoke what she'd felt towards a brother who – while she had been barred from romantic love and happiness – had consumed everything life had given him, with abandon?

Yet her distress concealed much more— the secret torment of Aaron's rebuff, the slights encountered throughout her marriageable years, and the endless gossip she had suffered since her brother's marriage. These memories, they had screamed at her and filled her with anger. But nothing, nothing had roared louder than that fountain whose ghastly mouth spewed waters with such force.

For deep in the fountain's gurgling throat, Vera knew not how, but she sensed echoes of something worse.

Vera startled. She stared out from the parlour, suddenly alerted by the sharp noise arising from the entrance hall. It was the din of metal on marble tiles. Again, she heard it. It resembled the high-pitched note a spoon or another metal object might make if dropped.

"Who's there?"

A fear that the parlour might not be as safe as she once thought overwhelmed Vera, and she rose from her seat. Her heart raced as she felt her way out towards the entrance hall, the lamp unsteady in her trembling hand.

"Is that you, Shannon?" Perhaps the maid had come out to check upon her. Vera stepped out of the parlour. She studied the floor and frowned. A tiny silver spoon gleamed on the tiles at her feet. Surprised, she lowered herself to pick it up. A violent blow struck her other hand and the lamp fell from her grip, shattering across the floor. Vera felt herself trip. She tumbled forward, landing on her palms with a gasp. The light had gone out. Only remained the moonlight seeping through the glass doors and into the entrance hall. Its beams shone onto another spoon that had caused Vera's fall. Alarm seized her. She raised herself and ran to the staircase. She climbed the stairs without looking back. She would not remain another day in Alexandra Hall. She'd pack her bag tonight and ask the gardener to take her to Reading Town in the morning.

As she reached Calista's portrait halfway up the stairs, Vera froze. She thought she saw the Greek girl grin back at her. There was something hard under her foot. Clinging to the banister, Vera reached for the object. Another damned spoon. And another…over there…on the previous step.

And below it, reaching out towards her, there was…

Vera tried to scream but her throat felt tight. She opened her mouth, but no sound came.

Chapter 2

Maurice Leroux

"YOU don't let me find you, Maurice. Don't let me find you. Because if I find you, you bet I'll whip you so hard you won't forget it."

The woman he called mother spun upon her feet and strode back towards the kitchen.

"Maurice! You come out now."

She opened the pantry cabinet, peered in. Did she not know, it was the last place where he would have hid? He'd rather get caught than be trapped in there. She slammed it shut.

"Where is he? Where has the little demon got to?"

Maurice's heart leapt in his chest as he watched Therese's stained clogs move past the kitchen table. Therese had nasty powers. She could change the manner in which she spoke at will. "Come out Maurice. Mummy won't be mad."

It always made him sick to the stomach to hear her take on that sweetened voice. If truth be known, he preferred it when she screamed at him.

Therese always went everywhere with her imaginary friends, women that you could count upon, women that never let you down and who, like Therese, fought their way into the world. There was no one else in the room, but she muttered bitter words under her breath. "What did I tell you, girls? Just like his father. A mouth to feed and nothing in his little pea-sized brain. Little runt will get what he deserves. And when I catch him…"

Her steps became frantic. She agitated herself. Now she was mad.

She had eyes everywhere. Nowhere could he hide. For this was home.

At four, he was too young to understand that no matter how dearly he wished it, sitting still, crouched into a ball with his knees tucked in beneath his belly, even halting his breath and shutting his eyes did not make him disappear. No one could achieve such a feat. If he could, he might have merged into the rug, taken on the crimson of the fabric, become one with the splintered wooden slats. He would have…

Calloused hands reached under the table. They grabbed at him. He smelled the strong ale on her breath, the sweat of her armpits.

"Open your eyes Maurice!" she barked.

He couldn't. He couldn't face her. He had to do it: he had to disappear, now.

Until the blow to his head startled him. His jaw slackened but he was tongue-tied. He blinked, then stared breathless at her flashing eyes between two chair legs. She made a triumphant snarl that promised more cruelty. She was all teeth and eyes and she roared, dragging him with force to his feet. A splinter dug deep into his knee.

In her high-pitched honey voice, the voice he dreaded, she launched into her fury.

"I told you I'd find you, didn't I? What did I promise you? A good belting. Yes, that's right."

With one hand she clutched onto his locks, her grip, fierce and unyielding. With the other, she felt against the hearth and found a long metal rod.

Over the years, he had discovered ways to grow numb when she struck. Blow after blow, he'd learnt to leave his body. One. That's how he did it. Oh it hurt, but he was long detached from his own skin. Therese's long entangled hair danced savagely around her head as she struck him. In her eyes, malicious sparks were set alight. Two. Three. While she gripped his arm and he watched her fly into her mad dance in which he was but a prop, he would wonder at the curious blend of rage and pleasure in her eyes. Four. Five. The froth bubbled at the corners of her mouth and he would feel only repulsion. But as horrifying as she was, once she had found him, the images moved so fast that for all his tears, Maurice no longer heard, no longer feared. Six, seven, eight... countless blows. He was numb to them all. For the chase is what he feared most. Always the chase.

And the neighbours heard, how could they not? For their street was narrow and each home abutted the wall of the other. And when the Parisian rain did not wash away the slurry of household waste, each home swam in the refuse of the other. The blank faces he'd see the next day told him that no help was coming, for Therese was all he had, all he could expect. And the look in their eyes as they stared – at his bruises, at his blackened eyes – then turned their faces away, brought him only shame.

"Inspector Maurice Leroux," began the lawyer, "I'm delighted to meet you." Maurice's memories vanished. He reached out to shake Mr. Wilson's hand.

He had been standing in the stuffy office for some time, watching the rain pelting against the window, when scenes of his childhood had entered his thoughts.

Unfamiliar places, new experiences, new faces — they brought back these unsettling incidents. He felt proud to gain courage from his past, to reflect on what he had endured and overcome, despite feeling entirely alone with his memories. For some things were not spoken.

"I am in a delicate situation, Mr. Leroux," began Mr. Wilson as they sat in his study. "Before he died, my client appended stringent stipulations to his will and I am bound to abide to them. Did you read what I sent you?"

Maurice launched into his college-level English with only a rare touch of a French accent. "I understand Mr. Nightingale was an eccentric," he said.

"As eccentric as they come."

"Why me?"

"For the utmost discretion. We felt it best to invite a French national to work on the case. You have a fine reputation in Normandy and one of Mr. Nightingale's medical colleagues, a man he met in France on several occasions, recommended you."

"Do I know this Frenchman?"

"It hardly matters, does it? He knew you and your work in private investigations. I shan't reveal his identity. We would like to work quietly, as you'll appreciate. While you remain here, in England, I will hold on to your passport. It will be returned to you when you wish to journey back to France."

"I can assure you my work ethics are exemplary."

"It is a simple formality. Mr. Leroux, if it wasn't for Mr. Nightingale's secretive nature, you would not be here. There's no reason for me to distrust you. I am in your debt. Few French inspectors speak English as well as you do and I can't see them being much inclined to brave the Channel with all the upheaval back home. Uncertain times in France."

"I acknowledge that we have had an interesting revolution. But it is largely over, now, since June."

Mr. Wilson smiled. "That's quite an understatement. This is the second time you depose of your monarchy. Napoleon Bonaparte must be laughing in his grave. But let's return to the facts. After her brother's death in August, Aaron Nightingale's sister approached me. She told me she wished to visit the estate and settle some matter. Due to the family ties, I did not see a problem. I gave her a set of keys and notified Mrs. Jane Cleary, the housekeeper."

"Is Mrs. Cleary also a suspect of this investigation?"

"Everyone at Alexandra Hall is a potential suspect. Aside from Mrs. Cleary, there is a cook, a gardener and four maidservants. Since Aaron Nightingale's passing, they remain at Alexandra Hall. When six months have elapsed, Aaron's younger brother, John, will be permitted to move into the estate with his family. He will either re-appoint the staff or dispose of it."

"Why the six months delay?"

Mr. Wilson cleared his throat. "The deceased willed it," he replied with an evasive gesture. "Perhaps Mr. Nightingale wished to leave his home empty for a period. My role as his lawyer is to respect his wishes. Nothing is to change for half a year. Alas, he could not have foreseen the murders. One of these took place last month and the other, two weeks later – both of them after Mr. and Mrs. Nightingale passed away earlier this year."

Maurice winced. "Are we then speaking of four deaths having taken place under the one roof over the course of a single year?"

Mr. Wilson nodded. "Unsettling, wouldn't you say? Following the death of Mr. and Mrs. Nightingale, there were two murders.

The first victim was a maid, Sophie Murphy. The other victim was Vera Nightingale. As you can imagine, John Nightingale fears for his wife and children. He summoned me to have someone investigate before he moves in next year. Now you understand my position. How do I come to John's aid while respecting the wishes of his deceased brother? During this six months period, I am entrusted to protect the Nightingale estate and safeguard the owner's reputation. That's where you, Mr. Leroux, discrete Frenchman with no ties in England, are a godsend. I've written to Mrs. Cleary to let her know you're to have free run of the house. And I've provided you with the details of each staff, here."

Maurice opened the leather folder. He leaned over several files describing the members of the household and the circumstances of each murder.

Wilson found himself a cigar from his top drawer and lit up. "What do you think, Mr. Leroux?" he asked, blowing a puff of smoke.

"Was anything reported missing or lost?"

"No theft seems to have taken place."

"Do any of the staff have a criminal record?"

"I await further information, however Alfred Fitzpatrick, the gardener, did spend some time in a local jail in his youth."

"I see. Something else comes to mind, Mr. Wilson. For Mr. and Mrs. Nightingale to have both passed away in a matter of a few months would have been distressing for Miss Vera Nightingale. A house of mourning is not a pleasurable prospect for a lone woman. Why would she choose to return to the house? I find it perplexing."

"As do I, Mr. Leroux. At the time, I honestly believed she was sorting through her finances and wished to see those items Aaron had passed on to her."

Maurice reflected on Wilson's words.

"Aside from you, who knows of these murders?" he asked.

"Local Berkshire police were sent. They are well acquainted with the family. Post-mortem operations were performed. Nothing else."

"What were the results of the post-mortems?"

"I am glad you asked. I have organised for the physician who performed the autopsies to visit Alexandra Hall so that you may ask questions. He believes he should have some time on Thursday to discuss the details of the inquest. What we do know is that the maid bore a fatal head injury. As we hoped to avoid a scandal, her family has been handsomely compensated and discouraged from disclosing the details of this sad affair. That being said, the official explanation for these deaths is that both women fell down the staircase."

Maurice raised an eyebrow. "And what is the truth?"

"Sophie Murphy did die of a head injury. The cause is unknown. Vera Nightingale was found at the bottom of the staircase, yes. But a fall is not what killed her. She suffocated."

Chapter 3

Monday

NO marks on Vera Nightingale's body. No sign of loss of blood, concussion or struggle. Strangulation was ruled out. How then, had she died?

Maurice contemplated this mystery during the four-hour coach ride from London into Berkshire. The journey was pleasant enough, though any hopes of admiring the countryside had been stifled by a thick fog that only lifted once they were past Reading.

As the stagecoach reached the grounds of Alexandra Hall, swollen clouds smothered the last of the timid afternoon sun. Sweeping grey skies stretched above the estate as far as the eye could see, adding to the desolation. In the distance, the Nightingale house rose from the mist.

Swaying poplars lined each side of the road, all the way to the mansion's gate. After hours of being tossed and jerked around in a carriage, Maurice welcomed the smooth path. His weariness dissipated the moment his eye fell on the four majestic Doric columns gracing the house's entrance.

A fierce autumn wind blew as they drew near, and when Maurice tilted his head through the carriage window, he saw how violently the trees shook.

By the time the horses came to a halt, Maurice felt the November chill deep in his bones. He regretted that his larger coat remained in his trunk, which was tied to the back of the carriage. Shivering, he stared ahead. Two glass doors opened wide. A group of women stepped out, holding their bonnets in place as the wind flapped through their long skirts. A few meters away, a man in his sixties followed behind them along the narrow path towards the road.

As Maurice dismounted the carriage, these staff members aligned themselves along the side of the road to greet him. Leading the group, was a tall wiry woman who looked to be in her late fifties. Hers was the face of disdain and quiet resignation all blended into one, such that the onlooker knew not whether to dread or pity her. This austere being whose sunken eyes were so tiny they seemed like little black holes, was flanked on either side by four women clad in black.

Much younger, they each wore a full-body white apron of cotton and lace over a black dress. Their hair, piled high above their necks, lay tucked underneath white bonnets. The tallest was a fair redhead who seemed to mimic the dignified airs of her housekeeper. By her side and glowing with confidence, a brunette peered with curiosity at Maurice. The third maid, a sickly looking waif, shivered so intensely that Maurice could hear her teeth chatter from where he stood. Beside her, what appeared to be the youngest maid, stared absent-mindedly as though absorbed in a daydream. These young women stood at the ready while the housekeeper studied Maurice with an unflinching expression.

She dressed in a similar attire as the other maids but unlike them, wore no apron. All that black taffeta lent her a severe appearance and failed to conceal her bony shoulders and elbows. Her long puffed sleeves billowed under the wind, yet not a hair moved on that grey bob sitting high over her brow.

Affixed to her leather belt was a chatelaine where hung keys of all manner of shapes and sizes. Upon sighting the numerous dangling keys, Maurice guessed at once who she was.

“Mrs. Cleary, is it?” he asked, meeting her stern glare.

She nodded. “Welcome to Alexandra Hall, Mr. Leroux. I trust you had a safe journey.”

The women by her side curtsied, then clasped their hands primly together.

“You find this house in deep mourning,” said Mrs. Cleary, ever slowly, as though she wished to impress a sullen mood to the visitor. “In the last year, we bore witness to the passing of four people. Indeed, nothing has been the same since Mrs. Nightingale suffered an unfortunate illness in January this year..."

As she finished speaking, a cold gust shook the nearby trees and nature's moans rose above Maurice's kindly response. Mrs. Cleary shirked back and stared ahead. To Maurice, she appeared horror-stricken.

He watched Mrs. Cleary cast a furtive glance at the house then rub her arms as though unsettled. She turned back to him and inhaled deeply.

"I shall show you your room. Please, follow me."

The housekeeper's accent might have been Irish, pondered Maurice, but she did her best to disguise it. Maurice followed the women in silence.

The case of the ceramic bust

ALEXANDRA Hall was stately. Wherever Maurice's eye fell, Georgian perfection greeted him: lofty ceilings, majestic windows, elaborate mirror fixtures, flowers painted upon wallpapers, and expensive portraits. From the checkered tiles in the entrance hall, to the gold acanthus mouldings on the ceilings' edges, it was the sort of house where echoes graced the rooms as one spoke, and where one might not glimpse another soul throughout the day. He ascended the magnificent staircase and followed Mrs. Cleary to his room at the far right of the landing.

He dropped his bag by the door and gave the guestroom a quick glance. A large window to his left gave an excellent view of the gardens. A lacquered ebony desk stood by the window and in the closet to its right, were water amenities and a porcelain basin.

"Ellen has filled the water pitcher for you. She'll come by to empty your basin twice daily."

"That will be perfect."

"There are bell cordons on the side of your bed, should you require anything to be sent upstairs."

"Thank you, Mrs. Cleary. Is there a room where I might conduct interviews for my investigation?"

"You are welcome to carry on your work in this room," replied Mrs. Cleary. It sounded more like an order than an invitation. Maurice sensed her protectiveness over the late owners' home. She seemed like the sort of person with a strong need for control.

"That will not do unfortunately," he insisted, conscious of the tightening in her jaw. "I much prefer a separate room where I might question the staff members in private. Perhaps a study?"

"I suppose…there is Mr. Nightingale's study."

"Splendid. Please take me to it." He hoped she would grow more cooperative over the coming days.

"Quite. Whatever is more agreeable to you, Mr. Leroux. Please follow me," she replied in an icy manner. She gestured to a room three doors from his, and Maurice followed.

"This is where Mr. Nightingale wrote at night when he was still with us. His sister spent some time here before she died, but everything should be in the place he left it."

As Maurice stepped into the study, thick oriental rugs absorbed the sound of his footsteps. Scarce light penetrated the narrow stained-glass windows. The heavy oak furniture and the wine wallpaper absorbed any rays that dared reach this room.

To Maurice, who lived alone in a stone cottage and who, since his escape from Paris to Normandy, enjoyed long walks along the beach, this study felt stuffy and oppressive. It gave him the impression that Aaron Nightingale preferred whiling the hours of the day in near darkness. The Englishman had jealously guarded his privacy.

The tiredness that had overwhelmed him during his journey to Alexandra Hall soon vanished as Maurice's curiosity took over. His eye fell on scattered documents across the desk, where dust had settled. Drippings of hardened wax had grown fat round the remnants of a candle. It seemed as if only yesterday, Aaron Nightingale had sat there and poured over his notes and his books. The tall-back regency chair seemed to await its owner.

A bookkeeping journal lay open on the desk and Maurice glimpsed the headline of *August 1848*, the month of Aaron's passing. A disordered pile of books towered beside this register, and atop the heap, a thick volume remained open. Maurice's gaze flitted across a chemistry passage. He sensed Mrs. Cleary's watchful eyes upon his back.

A small ink bottle had tipped over, staining the journal's right edge. Maurice felt the paper and frowned. The ink had barely dried. The remaining writing implements were laid out on the left of the desk.

"Was Mr. Nightingale left-handed?" he asked, wondering if anyone had re-arranged the objects on the desk since Aaron's death which would surely account for the spilt ink.

"Yes, he was. He used to say that boarding school had taught him otherwise, but he preferred to write with his left hand. So did she."

"She? You mean, his wife?"

"Yes, Mr. Leroux. Mrs. Nightingale learnt to keep accounts over time. Mr. Nightingale had a tutor come by during her first years in England. For years afterwards, Mr. and Mrs. Nightingale worked together."

Discarding the stained journal, Maurice sighted a white ceramic bust sitting upon the raised portion of the desk. He had not noticed the statue until now because it seemed partly hidden, its face turned away against a pot of dried plants. He reached for the bust, his sense of details stirred by the odd feeling it had given him.

The generous bearded locks had gathered dust. Maurice stared avidly into the face. He noted the wavy fringe, the broad, handsome features with two horizontal lines on the forehead. The bridge of the nose seemed narrow between the man's small eyes, and the mouth appeared to clamp shut. A thinker, the owner of that face was in his late forties at most.

Where have I seen that man before, he wondered, as he replaced the ceramic bust. His eyes shifted to the back of the room.

Bookshelves filled the entire wall behind Mr. Nightingale's desk. On each row, expensive science and medical volumes with gilded leather spines were arranged in alphabetical order. An entire row dealt with the animal kingdom. He glimpsed a volume by a certain Georges Cuvier, another by a Professor Edward

Forbes. Maurice ran a finger across the top of one shelf, then brought it to his eyes. No dust.

Up to now, Mrs. Cleary eyed him intensely. He had even sensed her distress when he had picked up the bust ornament.

"Anything wrong, Mr. Leroux?"

"Has anyone entered this room since Mr. Nightingale passed away?"

"Miss Vera came in briefly to look for correspondence. Other than that, the girls dust the shelves once a week but I assure you they do not touch anything else."

"And what about this week, or just today?"

"No one has entered this room since Miss Vera Nightingale passed away, Mr. Leroux."

Maurice eyed the spilt ink once more but kept his thoughts to himself. He studied the rest of the room.

"What sort of correspondence do you think Miss Vera was looking for?"

"That is why you are here, Mr. Leroux. I am afraid I cannot help you," replied Mrs. Cleary drily.

As the housekeeper spoke, Maurice's eye was drawn to the glass cabinet, opposite the window. On the top shelf, he could make out maps, weighted down by another ceramic bust. The sculpture's face was turned away, facing the wall.

Maurice walked to the cabinet and tugged at the latch to open the glass panel. The panel resisted.

Mrs. Cleary's eyes grew sharp.

"What are you doing? This cabinet is locked."

"Do you have the key?"

"Mr. Nightingale may have kept it in his first drawer."

Maurice returned to the desk and rummaged through the first drawer. He stood back, a little startled at the numerous glass vials inside it. The tiny bottles were filled with a curious liquid. Maurice reached past them, then carefully felt towards the back of the compartment.

"I think I've found the key."

"What exactly are you looking for, Mr. Leroux?"

"I want to see those maps," he lied. She would have to learn to trust him while he performed his work. Her manner was suffocating.

He inserted the matching key and opened the glass pane. He had no interest in the maps. The ceramic bust troubled him. Why was its face turned away, exactly like the bust on the desk?

He reached for it and recognised the features. The same man. Maurice searched through his memory. Handsome, broad cheeks, profuse beard, wavy locks…

"That will be all, Mrs. Cleary. I shall be delighted to work here from time to time."

Her jaw tightened as she nodded.

"Then I shall ask Gerard, our cook, to prepare dinner."

But as Mrs. Cleary spoke these words, she no longer looked at Maurice and her gaze lingered instead to the back of the room.

Sensing the housekeeper's uneasiness, Maurice followed the direction of her eyes. In the last instants, the sun had set and Aaron's books were cast in darkness. Yet aside from the advancing night, nothing seemed out of the ordinary. When Maurice turned around, Mrs. Cleary had left.

Dismissing her odd behaviour, he retrieved the topmost map and studied it as though he were peering into Aaron Nightingale's secrets. He recognised the land formations. It was an antique map of the Mediterranean, nothing more.

Maurice replaced the map in the cabinet and weighted it down with the bust, this time with the face turned outwards.

The infernal

MAURICE longed to rest after his day's journey but the night saw him stir and awaken at ten o'clock. Staring up at the high ceilings, then at the oil portrait on the wall across his bed, he met the stern face of a black-clad conquistador gazing down upon him.

In this bearded Spaniard's gloved hands, the tropical parrot seemed to come alive. Its large eyes circled before glancing back at Maurice. Maurice blinked, still half-asleep. The parrot looked to the window as it always had.

Outside, wispy clouds occluded all but a sliver of the full moon. An eerie glow poured through the veiled window, casting its blue rays on a frayed rug.

It was always a struggle to fall asleep in odd surrounds, breathing in musty odors. It all worsened when he suffered nightmares. Maurice cocked an ear and understood what had disturbed his sleep. There was a dull mechanical noise emanating from his bedroom door.

Where this door had been ajar at the time he had fallen asleep – for Maurice feared closed in spaces – now it was shut. He could hear the engaging clicks of a metallic lock. Once. Then twice. For reasons he could not imagine, Mrs. Cleary had locked him inside his own bedroom.

It had to be Mrs. Cleary. No one else in Alexandra Hall possessed a set of keys to the rooms. Did she not trust a Frenchman?

"Mrs. Cleary?" he called out. Alarm seized him as he stared in disbelief at the locked door. Confused, Maurice pondered over the housekeeper's strange behaviour, until at last, overcome by the day's efforts, he succumbed to sleep with the welcomed afterthought that he might solve this mystery in the morrow.

Stillness enveloped the room. The door remained shut. Night clouds rolled across the sky, unveiling the moon whose light soon bathed Maurice's face. Close to midnight, a persistent rattling at the door's hinges stirred Maurice. He opened his eyes. He could see that the brass handle had shifted from its resting position. Someone was attempting to pry open his bedroom door. He held his breath, wondering why Mrs. Cleary would seek to open a door she had locked herself, hours earlier. Forceful, but in vain, the furious grip worked at the handle until at last, it gave up.

The room fell silent once more. Maurice pulled the coverlet up to his chin and turned to his side, determined to sleep. Alexandra Hall plunged once more into silence. The portraits in the parlour lay motionless. The clock on the parlour mantelpiece ticked on. The embers in the fire blackened to cinders. Nothing stirred on the grand staircase.

Fewer than ten minutes had elapsed since the attempt on Maurice's door, when out of the darkness, the clank and clatter of copper and brass pieces resonated from the kitchen. Tentative at first, then in violent outbursts, the clamour intensified, rising to thunderous proportions.

The sound of shattered glass reached Mrs. Cleary's bedroom. The housekeeper's eyes snapped open, dull and bloodshot. She awoke in gasps. A look of dread distorted her features as she heard the malignant presence downstairs. She had guessed its nature long ago.

She leapt from the bed. Her eyes were wild with fright, and her lips moved as though in a trance as she uttered a prayer beneath her breath. There was no order, or resolve in her movements as she felt for her robe in the dark. The haggard housekeeper resembled nothing of the well-do-do figure she cast in daylight. Trembling with fear, she wrapped the robe round her thin shoulders and pushed her feet into slippers.

Under her claw like fingers, the door swung open and Mrs. Cleary stepped outside, lamp in hand. She stared at Maurice's door across the stairs. It lay shut. She hoped dearly that he remained fast asleep and heard nothing.

The noise…she had to make it stop. A shrewd expression lit her eyes which were so inflamed that it seemed she might weep blood. Yanking her robe tight around her, she descended the staircase, a thin figure, propelled by a devilish force that belied her sixty years.

She'd reached the landing but the sound, far from ceasing, seemed louder and more menacing. Mrs. Cleary felt faint. She crept towards the kitchen, her heart pounding in her chest. Then, fearful of what lay within, she stopped short, three feet from the entrance. She could not bear to see what might be inside the room. And as the malevolent clamour continued, Mrs. Cleary reduced to a pitiful state. A terrifying notion that she had been right all along, robbed her of her breath.

Behind the kitchen's French doors, an unstoppable being smashed pots against the windows. It hurled utensils overhead and they flew across the room in all directions. Mrs. Cleary clasped her mouth, suppressing a desire to scream. At last, unable to bear it any longer, she let out an agonising plea.

"Stop it, please! Please, leave us alone!"

And then all at once, the noise ceased.

In disbelief, Mrs. Cleary dared a horrified glance inside. She could make out nothing. Her lamp shone through the French doors and onto the back wall. She caught a movement, both monstrous and inhumane. A shadow and nothing more, but its demonic shape unfolded and grew in size as the figure came forth.

Mrs. Cleary's courage failed her. She gave a horrified yelp and dropped her lamp. Within seconds, she had fled upstairs. Behind her, the French doors burst open. But Mrs. Cleary had reached her room and bolted herself inside.

Chapter 4

Tuesday

"I THOUGHT we might give you breakfast outside today," voiced Mrs. Cleary. Behind her, an attractive maid carried a tray of freshly baked oat scones.

Despite her cheerful disposition, Mrs. Cleary looked as though she had not slept. Maurice observed ghastly dark circles beneath her eyes while her delicate complexion seemed ruddy even under the gentle autumn sun.

The maid lay the platter before him, together with strawberry jam, a little butter from the ice cellar, and a pitcher of heated milk. She sported an audacious smile on her lips and seemed to linger a while, as she arranged cutlery along the porcelain cup and saucer.

"That will be all, thank you Madeleine," cut in Mrs. Cleary. A touch of cynicism flitted across the maid's face but she nodded and hurried off. Mrs. Cleary began to serve Maurice and he noted with surprise that her hand shook as she poured the milk.

He still brooded over why he'd been so rudely locked up during the night. At eight this morning, he had found the door sensibly unlocked. Maurice cleared his throat, preparing to confront Mrs. Cleary but instead, seeing her in such fragile state, he changed the conversation.

"What are those? They look delicious."

"Have you not had scones, Mr. Leroux?"

"Scones. No, I don't believe I have. Are they an English delicacy?"

"Hardly. They are the talk of town ever since her Majesty Queen Victoria adopted them for afternoon tea. But they are from Scotland, I believe. Something of the sort. I would normally ask Gerard, our cook, to whip up some cream but we've had an accident overnight. Gerard rose early to busy himself with... something in the kitchen."

"Oh, is that what it was? I overheard strange noises last night."

"Noises? I'm sorry to hear that. It was likely Alfred and his rusty wheelbarrow," dismissed Mrs. Cleary.

"I'm relieved. At least it's not like those rats in Paris," he chuckled, hoping to cheer her up.

Mrs. Cleary laughed and to Maurice's surprise, it sounded forced, almost hysterical. Maurice watched her regain her composure.

"Rats!" she repeated. "Fancy that. Dear God. No, nothing of the sort. Gerard would certainly know how to deal with those. Would you believe, Mr. Leroux that Alexandra Hall has not had rats in the last year."

Maurice munched into the buttery scone which he had slathered with jam.

"No rats. Really. That's splendid news. I am glad to hear it. In that case, I shall need no chaperoning as I visit every room of this house today. You have been most kind to show me Mr. Nightingale's study, and I intend to further my investigation by sifting through all remaining rooms and see if I might uncover anything unusual." He eyed her keenly, certain that her reticence would show. She had made her distrust clear by locking him in so ruthlessly.

But Mrs. Cleary only nodded. She lifted the heavy set of keys that hung from her chatelaine and after artfully removing an old copper key, she handed the rest of the set to Maurice.

"Please let me know if you require anything else," she said. Maurice stared at the lone key in her hand. Larger than the others, it appeared to have been crafted a century ago.

Mrs. Cleary slipped the key into a little pouch.

Maurice cleared his throat. "Won't you have a scone, Mrs. Cleary? I feel awkward eating these alone. They are a little dry but I could almost get used to living away from France."

"I'm afraid I can't do that."

"I insist. I'd be delighted if you could join me. At least have some tea."

With pursed lips, she sat across him and reached for the porcelain teapot.

"So the kitchen I understand is out of bounds today."

Mrs. Cleary replaced the tea pot abruptly.

"I think that would be best," she uttered drily.

Maurice gazed at the garden and the gentle yellowing on the leaves. "What was she like? Calista Nightingale…"

Mrs. Cleary's stern expression faded away. "You must have noticed her portrait along the staircase," she replied.

"The portrait? Oh, you mean the one you were dusting yesterday afternoon?"

"Yes."

"It is charming. But what was she like as a person?"

"Well, she wasn't from here. I mean, England. Mr. Nightingale liked to receive exotic parcels from all over the world and I imagine in his romantic inclinations he searched for that rare pearl. His adventures led him to Greece. And that's where he found her."

"How remarkable."

"Yes, I think so."

Mrs. Cleary sipped her tea. A dreamy expression painted itself on her previously tense face. Maurice intuited that she had been fond of Calista Nightingale and missed her. Her reticence had eased the moment she had begun speaking of her.

"What did she do all day?" asked Maurice. "It's frightfully dreary here without children. I imagine she pined for her family in Greece."

"I know what you mean. She was certainly a different sort of woman. Mrs. Nightingale always used to say she had grown up in a village by the sea and that she missed it. It was on an island that he first met her. I forget its name. But there are so many of those islands, you know. I mean I wouldn't know, but I've heard it said."

"She told you that? She must have trusted you," said Maurice. He had seen from Mrs. Cleary's eyes that she seemed to be revisiting kindly memories and hoped she would share more.

"Oh, yes. She told me once that she swam often as a young girl. She described the sea and her eyes would light up. 'You see this aquamarine, Mrs. Cleary,' she said to me one day. She was showing me her engagement ring. 'You see this blue colour? In my village, that is the colour of the water,' she said."

Mrs. Cleary had now forgotten her tea. She gnawed at her lip. "I daresay, if I had been in her place and lived nearby to a pool of water of that colour, I would have done my best to remain there and never come to England." The housekeeper seemed bitter. As she spoke those last words, Maurice detected that her Irish accent had grown more pronounced.

Mrs. Cleary rose. She seemed agitated as though the idea of drinking tea with the French inspector tarnished her efficient image. "Well, I should call on Shannon to clean up, now," she said.

"Already? But *madame*, you've not finished your tea. Mrs. Cleary, in France, we like to take our time with our meals. As for me, I'm going to have a second scone. Please, won't you sit back down?"

The housekeeper dusted off imaginary breadcrumbs from her taffeta dress, then resumed her seat. She sat upright as Maurice piled on strawberry jam onto his scone. The red of the jam, its resemblance to blood, reminded him of a question he'd long wanted to ask.

"Pardon me, what did she die of?" he asked, perplexed by Calista's death earlier in the year.

A darkness passed over Mrs. Cleary's face.

"The winter. She fell gravely ill one evening and didn't leave her bed for weeks. Her cough worsened over Christmas. We all believed she had caught a cold. She had done so many times before. She didn't wish to see a doctor at first. She asked to see Miss Vera. It was… odd."

"How would this be odd?"

"Well she'd never seen Miss Vera since the wedding ten years ago. The two never got off to a proper start. In France you may speak of equality, but here, in England, one should know one's place. Respectable Englishmen do not marry peasant girls. And certainly not from the Greek countryside."

"I see, now. Do you think Miss Vera didn't think much of her brother's wife then?"

"Well, it's not for me to say. All I know is she remained a spinster due to local gossip. If she resented her sister-in-law, I wouldn't know. Yet, as Mrs. Nightingale's illness worsened, I know for a fact that she dispatched a letter, and confessed to me that she hoped Miss Vera would come quickly to Alexandra Hall."

"I can understand that Calista might have wished to speak with another woman. It's quite lonely here at Alexandra Hall. So what happened? Did Vera come?"

"She did. For a while, Mrs. Nightingale regained her appetite. Miss Vera spent time with her in her room and I think her presence did much good. But then her cough worsened. She had much difficulty breathing. Before Mr. Nightingale could fetch a doctor, he found her dead one morning. It was dreadful."

Mrs. Cleary's tea had grown cold.

"Was she buried in her home village, back in Greece?"

Mrs. Cleary attempted to hide her discomfort. "Sadly, no. Mr. Nightingale was in no way inclined to make that journey. Imagine, setting off to France to board a ship from Marseilles and sailing all the way to Athens. Then yet another ship to her island home. Oh, no. Mr. Nightingale was adamant that he had an important project to attend to, and could not absent himself from Alexandra Hall, not even for two weeks." Resentment tinted Mrs. Cleary's voice. "Even his sister who had visited him for the first time in years failed to part him from his work. I remember it well. We were in mourning. Miss Vera entered his study and they talked for hours. He lashed out at her and told her to mind her own business. Then he sent her packing. A day later, we buried Calista in the garden."

"I see. Now that you have mentioned Mr. Nightingale, I must tell you this. It is out of character for a man of learning, one so passionate about his work, to give up on his desire to live. I am alluding to his sudden death in August. Rather odd, don't you think? Do you think he felt guilty when his wife died? And that he let himself die?"

Mrs. Cleary thought for a moment. "Mr. Nightingale was never quite the same after his wife died. He used to walk through the house with a worried look on his face. At the time, I gathered his work troubled him."

"It must have been important work for him to deprive his wife's family of attending the burial. What was he working on?"

"Oh, I wouldn't know." She waved a hand and turned her face away, avoiding eye contact.

"Where did you say he conducted that work?"

His question remained unanswered. A tall maid with ginger-coloured hair had come forth, and upon seeing her, Mrs. Cleary promptly stood.

She cleared her throat and gave orders.

"Shannon, I believe Mr. Leroux has finished his breakfast. Hurry up and clean the table and bring a water carafe to the study."

"Yes, Mrs. Cleary."

Mrs. Cleary turned to Maurice. "If you'll excuse me, I will see that the cook has everything he needs. Let me know if you'd like some sandwiches for lunch. I'm sure we have some ham in the larder and I'll ask Gerard to make a fresh loaf of bread."

"That will be lovely, thank you."

She stared at him as though collecting her thoughts.

"Mr. Leroux. You'll find Alexandra Hall a fascinating place. At times when you examine all the art work and the exquisite objects that Mr. Nightingale so loved to collect, you might overlook details the first time round. Colours and shapes have a habit of changing in this house, in a most unusual way. When you think you have grasped what you are seeing, you find it is all an illusion, and things take on quite another form."

"I don't understand what you mean, Mrs. Cleary. But I'll keep an open mind," said Maurice.

"Oh, no. You'll understand what I mean, in time." She hastened away.

Maurice began his inspection of the house by visiting Calista's bedroom upstairs. Soon after breakfast he headed to the room diagonally from his.

As he unlocked the door and stepped inside, a lingering feminine scent wafted to his nostrils. It was soft, jasmine like, and a mournful feeling tugged at his chest as he inhaled. The large bed, untouched since January, was painted in white and gold. Silk blue sheets mirrored the azure of the ceiling. Within this celestial artwork, naked cherubs looked down onto the bed. The room's serene atmosphere was enhanced by the pink pastel blooms adorning the walls.

Maurice's eye lingered on an antique vanity table to his right. Mrs. Cleary's obvious fondness for Calista had moved him. A wave of sadness rushed through him as he sighted the objects on the table: a silver casket, a porcelain brush, a handheld mirror and numerous perfume bottles. But upon lifting the casket, he was struck by its contents— coral and bead necklaces, in a style that he'd never seen. Inside the drawers, he found no letters, only paper and ink. And then more strange beads, many of them, blue.

Maurice opened the tall 18th century double-door closet but instantly shirked back, clamping his nose. Upon recovering from his surprise, he peered in to examine the long, full dresses until he understood the reason for the odour. At least five of these gowns looked horribly stained. He wondered what to make of the stark contrast between Calista's refined room and the coarseness inside her closet. Then he shut the doors.

Perhaps all might be explained once he understood more about the house's occupants.

Gerard

MAURICE entered more guest rooms to the right of Calista's bedroom. His search led him back to the stair landing, then to Aaron's study.

As he passed the space between Aaron's study and his guestroom, he noted a wet trail on the floorboards and on the rug in the corridor. A glistening liquid had been smeared there. At first, he feared that his own shoes might be stained, but upon inspecting them, Maurice saw they were not. Finding a towel in his room, he used it to dab the moisture on the floorboards, keeping an anxious eye on the stair landing to check that none of the maids saw him. He did not wish to be a grubby guest. There. Mrs. Cleary would not notice a thing.

Relieved, Maurice proceeded past his room. Finding the correct key, he entered a spacious carpeted library filled with antique volumes and leather-bound classics. Wooden shelves reached the ceiling, covering every wall. The scent of dark cedar filled his nostrils. Were he not working on a case, he would have loved nothing better than to explore these treasures at leisure. He regretfully sighed and left the library.

He had now reached Aaron's bedroom at the far corner of the second floor. Maurice unlocked the door and stepped inside.

The richness of the furniture was astounding. There was even a fireplace finely carved in sandstone. An opulent Persian rug covered the floorboards. A rustic chandelier in blackened metal hung from the wooden ceiling. Maurice gazed up at the Renaissance coffers. It was a style, he had only seen in the grandest homes.

Dominating Aaron's room, was a four-poster Renaissance bed in maroon oak. Its headboard was hand-carved with rosettes, foliates, and a scene of merry musicians. Atop the bed lay a gilded coverlet and dozens of silk cushions.

A large leather chest abutted the foot of the bed. Maurice lifted the lid. Personal clothing, two leather caskets, shoe boxes, and dusty books filled the trunk. His eye lingered on the smaller sized casket which bore a distinct medieval emblem. It was locked, but Maurice admired the courtly love scenes where a troubadour and his lady, both painted in red, exchanged affirmations. Before closing the trunk, he wondered where Aaron had obtained such a rare treasure.

Turning to a grand armoire, Maurice peered into Aaron's wardrobe. His lips curled with a smile. On the surface, Aaron Nightingale might have resembled a dandy, but to Maurice, he evoked a chameleon like image, dressing in various styles at whim. Perhaps Aaron had even fancied himself as a Renaissance man, mused Maurice, a man with boundless abilities…or a god. Maurice reflected on this idea.

He exited the room and headed downstairs. Halfway down the staircase, he paused at Calista's regal portrait and for a moment, he could not lift his eyes from her. He was reminded that it had all begun with this Greek woman's death. Calista first, then Aaron, followed by the maid and Vera. He'd been called upon to solve two murders, but he was not prepared to overlook four deaths in one year.

Having reached the kitchen, Maurice decided to sneak inside and interview the cook. He cast a quick glance around him. Mrs. Cleary was nowhere in sight. He pushed open the French doors.

Gerard O'Malley knelt before the giant stove oven in the heart of the room. He worked at blacking its surfaces.

As Maurice entered, he startled. "Jesus, Mr. Leroux. You frightened me."

The Irishman interrupted his work and rose to his feet.

"So I hear you like my scones, Mr. Leroux," he said. He spoke with a thick accent and with English not being his first language, Maurice strained to understand him.

"Delicious, thank you," he replied. "Is there something wrong with the oven?"

"That old thing. Nah, she's right. Just weekly routine. Real bastard of a job. Makes it worse when you have to wake up at four in the morning." Gerard wiped his nose, smearing a little grease upon it. He found an old rag and wiped his hands on it.

"That early! Mr. O'Malley, I hope it was not the scones that you had to bake on my account," said Maurice.

Gerard continued to wipe his hands, giving the impression he had not heard. He seemed reticent to speak.

Spotting nicotine stains on the cook's fingers, Maurice dug into his vest and began to light a cigar. "Would you like one?" he asked, presenting his cigar case.

"Oh no, I shouldn't. Mrs. Cleary won't like it."

"I've closed the kitchen doors. She won't know a thing."

Gerard reached for a cigar. Maurice leaned across to light it for him. "I'm investigating the deaths of Sophie Murphy and Vera Nightingale," he reminded the cook.

"I know. I just don't think I can be of much help to you."

"Well you can start by telling me what happened here," said Maurice, as he glimpsed the shattered glass on one of the windows.

"I don't think Mrs. Cleary would like that much, sir."

"Mrs. Cleary doesn't have a choice. I am working at the behest of John Nightingale. Don't worry, you won't lose your job by speaking with me."

Gerard looked worried. "Just between you and me, then."

"That's right. Nobody has to hear it."

"Well in that case..." Gerard leaned in to confide in Maurice. "You should have seen the state of the kitchen this morning, Mr. Leroux," he whispered. "Like a blasted hurricane went through it. My crockery smashed to pieces. The saucepans in such a state. It's a wonder the French doors are in one piece. You'd best watch your step unless I missed a piece of glass."

"Has someone tried to break into the house?"

A look of dread passed over Gerard's face. "Afraid not. It's much worse than that. Look, I don't want to say."

"I'm sure you're bursting to say it though," observed Maurice.

"Sure I am, but she might hear us. Mrs. Cleary…"

"Nobody can hear a thing. I've closed the doors, Gerard," reminded Maurice in an encouraging tone.

Gerard lowered his voice. "Alright, where do I start? She's been acting strange ever since Calista Nightingale died. Oh, she says there's a haunting in this house, but I ain't so sure. I ain't buying it. I've seen her tantrums."

Maurice frowned. "Mrs. Cleary never mentioned any haunting. It's the most ridiculous idea I've heard."

Gerard fixed Maurice as though weighing up whether to speak further. He peered through the French doors to make certain that no one was passing by.

"She won't mention any of it to you. The lady has gone insane, if you ask me. But what choice do I have? I answer to her. I do what I'm told. Don't want to lose my job when Mr. John takes over. Though I'm sure he'll straighten her out. I think she's just showing you her good side." He paused. "For now."

"You said she thinks there's a haunting. Can you explain what you mean?" asked Maurice.

Gerard looked askance through the windows to check that no one was watching him from outside. He turned to Maurice. "She's been saying Vera Nightingale was murdered by Calista's spirit. That she died of fright. That's the way she said it."

Maurice blinked. "Murdered by a ghost? That's absurd." He'd not expected Mrs. Cleary to be the sort of person to fall prey to superstitious thoughts. "Alright then, about Vera Nightingale. Tell me more about that night. What were you doing?"

"Sleeping, sir. I got up the next day before everyone else. Now I found Vera Nightingale by the stairs that day and to be sure, I remember the horror on her dead face. She sure did look frightened to me. But I think anyone who was close to death would find themselves in a little panic, don't you think?"

"You found her?"

"I did. I asked the gardener to ride into town and summon the police."

"What else did you see that day?"

"There were spoons scattered across the stairs and down below. I didn't want no one tripping on them so I put those nasty things away. The police didn't like that much. They spoke to me like I had tampered with the evidence."

"You think someone might have placed them there on purpose and caused her to trip?"

"No one here would do such an awful thing. I think maybe she was carrying them and they slipped from her hands when she fell."

"What was Vera Nightingale doing with spoons in the middle of the night?"

"Well…I…I don't know."

"What happened afterwards?"

"Oh, the usual drama. Mrs. Cleary was no use. She'd been running errands in London the day before, and didn't show up until the evening after I found Miss Vera Nightingale. I had to do everything myself. The girls were in tears. The coroner asked everyone what they'd seen. What could I tell them? Nothing. I heard nothing that night. I think Vera Nightingale gave herself a fright and fell down the stairs."

"Do you truly believe that?"

"Why not? It wouldn't be the first time Alexandra Hall made someone's blood run cold. What with all those portraits crowding the walls. Bunch of ghouls. Even I get frightened at times the way those people with their stiff airs look down on you."

"I'm surprised both you and Mrs. Cleary believe Vera Nightingale died of fright. You should already know that she suffocated. The fact is, somebody smothered her."

Gerard grew pale. "No one here would do such a thing. I already talked to the police and they said the same thing you did. But I don't know, I still cannot believe it."

"Where did you say Mrs. Cleary was all this time?"

"Like I said, in London, running errands. Between you and me, she wants to emigrate to Australia. She hates it here."

"How do you know so much about what she plans to do?"

Gerard had poured some flour in a bowl, made a well and added in a little yeast paste with salt. He walked to an internal pump and filled a water pitcher. "Well, she used to confide in Sophie. Sophie Murphy."

"The maid who died two weeks before Miss Nightingale."

"Yes. Sophie let it slip. Not much that girl could keep secret. But anyhow, it doesn't matter now, does it?"

He looked suddenly dispirited as he kneaded the dough to prepare a bread loaf.

Maurice reflected upon the cook's words. "You haven't answered my first question. Who do you think created havoc in your kitchen, Mr. O'Malley?"

Gerard's ears blushed red. He shook his head as he pounded a fist into the dough which he then flipped over and gave another spray of flour.

"I ain't saying it, Mr. Leroux. Don't want to get myself dismissed. Who else is going to hire an old man like me?"

"Well you seem a little troubled by it all. Maybe it might help you to bring someone into your confidence."

"You're a smart man, sir. And you're right, it's been bothering me. Do you really want to know what I think? I think it's Mrs. Cleary. I think she's doing it herself. She's got so much anger bottled up within her that it wouldn't surprise me."

Gerard's pounding grew harsh, his fingers clawed at the dough before slamming it loudly on the bench. "This is not the first time," he muttered under his breath. "If it happens again, I'll have her send out for new crockery and get me another set of copper pans. Haunting! What bullshit. The woman is a tyrant. And a mad one at that!"

As he uttered those words, the French doors were pushed open and the eldest maid strode into the kitchen. Gerard hushed instantly. He hurried to the sink to put out the cigar he'd half-smoked.

"I can smell tobacco," she said.

"It's nothing, Shannon. Inspector Leroux, here, wanted to have a talk and..."

"Mr. O'Malley's right. It was my idea," said Maurice.

Shannon crossed the room with an air of efficiency. Without a word, she moved past Maurice and reached out to open the windows.

Maurice left soon after. He was lost in thought. Returning to the landing, he resumed his tour of the house, entering a gallery of rooms. Some of these were not locked but when they were, he spent considerable time ferreting through the keys Mrs. Cleary had given him to determine which of them fitted in the lock.

Having reached a corridor, he heard a dog bark behind him. A voice, young, almost infantile, called out after it.

"Willy! Come back here, you. Don't pester Mr. Leroux."

Maurice turned around and saw a young maid hurry off with a tiny Bolognese under one arm. She held a duster in her other hand.

Save for the housemaids' routine cleaning, it seemed these rooms had been neglected and uninhabited for a long time, possibly longer than a year. There was an absence of furniture which made settling in or sitting down almost impossible, but Aaron Nightingale more than made up for it with artefacts. Portraits left not an empty space upon the walls.

Maurice neared a room whose door had been left unlocked. Noticing a curious odour, he peered inside. He inhaled the scent of wood, and...something else. He could not describe it.

The treasures in that room were overwhelming: Abyssinian wooden stools covered with hides; long deadly arrows and feathered bows from presumed wanderings in South Africa; carved shields; and leaning against the golden wallpaper, were noble African faces carved into long ivory tusks.

Elsewhere he saw embroidered leather poufs and fancy cushions from the Sahel lands and from Egypt, a low damascene table for playing Arab checkers, an oriental lamp with filigree details, then scarabs upon scarabs in blue, turquoise and gold, all heaped into a dusty Moroccan leather box.

Aaron Nightingale had possessed untold riches but he seemed to have never touched any of it. Everything lay frozen, exactly as it would appear in a display window or souk. Rich leather scents filled Maurice's nostrils; and once more, a curious odour, but he could not make it out. It was a malignant smell, as though something rotted inside the room.

Maurice was about to leave, when his eyes caught the largest of the African masks, set against other gilded objects. For a second it seemed to him that the mask had come alive, that its features had shifted like a gleaming mass. Its crown of hair had seemed to unfurl. Maurice squinted. He stared again at the mask but saw nothing out of the ordinary. *Colours and shapes...* Mrs. Cleary was right. Dismissing what he had seen, he left the room.

His steps echoed in the long corridor. He passed further rooms and yet more portraits hanging upon the walls. At last, he came into large billiard room with heavy red carpet. An imposing brass chandelier hung directly above the wooden felt-covered table. Everything looked new, untouched. Had Aaron ever played billiards at all?

On the face of it, one could imagine Alexandra Hall and its contents to be nothing more than a projection of Aaron's ego and his vain pursuits. The entire house could be considered a cabinet of curiosities. There was an unease as one stepped inside its rooms. The luxury and decadence unsettled. It spoke of the soul of a man with an insatiable lust for possessions.

But a disquiet of another nature haunted Maurice: aside from her bedroom, there was a near absence of Calista Nightingale's feminine touch, as though she had never existed.

For wherever he looked, whether it was the billiard room or the numerous chambers filled with exotic art, or even the parlour with its heavy empire furniture and its grand yet zoo-like portraits, there was no evidence a woman had lived here, nor that her personality had been permitted to make its mark.

Alfred and the gardens

IT was almost lunchtime, when Maurice returned to his room with a flash of inspiration. He wrote it down in his journal.

I keep thinking about something I saw that, to most, would appear innocuous – a ceramic bust in Aaron's office and which I've now identified. Aaron Nightingale was once fond of Aristotle it seems.

There are those instances when you can't bear to face a person – be it from shame, or even fear, and when you naturally wish never to have their eyes fall upon you.

This is the impression I have of Mr. Nightingale and his relationship with the Greek philosopher, Aristotle. Aaron owned two ceramic busts whose faces he turned away. I wonder why.

Then turning to the stationary provided at his desk, he wrote the following letter.

Mr. Wilson,

I arrived yesterday and all is well. I shall remain in Alexandra Hall for a few more nights at least. Aside from some expected hostility towards an inspector, and a few odd superstitious beliefs, I've so far encountered nothing out of the ordinary.

It appears that aside from the cook, the gardener, the four housemaids, and Mrs. Cleary, we are quite alone on this estate.

I plan to interview the housemaids tomorrow.

I shall also endeavour to learn what I can about Aaron and his activities in the event it bears on this case.

I shall keep you informed of my discoveries.

Inspector Leroux

Maurice slid the letter in an envelope to which he affixed a Penny Black.

He went downstairs, opened the front glass doors and walked up to the pathway towards the road. He handed over his stamped envelope to the errand boy awaiting by the carriage.

"Inspector Leroux," he said, introducing himself as he shook the young man's hand. "How long does it take to deliver letters to London?"

"For London, sir? Delivery by the next day. I hand mail over to a postal boy in Reading Town while I busy myself with buying provisions."

"Once delivered, when shall I expect my response?"

"Depends on how quickly that person wants to reply. But if they reply straight away, you might get your response in a day, two at most, sir. As for me, I'm here in the mornings every day, even on Sundays, sir."

"And when do you usually leave?"

"Once I have Mrs. Cleary's shopping list. Usually by noon."

Maurice thanked the delivery boy and walked off, seeking the gardener.

As he neared the house, he glimpsed the young maid he'd seen earlier, with her dog in tow. She'd wandered off on the veranda. He imagined she might have been on a lunch break from her chores. He was about to wave in her direction when a flurry of black fabric stormed out of the double glass doors. He realised it was Mrs. Cleary striding outside towards the girl.

Maurice flinched, astounded by the housekeeper's face. She bore a rageful expression and her features were frightfully deformed. He saw the young maid turn and instantly startle as Mrs. Cleary yelled at her. Maurice could not make out her words, but he watched in fascination as the housekeeper yanked at the girl's sleeve and dragged her forcefully back into the house. For a moment, Maurice was uncertain about what he'd witnessed. Perhaps Gerard was right and Mrs. Cleary had all the manner of a tyrant. Feeling sorry for the girl, he shook his head and continued on.

Venturing towards the back of the house, he crossed a spacious lawn. In the spring and summer, it might have been lined with patches of continental flowers and scented rose bushes, but with the approach of winter, the stripped plants inspired something akin to despair. To his left was a fountain, and a little to the right, by the creek, he noticed a herb garden encircled by a tall hedgerow.

Maurice crossed the arched entrance of the hedgerow. Here, the garden was reduced to a dismal state where nothing worthy sprouted. In their original form, the leafy basil, the coriander, mint, chives, and thyme might have been Calista's joy. Now almost a year had passed and these plants had fallen into decrepitude.

Beneath an old cypress by the creek, Maurice noticed an abandoned grave covered with leaves and other debris from fallen branches. Brambles had grown across it, smothering the stone. He was appalled by this sight. What was so important for Aaron to have neglected the love of his life? Had they quarrelled prior to her death?

The brambles' sharp pins cut through his fingers as he forced apart the entangled branches. After multiple efforts, he was better able to see the stone beneath.

Maurice knelt. He read the inscription on the curved headstone.

Calista Nightingale
née Argyros
December 1814 – January 1848
πάντα ῥεῖ

She had turned thirty-three just prior to her death. Maurice was moved. There was a sea shell engraved beneath the Greek words and then nothing else. The tombstone was bare.

Maurice had never entertained the idea of travelling to the Mediterranean but he imagined how liberating it would have been for a child to swim in aquamarine waters under a generous sun. Calista had known a different life before arriving in England.

What had it been like for her to live with Aaron Nightingale, so far from home, without children to keep her occupied? To be buried here, a place so removed from the coastal village she had known, isolated in this dreary rural setting, seemed entirely unfair. And why was her tomb kept apart? There was no sign that her husband was buried nearby. Maurice guessed that Aaron's tomb might be found in a proper cemetery, perhaps in a family crypt. It only saddened him further.

The rustling of leaves drew him out of his reverie. He gave the lonely grave one last look, then stood.

Deep in thought, Maurice paced through the garden lawns where weeds seemed to have taken over. The only tended part of the grounds was the area near the fountain, right below the guestroom where he slept.

As he approached the fountain, he noticed a burly man in his mid-thirties emerging from a flight of stairs below ground, axe in hand.

His swarthy face and rippling forearms were streaked with soot. The rough cotton of his dark trousers hinted to his work as a groundsman. He must have been refuelling the boiler which controlled the fountain's steam pump.

"Good afternoon," called out Maurice as he neared the gardener.

"So you're that inspector," said the man who towered over Maurice. "The Frenchman," he added, a hint of mockery in his voice.

"My name's Inspector Leroux. I'm here to investigate the deaths in this house. You must be Alfred."

The gardener's eyes narrowed as he nodded. He gave Maurice's hand a brutal squeeze. "I wonder why you were brought in and not some English lad. The Nightingales likely don't want no countrymen snooping in their business. Smart lads." He grinned, revealing a row of crooked teeth.

"I'm a private investigator, Alfred. I've worked on cases in Germany and Spain in the past."

Alfred eyed Maurice from head to toe. In a provocative swing intended to intimidate, he hoisted the axe to rest across his shoulder. Maurice was made painfully conscious of the man's size and strength.

"Well it's nice to meet you, sir," said Alfred. He seemed eager to get away.

"One moment, Alfred," cut in Maurice. "I'd like to ask you some questions about these two murders. Just getting acquainted with everyone."

Alfred stopped in his tracks. He didn't look pleased. "That right? Just speaking with everyone like the police did." He stood upright, flexing his muscles.

Maurice held his gaze.

"That's exactly right. So you spoke with the police?"

"Sure did. Twice already. And I can't say I was any help. No chance I killed anybody. I'm not even allowed inside, see. Mrs. Cleary would die of fright if she saw my filthy boots plodding along on her tiles. Still, who knows, maybe you'll find what you're looking for. Sorry, I can't help you." He made a start.

"Be sensible, Alfred. I'm sure you don't want John Nightingale finding out you've made this investigation harder than it is. Two murders are not dismissed so easily. And so close in the space of time. Surely somebody has to take the blame for that," reminded Maurice.

The groundsman turned abruptly. His axe changed hands, much to Maurice's alarm. A mocking smile drew itself on the gardener's lips. "Accidents do happen," he said. "I'm told the two women were very near the staircase. And as I've told you, I've already given my statement to the police."

"Nonsense," insisted Maurice. "I'm hearing far too many fanciful statements. Mrs. Cleary thinks this place might be haunted. Now, here you are, evoking accidents. Too convenient for my liking."

The gardener's weathered face looked suddenly weary and he emitted a nervous laughter. "Blimey, how many times do I have to tell you? I ain't so sure myself what happened to those women. Never seen the inside of that house." He paused. "I tell you what, maybe what you ought to be looking into is family secrets."

Maurice startled. "Now why would I do that?"

Alfred glowered at him. "I'm sure you'll figure something out."

"Explain what you mean or I shall report you to John Nightingale for obstructing my investigation."

In response, Alfred fixed him. Maurice watched the gardener's thick fingers tighten around the axe handle but he stood his ground. "Now tell me, did you see something?" he repeated.

Alfred shook his head. "A feeling, that's all. Some folk you know just by looking at them that they don't belong here. Mrs.

Nightingale never belonged in Alexandra Hall. And that's the truth."

"That may be, but it was her home. What makes you say all this?"

"In all the years I've worked here that lady never looked happy to me."

"Explain what you mean."

"My little cottage, see, is not far behind the creek and a few times, months before she passed away, I'd see her come out of the house at night. Now I'm a big fellow, but it still gave me the shivers. That's all I know."

"You often peer at the women of the house, Alfred? Watched any of the maids recently?"

"I ain't saying that," thundered Alfred. "What I mean is I saw a lamp in the dark. So of course, I got curious. I looked through my window. There she was. Barefoot, like some wanton creature. She'd be dressed in a white nightrobe with her long black hair all loose down her shoulders. I was looking, you know, like any man would but, you know, minding my own business. I was curious, is all."

"Sure, you were. I know all about your past jail time. So you followed her, then? Did you touch her?"

Alfred's jaw twitched in anger. "I never touched anyone!"

"You expect me to believe that?"

"Like I said, I stayed out of her way. The first time it happened, I asked myself what business this lady had with going out like that, and in the middle of the night. And so I watched her. She crossed the garden and found the creek. She knew what she was looking for. Now, I'm not made of stone. It was a pretty sight, this foreign lady. But to me, she looked much like some weeping ghost. Yes, sir. So that's all I meant, see. If you're looking for your ghost, it's her."

"I don't believe in spirits, Alfred."

"Neither do I. But there's ways of haunting, see. I'm not speaking of some raving Scottish ghost with a sword and that. I'm talking another sort, the wronged kind. If anyone haunts this place, then that would be Mrs. Nightingale."

"That's a convenient tale," said Maurice. "You sure it was her and not one of the maids?"

"Oh no, it was her, alright. Scared me a few times. She'd just sit there, by the creek. I told myself she must like being near the water." Alfred reflected on that memory and shook his head. "That lady, I can tell you right now, there was something not quite right about her."

Maurice reflected on the groundsman's words. He had felt for Calista ever since discovering her grave.

"Plenty of unsavoury characters in these parts, Inspector Leroux," volunteered Alfred. "I'll tell you what, if anyone broke into the house to murder those other ladies, they most likely came from Reading Gaol."

"An escaped convict? I considered that already but no theft has been reported. I find it doubtful."

"Well, I'd best be going. That firewood ain't chopping itself."

Alfred picked up the tools he'd left by the side of the fountain and walked away to his cottage.

Maurice felt bemused by all he'd heard from the staff today. Had they all struck an agreement with one another to speak of nothing but hauntings?

He became drawn to the fountain's sounds. Water poured out of an enormous fish sculpture which seemed to leap over a shell-shaped pond. How was it, Maurice wondered, that only a hundred feet away, Calista's grave remained unattended while, here, was an entirely different story?

Maurice leaned over the large pool, the water's rush filling his ear. Beneath the water, the pond's surface glistened, set alight by tiny alabaster mosaics. Maurice had seen nothing like it before, not even at the Louvre. It was so beautiful that for an instant, he became oblivious to the grim deaths at Alexandra Hall.

The fountain was an astonishing work of art. Its bottom surface was a coloured mosaic of fish life with myriads of indescribable sea creatures shimmering under the light. Creatures that he could not name, and even the crest of blue waves appeared beneath the translucent pool, as though an entire ocean was depicted there.

No bugs. Not even a fallen reed. Not a leaf from the autumn-stripped trees that lined the garden. The pool's surface gleamed, exceptionally well-tended. One could almost forget there was a pump underneath, functioning perfectly. It all seemed magical, this clear water gushing out from the large fish's open mouth, flowing into the pond, the sea world beneath it coming alive.

Black and blue

THREE hours upon falling asleep, Maurice heard rapping at his bedroom door. He rose. Reaching for the handle, he was stunned to learn Mrs. Cleary had once again locked him in. It unsettled him. It brought up memories he wished long gone. He took in deep breaths and worked at calming himself down, focusing on what might be her reasons. It could not be due to distrust. She had given him a set of the house keys, after all.

A loud knock startled him.

Maurice lowered himself to the door handle. He inched himself close to peer into the keyhole. Into this shaft of light, he could make out the stair landing ahead. Who had struck his door? His heart beating fast, his eye pressed against the keyhole, Maurice waited.

He became aware of an unnatural odour. A long blackened face flashed into view, obscuring the corridor. With the light blocked, the figure became indistinct even as it drew closer and closer still. Before Maurice could discern any shape or form, a large eye was thrust before him, at the opposite end of the keyhole. A jolt passed through him. He held his breath. The eye, a glittering orb of black and blue, with a swollen pupil, stared back at him. It was grotesque. It might have been an illusion brought upon by the darkness, but it gave the impression its owner was ill or had ingested a nefarious substance.

The rapping at the door resumed with vengeance. Maurice recoiled in fear. He knew not whether to feel terror or outrage. He dared not peer again through the keyhole.

Now the door shook on its hinges. He stepped back, confused. It sounded as if multiple beings stood on the other side, and together they hammered at the panel from different angles. It was infernal. It seemed to scream, "*I have seen you. I know you are here.*"

Horror-stricken, Maurice fled to his bed. He covered his head with the sheets, and shut his eyes tight. The sensation of being locked in and the uncanny feeling the noise stirred within him brought back memories of his Paris home. He wanted to yell out but when he finally found his voice, it was choked with fear, childlike. "Be gone! I shall speak to you in the morning!"

The noise ceased.

Maurice opened his eyes. He heard a heavy mass drag itself away. Then all fell quiet. He could not imagine who had visited him or why they would wish to do so. The bedside clock told him it was past midnight. He recalled that it had been about this time when he'd heard the rap at his door the night before. He settled into bed but for some time, his heart raced and he could not sleep.

He thought of the eye and the curious shape and form it had. It was a rare colour but he could pinpoint it with ease if he were to see it again. Tomorrow while he questioned the maids, he would be sure to match the eye with one of the residents of Alexandra Hall.

At long last, Maurice found sleep but it was far from restful. For when the dream came, it rose from a place of despair and brought him back to Paris. He found himself, sitting in his childhood home. There, he lived with a woman whose eyes he feared most of all. For hers were cruel and when he looked into them, he saw only that she wished to tear him apart.

Under the glow of a single candle whose weak flame only enhanced the misery in the room, Maurice the child sat upon a wooden stool, one tiny hand upon the kitchen table while the other held a spoon. His tear-filled eyes were riveted on the ceramic bowl in front of him.

In the bowl, in that cold soup, that opaque milky stew, he watched the numerous maggots crawl, and the bobbing flesh of a bloodshot eyeball.

"Eat it now, Maurice," came his mother's menacing voice. Maurice dared not look at her. He clutched at his spoon and stared, against his wishes, at the ghastly bowl.

But now, the wooden table seemed infinite, like a creature with a mind of its own. How it stretched and stretched, how its timber planks seemed to elongate to astounding proportions, taking the shape it wished. And down the far end of this unimaginably long table, there was she. Therese.

Maurice shook his head violently and pushed the bowl away. "*Maman.* I can't…" he sobbed.

A mistake. A mean glint lit Therese's eyes. She seemed to suddenly awaken. The long strands of dull hair which hung about her face, lifted, flying all about her. She stared at him with a vicious snarl. Tears ran down Maurice's cheeks. Then he blinked. For in an instant, his mother's traits had mingled with those of Mrs. Cleary's. The resulting monster was at once austere and seething, distant and deranged, the eyes, both blue and black. He blinked again, unsure of what he was seeing.

"Eat it!" hissed Therese from the other end of the table. The candle light flickered, and before Maurice knew it, her hands and bony knees were upon the table, and on all fours, she crawled towards him. She was all beast. Each of her movements was a violent thump against the wood that sent vibrations down the entire table. Thump, thump, thump.

She called out to him, "I will take you to the guillotine, if you are bad, Maurice!" She gave a terrifying laugh, and the words she spoke became inhuman sounds in her mouth. "The guillotine!" she sang. "The guillotine!" That word seemed to vibrate endlessly in her throat just as Therese galloped across the table like a vengeful demon.

As she drew near, little Maurice was crippled by such a dread that he dropped his spoon. Therese's triumphant laughter was an inhuman shriek. She was going to reach him very soon, and when she did...

By enchantment, the table lengthened and lengthened again, increasing the distance between Maurice and his hateful mother. How far it seemed to stretch as Therese's angular limbs crept forth, faster and faster still. Thump, thump, thump, against the wood. He could do it forever; he could make the table stretch so that she would never reach him.

In his bed, Maurice's entire body sweated and writhed. His head shook frantically on his pillow. Thump, thump, thump. Again, Therese drew closer, but he would not let her. He would not.

Thump, thump, thump. A noise rose from beneath Alexandra Hall like a deep echo of the thumping in Maurice's dream. For underneath the stairs, below the ground, where no light shone, a restless presence stirred in the dark.

Chapter 5

Wednesday

"Mrs. Cleary, I must remind you not to lock my bedroom door," began Maurice the following day as he sat on the veranda for breakfast.

He was struck by her response.

"I am merely protecting you," she snapped, with that self-righteous tone she employed for effect. "What should happen if you were to roam around and suffer some accident?"

He had not imagined that Gerard might be right about the housekeeper's questionable sanity. For a moment he stared back at her, lost for words.

"I understand you do not mean disrespect, Mrs. Cleary. However I feel that your fears are misplaced. I can take splendid care of myself. I do not need to have my door locked for me like a child. Please, if you could leave it alone. I would much prefer to sleep in a room where I can go outside at my own whim. Imagine if I were to accidentally set the room on fire. You would be grieved to find my body set ablaze before anyone could open the door."

As he spoke to the housekeeper, Maurice became aware, even before she responded, of his increasing heart rate. He had felt the same agitation in the past whenever his mother was angered and was about to speak. He instantly pushed away the memory.

Mrs. Cleary flashed him an angry look whose sudden energy startled him further.

"Have it your way," she said. "Whatever was I thinking?" Then no sooner had she uttered those words than her eyes took on a dark glow. "You think you have it all figured out, don't you? You believe I am imagining things? Mrs. Cleary is a raving fool. That poor woman." She recollected herself, but Maurice saw that she shook.

"What exactly are you protecting me from, Mrs. Cleary?" he asked, adding sugar to his tea.

"Sooner or later, Mr. Leroux, you shall see," she breathed, her voice lowered. "Don't say I did not warn you."

"Warn me about what? That Calista Nightingale has returned to Alexandra Hall as a ghost?" asked Maurice in a mocking tone.

She was startled. "Who…who told you this?"

"I am not at liberty to say. But your fears have not gone unnoticed by the rest of the staff."

"I'll not have the staff gossip about me," she muttered, visibly insulted.

"I would not go so far as to call it gossip. Needless to say, this notion of hauntings is far-fetched."

Mrs. Cleary glowered at him but said no more.

He ignored her outburst, content that from now on, that bedroom door would remain unlocked.

As he drank his tea, he noticed with a certain dismay that Mrs. Cleary's eyes were not only far too small, but also black. There was not a trace of the mingled blue he had glimpsed last night through the keyhole.

So then, if it were not the prying housekeeper, whose eye had he seen? Maurice concealed his confusion and continued to eat breakfast.

In the meantime, a transformation had taken place in Mrs. Cleary and the distress she had revealed earlier seemed gone. She now smiled at him in a manner she thought sweet and conciliatory. Maurice shuddered, for reasons he could not explain, save perhaps that Mrs. Cleary behaved like his mother. For a moment he was reminded of his dream.

"You must forgive me," said Mrs. Cleary, as though nothing had happened. She sat quietly, looking newly composed. Save for the pulsating jugular on her throat, there was no trace of an earlier outburst.

At last, having poured her tea, she declared, mouthing each word slowly:

"Things go…awry around here. You must remain watchful." She nodded to herself. "Very watchful."

She averted her eyes and sipped her tea.

Maurice buttered another slice of fresh bread and tried to bring the conversation to something concrete that was nearer to the purpose of his visit.

"Well it certainly appears that death follows this house. Is that what you meant when you spoke of awry things?" he asked.

"No. You don't understand." Her voice was cold, almost aloof. "When Mrs. Nightingale passed away, and while her husband still lived, that's when it all began. Things would go missing."

"What kind of things?" Maurice bit into his buttered bread.

"All sorts. Bobby pins, my brooch, sugar cubes… teaspoons. I used to have quite a collection in the kitchen closet. Now they are mostly gone."

Maurice drank his tea. He was ready to wave it all away as the ramblings of a lunatic.

A glint flashed in her eyes. "I'll show you now, if you like." She stood firmly. "Come with me."

He stood, a little reluctantly. They walked across the veranda, stepped silently through the house and towards the kitchen.

Gerard was absent. He had left the French doors wide open. Maurice intuited he might have gone out to smoke.

Mrs. Cleary led Maurice to a large glass and mahogany closet at the back of the kitchen. "See for yourself," she said, gesturing to the bottom shelf.

Maurice inspected the cabinet. Behind the glass panel, a collection of silver spoons hung upon a wooden board. But where there should have been others, the slots remained empty.

"Yes," he nodded, still not convinced. "I do see that half these silver spoons have gone missing."

"They did not just go missing. It was her. She took them!"

"Why would any…ghost… wish to possess these spoons? Mrs. Cleary, I don't see…"

"Because she's playing with us. When Gerard found Miss Vera after she died, he said there were spoons scattered along the staircase and in the entrance hall. Don't you see?" She eyed him intensely with those black pupils, waiting for him to acknowledge what to her was all too evident.

Maurice sighed. "No, Mrs. Cleary, I do not see. If anybody took these spoons it was a person of flesh and blood. Did you report these missing objects to Mr. Nightingale?"

She stifled a mocking laugh and stood upright. "One must never, never disturb Mr. Nightingale. And after his wife passed away, well, he was a changed man. I mean, why would I bother him with spoons? Of all things. He was an awfully busy man. He fixated on whatever project obsessed him. Nothing else mattered."

"What about the other maids?"

"I already searched their things. It was not the maids."

"Perhaps Mr. Nightingale himself took away those spoons," offered Maurice, tired of her games.

"He would not…"

"What about Alfred? Oh, that's right, I forgot. He is not permitted inside the house."

"Don't believe a word that man says. If he were so inclined to come inside, there'd be no one to stop him."

Maurice was intrigued. Here was Mrs. Cleary insinuating that Alfred could not be trusted. As he pondered over this, a loud clamour of pots and pans rose from the front end of the kitchen. Mrs. Cleary was violently startled by this noise. Her eyes doubled in size and she gasped. Maurice heard a door slam shut. The housekeeper wailed and clutched at her throat. She appeared to swoon, before suddenly gripping the back of a chair, trembling, her face ashen, her lips blue.

Maurice dashed to the front of the kitchen. Gerard was nowhere in sight. Seeing that the French doors were still opened, he wondered what door he had heard slam shut. Had someone been eavesdropping their conversation? He stepped out. The passage was clear, yet the small white Bolognese growled by the stairs.

"Willy! What are you doing here?" cried a young voice.

A maid emerged from the corridor. She reached for the dog and swept it up in her arms. "You know you are not supposed to be here," she chided, burying her face into its belly. Conscious of Maurice's gaze, she shuffled away.

Maurice studied the empty staircase and wondered why the dog had growled at it. He re-entered the kitchen to find Mrs. Cleary slumped on a chair.

"Would you like a glass of water, Mrs. Cleary?"

"Could you please?"

Maurice grabbed the pitcher on the table and poured her a drink.

Her voice rose behind him. "Do you believe in Greek mythology, Mr. Leroux?"

It was an odd question. He walked to the pump and refilled the pitcher. "I studied a little of it during my years at the Sorbonne," he answered. "I remember that I enjoyed it."

"Did you, now." She nodded to herself, as an unconvincing smile twisted her lips. "So you would know all about the story of Medusa?"

Maurice startled. "Medusa. Well, I remember some of it, yes."

She sipped her water, still gazing up at him with her little black eyes.

Maurice tried to remember. "Medusa… Well, let's see. She was a gorgon. Wasn't she? Why are you asking about Medusa?"

"Perhaps you should return to your native France before you find yourself face to face with something you might regret."

"Is that a warning, Mrs. Cleary?"

She did not reply. She finished drinking her water.

Maurice drew out a cigar from a case in his pocket. He lit it impatiently. "You're wasting my time, Mrs. Cleary."

"All I know, Mr. Leroux, is that there is something in this house." She stood upright. "I feel better now. As I said, things go awry around here. But we won't need to bear it for much longer. Once John Nightingale moves in, I'm sure he'll set things straight."

She made towards the doors.

Maurice reflected upon her grasp of Greek mythology.

"Wait a moment, please. Would you know a little Greek?" he asked.

Mrs. Cleary turned. Her face had softened.

"Only a little," she said, regretfully. "It was Mrs. Nightingale who taught me. We use to…speak a little. Why are you asking?"

Maurice thought back to the words on the tombstone.

"What does… *panta rhei* mean?"

A sly smile drew itself on her face.

"So you've seen her grave."

"Yes, I strolled past. I studied some Greek decades ago but forgot most of it. I thought you might know."

"Everything flows. *Panta rhei….* It means, *everything flows*. It was Calista's favorite saying. In her first years in Alexandra Hall, she liked to read Greek philosophy in the library upstairs. There is a longer version. Let's see… *Pánta khôreî kaì oudèn ménei."*

"Which means…"

"Everything flows, and nothing stands still."

Shannon

MAURICE looked forward to questioning three of the maids. The fourth had been appointed in the week after Sophie Murphy's death and it was his opinion that she would be too new to be of any help.

On Maurice's request, Gerard had prepared biscuits. He thrust a heaped platter into Maurice's hands.

"It's a traditional recipe. All homemade, with real butter. Not like those horrible things from Mr. Joseph Huntley's factory."

Maurice smiled. On his way to Alexandra Hall, he had spotted the new biscuit factory in Reading Town. "Thank you, Gerard. This is perfect."

"Mrs. Cleary has already brought the drinks upstairs."

Maurice nodded. As he headed up to the study, passing the maids in the entrance hall, he sensed their fearful glances upon him.

Seated in Aaron's study, he began his first interview with the blue-eyed redhead whom Mrs. Cleary had introduced as Shannon O'Sullivan. As she sat down, the first thing Maurice noticed was her eyes, and he knew Shannon had not rapped at his door.

In her mid-twenties, she had been here as long as Alexandra Hall stood, and had even waited on guests at the Nightingales' wedding.

She answered without fuss while Maurice took notes. No, she'd not seen anything suspect on the night of Sophie Murphy's death. She was asleep. Mrs. Cleary had found Sophie lying by the stairs. Weeks later, she'd heard Gerard shout out upon discovering Miss Nightingale's body. In both cases, Shannon had run to the grand staircase like everyone else.

Had Vera Nightingale welcomed any guests during her stay? No. Was there any signs of an intruder at Alexandra Hall on that night? No. It was a night as ordinary as the one before it and the one previous to that.

"And did you get along with Sophie?" asked Maurice.

"I suppose so. As I told the police, she was the sort of girl to get along with everyone. She was lively. She could make you feel like you were her best friend."

"Everyone's best friend. I see. So…no arguments?"

"I overheard something but…it was nothing." Shannon shrugged.

Maurice sensed her reticence. He had already sensed that Shannon was keen to remain on good terms with the housekeeper at any cost. "Miss O'Sullivan, what you heard might be important. And be assured that nothing you tell me will leave this room. You have my word."

"Well, I heard Sophie and Mrs. Cleary one day. It sounded like they were having a row."

"When was this?"

"Maybe two months before Sophie died. It was to be expected, really. Mrs. Cleary was awfully upset when Mr. and Mrs. Nightingale passed away. Sophie was her usual self. She often left work unfinished and we all had to pick up after her."

"What were they arguing about on that occasion?"

"I couldn't hear. I do remember Sophie shouting at Mrs. Cleary. She was saying something like, 'you won't get away with it, Louise.' But I must not have heard properly."

"Why do you say that?"

"Mrs. Cleary's name is Jane, not Louise. Besides, I can't say Sophie was bothered by that argument at all. Much to the contrary. She was very happy. Right up until she died."

"You're telling me she was in high spirits before she died? Why? Did she tell you anything?"

"Did she ever! We were all treated to her airs. She was mighty proud of herself, prancing around like a queen. She gloated about having come upon some money and said she was going to leave Berkshire to live in London. She'd given her notice, you know."

"I see. I did not know that." He had noted Shannon's fondness for gossip and the envy in her voice. And something else: Shannon was ambitious.

"Tell me, Miss O'Sullivan. Why do you think Mrs. Cleary would believe this house to be haunted? Don't you find this odd?"

Shannon looked uncertain. She squirmed in her chair.

"Why would it be odd?" she asked.

"Come now, don't you find it convenient?" He knew Mrs. Cleary had been in London at the time of Vera Nightingale's murder and was less of a suspect. But he wondered if Shannon might take the bait, and turn against the housekeeper.

He was surprised by her response. A frown marred Shannon's freckled forehead.

"There is something in this house, Mr. Leroux," she warned. "Everyone, save for Mary and Gerard has felt it. Well, the new girl hasn't, given she's only new. But it won't take much longer for her to see it. Even Miss Vera was afraid."

"How would you know what Vera Nightingale felt?"

"I attended to her room on the nights before she died. I'm quite sure she sensed something in the house."

"Did she tell you anything?"

"Well the nights before, she kept asking questions. Things like, are you certain the doors are properly locked? Then she made me go downstairs near the servant quarters and she'd tug at the bell cordons in her room to ensure I could hear her ring. She was terrified the bell might not work. It wasn't just her incessant questions. I caught her staring around her room like she might find something hiding there."

"Are you telling me Vera Nightingale was troubled by a presence she had seen in the house previously?"

"I don't just think it, Mr. Leroux. I know it. She was afraid."

"Why was she not in her room on the night she died?"

"Well, she was at the start. I'd brought her a bed warmer to heat up her sheets and she told me she'd not stay in her room that night. She preferred to remain in the parlour. I didn't think it was a good idea but she looked so frightened, and she claimed she couldn't remain a moment longer in that bedroom."

Maurice took note. "Anyone else aside from you know that she was in the parlour that night?"

"I don't think so." She paused. Her voice darkened, "I say, Mr. Leroux, it astounds me you've not noticed a thing yourself. Don't you feel even a tad disturbed by the sound of that fountain at night?"

"I hadn't noticed the sound."

"It drove Miss Vera crazy. Earlier in the year, she asked for it to be turned off but Mr. Nightingale said no. He wanted it on all the time."

"It's never been turned off?"

"Never. For as long as I've been here, Alfred feeds the boiler with coal." She was dreamy for a moment. "A real shame," she added. "Nobody else gets to visit Alexandra Hall to admire it. There's really no point to it at all."

"Perhaps Mr. Nightingale ordered this fountain as a gift to his wife," dismissed Maurice.

"Not that I remember. It was Mr. Nightingale who was awfully pleased with it. Like I said, he wanted it on at all times."

Maurice reflected on those words, then shifted the conversation back to his case. "Is there anything else you think I should know, Miss O'Sullivan? About the murders in this house."

Shannon glanced back nervously at the study door. "I'm not sure I should tell you this… I wouldn't want, you know, Mrs. Cleary to hear," she whispered.

"I'm certain that no one will hear. The door is shut. Please go on."

"Well to be perfectly frank, Mr. Leroux, I've had a bad feeling in this house long before anything happened to Sophie Murphy or

Miss Vera Nightingale. Take Mrs. Nightingale for instance…" She lowered her voice. "She was mostly quietly spoken and a demure sort of lady. But around two years before she passed away, she changed an awful lot. I'd never seen her like that."

"How do you mean?"

"Well, mostly temper. Like I couldn't do nothing right. She never complained about me to Mrs. Cleary, thank goodness, but she was bitter and unhappy with everything."

"What exactly did she die of?" asked Maurice, wanting to hear it from Shannon's lips.

"Didn't they tell you? She had a fever. And…" she bit her lip. "Months before, I'd seen her brooding at Mr. Nightingale at dinner and I'm not deaf, I knew there was something off between them. She used to smile a lot when they first got married. She gave us kindly encouragements and often we'd hop on the carriage with her and she'd buy us ribbons and girlie things in Reading Town. But in the last year or so, I noticed that she'd become cold with everyone."

"How would you know this?"

"Well… She no longer went out to the boutiques in town. She'd lock herself up in her room and see no one for days. And I caught her many times at dinner avoiding Mr. Nightingale's eyes, like…I don't know… I suppose, almost like she was afraid of him, or something."

"Married couples argue and fall at odds with each other at times. Perhaps the Nightingales had a disagreement."

"Well yes, and no," cut in Shannon, raising her voice. "If they had a disagreement, it would have ended. But no, it's not quite the same. She was, I'm quite sure, afraid of him. I don't see why. He was so nice."

A long shadow passed underneath the study door. Maurice paused. Was Mrs. Cleary listening in? He waited until the shadow faded away.

Maurice cleared his throat. "Afraid of her husband? Well, that's a hasty judgment, *mademoiselle*. Perhaps she was upset at him. It happens."

Miss O'Sullivan scowled and shook her head.

"But they worked together, didn't they?" insisted Maurice, conscious of the impatience on Shannon's face. For an instant, he wondered if the maid's temper could have led her to commit murder. "Husband and wife," he continued. "Quite an unusual pairing. They were working on some project. So surely they must have remained on cordial terms. That's what Mrs. Cleary told me. An important project of some kind…"

"Oh, yes. That they did. Disappear into the cellar almost every day… Such a long day. When she'd come out she was always tired. I don't think she fancied working very much. Come to think of it, maybe that's what did it." Her voice had trailed off and she fell silent.

Maurice caught her distant gaze.

"What's that you were saying, Miss O'Sullivan?"

"Well I can't be sure," she shrugged. "But my honest feeling is she dreaded going down there…you know, in the cellar."

Maurice leaned forward in his chair. He tried to suppress the excitement in his voice. "What's into the cellar?"

Shannon's eyes widened in alarm. "I've never been there myself. Mr. Nightingale was very strict that none of us should go down there."

Maurice nodded. "Then I shall ask Mrs. Cleary to take me there," he said. He jotted down a few notes. He had to ascertain the nature of Aaron Nightingale's work. "Was there anything else you wanted to share, Miss O'Sullivan? Something you think will add to my investigation." He had just noted a jagged scar on her right hand. It was recent, perhaps only a few years old.

She looked suddenly uncomfortable and concealed her hands. She stared at him. "I'm surprised you've not noticed the haunting in Alexandra Hall," she confided. Her voice was thick with warning.

Maurice suspected that Miss O'Sullivan belonged to that class of impressionable unmarried women who derived a certain mystical pride from her intimacy with supernatural happenings.

"No, nothing of the kind. The idea that in some shape or form, Calista Nightingale haunts this house, is to me highly implausible."

Shannon had grown quite pale. She shook her head violently. "I've seen it, Mr. Leroux. You should ask Ellen. Like me, she will not forget what she saw."

"Thank you, Miss O'Sullivan. I will call on you if I need anything else. You may go, now. Please call in Ellen."

Ellen

ELLEN was a short brunette with equally brown eyes and a quiet manner. Hanging round her neck was a tiny Christian cross which she often clutched nervously.

She was eighteen but appeared younger due to her frail and slightly malnourished frame. Never mind the colour of her eyes, thought Maurice, so unlike those he had glimpsed through the keyhole. He was disappointed. Whose eye had he seen last night?

He retrieved a case from his pocket, found a cigar and lit it. This promised to be a long day.

"Would you like some biscuits, Ellen?" Maurice pushed the plate of rich shortbreads in front of the young maid.

She blushed and reached for the buttery treat.

"Thank you, Mr. Leroux."

"I had Gerard make these. There's a glass of milk here also if you feel like something to drink."

"Thank you, sir."

He watched as Ellen took tiny bites of her buttery biscuit and tried instantly to brush away any stray crumbs. The girl was highly self-conscious. He wondered at first whether it might be an act.

"What do you remember of Sophie Murphy before she died?"

"I think…she was fine, sir."

"Did she seem upset to you?"

"No, sir."

"Did she seem on good terms with everyone?"

"Yes. She was cheerful. She showed us her new hat."

"A new hat?"

"Yes. She bought it from Reading Town. An expensive one, sir. Shannon even said she was surprised Sophie could afford that sort of hat."

"I see. Thank you, Ellen. Let's talk about Miss Vera Nightingale now. Did you see or hear anything on the night of Vera Nightingale's murder?"

Ellen shook her head.

"Nothing, sir. I was in bed. Shannon took care of Miss Nightingale that night. The rest of us were asleep."

"Did she see any friends or anyone else the day she died?"

"I don't think so."

"Where was Mrs. Cleary on that day?" He wanted to know whether Ellen would confirm what Gerard had told him.

"Mrs. Cleary had gone, sir."

"Where to?"

"I saw her take the spare carriage and ride off herself. To London, I think it was."

Maurice nodded. The vision of the thin housekeeper travelling alone and manning horses startled him somewhat. Perhaps Mrs. Cleary was stronger than he had assumed. "So Mrs. Cleary returned the next morning, is that right?"

"No, much later. She was gone for two whole days. She was back in the evening after we'd found Miss Vera."

"What about the gardener? Shannon said Miss Vera disliked the noise from the fountain. Perhaps she spoke to the gardener the day before she died. Think back. Try to remember."

"She might have, sir. Alfred came in that day."

Maurice blinked. "Alfred was inside the house?"

Ellen blushed profusely.

"Yes, sir. He came in through the servant quarters. He wasn't inside the house for long. Shannon saw him waiting for Miss Vera. She pestered him to leave."

"And then what happened?"

"He said he only wanted to talk to Miss Vera. He argued a bit and got cross."

"He got cross, did he?"

Ellen lowered her gaze and nodded.

She had now finished her biscuit. She clutched her hands so hard together that the white of her knuckles showed.

Maurice knew he had to make the young maid feel more at ease.

"How long have you been at Alexandra Hall, Ellen?"

"Two years sir. I came not long after the famine began."

Maurice tilted his head. "The famine?"

"Oh yes, sir. In Ireland."

"The famine in Ireland, I see. That's disheartening. I've learnt it has carried on for quite some time now. You must be so glad you are here in Alexandra Hall, then."

Ellen smiled timidly. "Oh, yes. Mr. Nightingale was awfully nice to take me in. He was a kind man. So sad to have him pass. And so quickly after his wife."

"So you like it here, in Alexandra Hall?" asked Maurice, watching keenly for her reaction.

Ellen's eyes looked sideways.

"I do an awful lot. Except that…"

"Except what? Do you girls argue with Alfred often?"

Ellen shook her head. She reached for the glass of milk before her and drank.

"Does Alfred come into the house often? What about that delivery boy?"

"He's fine, sir. It's not that."

"What is it, then?"

"Sometimes…I am afraid," she said at last, still holding the glass in both hands as though it were a shield and she felt safer with the object in her hands. "I only told Shannon of it. I've not told Mrs. Cleary, sir. I wouldn't want to sound silly and lose my job. You see, I can't go back home because of the famine. My parents can't take me."

The look of distress in her eyes reminded Maurice of the poverty he had seen in the streets of Paris. "I won't tell a soul. I promise. What are you afraid of?"

"Oh dear, no. It is too ungodly for me to speak of it. I cannot. I fear that I might go to hell if I even think of it."

In saying this, she clutched tight at her cross as though it might protect her.

Maurice was unsettled. A cloud of smoke thickened around him as he puffed at his cigar.

Whenever he interrogated people, silence was his ally. Most people were discomforted by silence and with little coercion, they spoke up to fill it. Sometimes they said irrelevant things and Maurice would then edge them in the right direction until they disclosed useful information. With the quietly spoken Ellen though, silence had no effect.

"Have you seen a ghost, Ellen?" he blurted.

Ellen stared back at him. A flash of recognition stamped upon her face.

"I…I don't know," she said. "I saw something, yes."

"Is it a person?" asked Maurice, more and more dubious.

"I don't know. I've had it enter my room once. I was so afraid that I closed my eyes."

"When was this?"

"The night after Sophie Murphy passed away."

"And what happened?"

"I was lying still in my bed. Mary, the girl I sleep with, was fast asleep. But Willy, her little dog began to bark. It woke me. So I opened my eyes and…it was too dark, I couldn't see anything. But something grabbed my arm…"

"Did you have a look at it?"

She shook her head. "I couldn't. Please sir, I don't want Mrs. Cleary to find out what I said. I don't want to make a fuss. I know what happens to us if we make a fuss. The government, they sent my brother to an Australian penal colony. I've no one else in London, now."

Maurice had heard of Irish outlaws being transported on British convict ships. Some of these poor souls were sent away for the pettiest crimes.

"I'm sorry to hear of your brother. It must have been hard for you."

"He didn't mean to steal. He only wanted to get a warm coat for me. We'd no money. We're not bad people, Mr. Leroux. He just didn't want to see me cold. But they called him a thief and sent him to Australia."

Ellen was on the verge of tears.

"That's quite alright. I don't think for a moment that you're a bad person, Ellen. I'm sorry to hear of your brother's fate. Listen, you've done nothing wrong. We don't need to tell Mrs. Cleary anything you've shared with me. I promise you. Now tell me again. Are you sure you didn't see anyone in the room that night? It might have been someone else that grabbed your arm. Perhaps it was Alfred? Or even Gerard?"

"Oh no, sir. Mr. O'Malley wouldn't. And it was not Alfred. It felt... repulsive and so cold and... At first, I struggled but it kept holding on to my arm. It wouldn't let go. I shut my eyes, wishing it to go away. I thought perhaps it would kill me. And then all of a sudden, Willy stopped barking. Then everything went quiet. I felt it slide off my arm and then..."

"What?"

"I heard the door shut. When I opened my eyes, it had gone."

"And you didn't see anything?"

"Not this time."

"There was another time?"

Ellen's lips were quivering.

Maurice felt far from France. How deeply he seemed to have sunken into the superstitious English countryside. Ellen was so malnourished that she had reached a state of hysteria. He'd often seen delusions of the sort back home.

"I'm sure it was nothing, then" waved Maurice, hoping she would reveal more. "Nothing to be afraid of."

Ellen looked pale. Her voice was hoarse as she spoke up. "There was, sir. About a month ago. I'd taken Willy for a walk by the road. I returned to the house. I looked up and..."

"And what?"

"I saw a greyish face by the window. It was in Mrs. Nightingale's bedroom. It was...horrible."

Maurice frowned. "You saw a face? Well, it might have been Mrs. Cleary's."

"Oh no, sir. Mr. Nightingale had that room locked up since his wife died. Besides, it was not that kind of face."

"Well what sort of face was it, then?"

"Something quite evil. Wrinkled and dark. It was too far so I couldn't see it very well. I mean, yes, it had eyes but... it looked nothing like you or me. I can't... I can't describe it..."

She reached for the glass of milk and gulped it down.

Maurice had been frustrated up to the point where Ellen described the face in Calista's bedroom. He thought back to Mrs. Cleary's own admission. Two women in the house, who seemingly had never revealed their fears to each other, had each confided having seen a ghostly apparition in the house.

Maurice crushed the last of his cigar in the ashtray and stared at his notes. Something about Ellen's account had drained him.

"Don't concern yourself, Ellen. I won't tell anyone."

"Can I go, sir?"

"Yes, you may. Please send Mary through."

Mary

MAURICE sat alone in the study, drinking tea. He was perplexed to realise that none of the staff he had so far spoken to and who slept at Alexandra Hall possessed the large black and blue eye he had seen through the keyhole overnight. This left Mary and the new maid. Though he could not imagine that the new girl would have dared to come knocking at his door in the middle of the night.

The study door opened and Mrs. Cleary marched in. "Mr. Leroux," she began. "There is something else I should have mentioned."

"What is it?" said Maurice, looking up.

"It's about Mary, the maid you've asked to speak to."

"Yes, please bring her in."

"Well I think you ought to know a little bit about her."

Maurice took out a file he'd been given by Mr. Wilson and summarised it as he read. "Mary is an orphan. She arrived at Alexandra Hall shortly after your appointment. From the information I have been given, the young girl suffers from a sleep condition and the presence of the dog ensures she does not harm herself while sleepwalking. I believe it says here that she's also a far removed cousin under your charge. Was there anything else Mrs. Cleary?"

The housekeeper eyed him sternly.

"You're well informed," she replied. "But that is not why I wished to speak with you."

She neared the desk and lowered her voice. "She's a simpleton. Do please be careful how you speak with her. And don't let the girl lead you astray. Mary is easily impressed. She confuses everything and makes things up."

Mrs. Cleary went on to describe Mary's limitations. At fifteen, Mary's tasks consisted in folding clothes and collecting dirty linen, sweeping and mopping the floors, and running errands around the house for Mrs. Cleary.

"You must understand," continued Mrs. Cleary, "I see to it that her tasks are of a less urgent nature. Mary cannot not do anything fast. She's not a reliable sort. If you get my meaning."

"Very well, Mrs. Cleary. Please show her in."

It could have been his imagination but he glimpsed a brief annoyance in the housekeeper's eyes as she left the study.

Shortly after, Maurice heard barking as Mary walked upstairs. She dawdled like a much younger girl along the corridor, her white Bolognese tagging along behind her.

As Mary sat across from Maurice, she lifted the dog to her lap and began to swing her legs happily. She was a little plump and like Ellen, her eyes were brown, almost hazel.

Maurice noted this with disappointment. It appeared it was not Mary who, whether by intention or through a sleepwalking trance, had hammered his bedroom door last night. Then who was it?

Growing more perplexed, he attempted to recall the gardener's eye colour. He would have to talk to him again and see for himself but he was certain his eyes were brown.

Meanwhile, Mary had already helped herself to shortbreads. She piled three on her lap and left the plate empty. She began to hum a song as she spoke to Willy in a maternal voice.

"You be a good boy today, Willy. A good boy!" she cooed in between the melody.

"Good morning. It's Mary, is it?" began Maurice.

She nodded. She seemed suddenly self-conscious.

"What do you think happened to Sophie Murphy? We haven't seen her around here for a while," said Maurice, his pencil in hand.

"Sophie was a lovely girl. She would give me caramels."

"Caramels, that's nice."

"She died."

Maurice flinched at Mary's bluntness.

"That's tragic news. I'm sorry to hear of it."

He thought for a moment.

"Do you remember what you were doing on the day she died?" he asked.

"Hmm… dusting mostly." She bit into another biscuit.

Maurice dreaded that all this questioning might grow painful due to Mary's limited understanding.

"Do you remember anything at all on the day when she died? Or perhaps, afterwards?" he asked.

"No."

The insouciant expression on her face jarred Maurice.

"Alright. What about Miss Vera Nightingale?"

Mary stifled a giggle and bit her lip.

"What's so funny?" asked Maurice.

"She died too."

"That's correct."

Mary was still grinning.

"Why did you laugh, Mary?"

"Because I know how she died," she replied matter-of-factly.

Maurice frowned. "You…think you saw something?"

To his astonishment, Mary shook her head fast.

"I didn't see anything! I promise!" she protested with pleading eyes. Her expression had turned fearful.

"You just said before, that you think you know how Miss Vera Nightingale died?"

To his dismay, Mary turned all her attention to Willy, brushing the dog's hair with an unsettling nonchalance.

"Oh, Miss Vera. Sweet auntie Vera. She didn't much like Willy. And Willy didn't much like her. Yes, I told you the right thing, Mr. Leroux, I did. I remember it all now," she said with a seriousness that bordered on comical. "I think Miss Vera was smothered with a pillow."

"Smothered with a pillow?"

"It would make perfect sense, don't you think?" said Mary with a cheer.

"Why would you say that, Mary?"

Mary did not respond. Instead, she took a mouthful of shortbread biscuit. The room soon filled with her loud chewing noises.

For an instant, Maurice had a vision of Alfred creeping inside the house and smothering Vera with a cushion from the parlour. The absurd image vanished.

It took some time before he could formulate easily understood questions that Mary could then comprehend, but he eventually got there. He discovered nothing more.

"Willy likes you, Mr. Leroux," Mary said at last. Her voice echoed the relief Maurice felt knowing the interview had terminated.

"Well I'm glad to hear that. You've always had this dog, I hear?"

Mary nodded with a smile. Maurice could not shake the sentiment this stirred. Had Mary's sudden sense of peace arisen because her questioning had ended? If so, what was she hiding? And did she even understand its meaning?

"Does Willy help you with house tasks, Mary?" asked Maurice, more and more disturbed by the young woman's newly found joy.

Mary abandoned herself to a burst of enthusiasm he had not expected. "Oh yes!" she chirped. "He's such a good dog. He follows me wherever I go. He's never far away. We like each other very much. He even helped Mr. Nightingale."

"He did, did he? What a clever dog."

"Oh, but he was very naughty one day. He disappeared for a whole day. Didn't you, Willy?"

Willy had now taken to bouncing joyfully on her lap. It stood on its back paws and nuzzled against Mary's neck. For the first time, Maurice noted several purple bruises on the girl's throat.

"Oh, you silly thing. You were so naughty," she chided.

And then Mary's youthful expression was suddenly torn from her face and Maurice witnessed an uncanny transformation. With her lips pinched tight, Mary now looked frightfully like Mrs. Cleary. Even the tone of her voice rose, and before Maurice could understand it, Mary's upper lip twitched and she began to yell at her dog. "Oh, you were nasty that day. We told you never to go into the cellar. And you wouldn't listen! You were bad, Willy!"

Outside the room, Maurice heard the housekeeper's hurried footsteps. The study door flew open. Her face twisted in a rage,

Mrs. Cleary burst in and glowered at Mary, but the young girl saw nothing and continued to scold her dog in a loud voice.

"What a mean dog you were, Willy! Never do it again! Never, never go back to the cellar!" Mary all but screamed at her pet, seizing the dog's front paws and forcing it to face her.

Mrs. Cleary's voice rose above the maid's hysterics. "Enough!"

Mary's mouth snapped shut and she jerked back so violently against her chair that Willy leapt from her lap and niched itself between Maurice's legs, under the desk.

Mary looked greatly alarmed. Mrs. Cleary turned to Maurice.

"Mr. Leroux, are you finished?" she asked icily.

"I believe I am," nodded Maurice.

"Good."

She then looked upon Mary with a hardened gaze. "Return to your tasks, miss."

Mary stood sheepishly. "Well, I should be getting on with my chores, then," she said.

"Not another word. Be gone," hissed Mrs. Cleary.

As Mary disappeared with Willy closely in tow, Maurice cleared his throat.

"I can assure you that she was quite harmless."

"Nonsense. That girl is full of ideas. She's an embarrassment."

"Not at all. You were unnecessarily cross with her. She was only distressed at Willy for some past incident, that's all."

Mrs. Cleary's nostrils flared. "An incident?"

"Yes, something about Willy accessing the cellar."

Maurice fixed Mrs. Cleary, stressing the word, cellar.

"A figment of her imagination. As I've made perfectly clear, Mary is unreliable at best. She confuses everything."

"That may be so, Mrs. Cleary, but the cellar is no figment of anyone's imagination. It exists. And I intend to have a look inside it. I will need you to show me where it is."

Mrs. Cleary looked shaken. Her assurance lessened.

"The cellar…but… has Mr. Wilson not told you?"

"Told me what?"

"Mr. Nightingale made it perfectly clear in his will that we are barred from the cellar for at least six months. Mr. Wilson read the will back in August. Everyone was present. I am afraid it might not be until February until you can enter. What a pity, as I'm sure you'll have returned to France by then."

She almost smiled at those last words.

"Mrs. Cleary, that is all fascinating. But would you believe that Mr. Wilson also wrote me a letter, upon my appointment, and which I have here." He retrieved a stamped note from his leather folder and brandished it in front of the housekeeper. "It says, right here, that Inspector Leroux should have access to every room in Alexandra Hall if it is to further his investigation. Now I don't care what Mr. Nightingale stipulated in his will. That was then. This is now."

Mrs. Cleary pursed her lips and stared at the signed attestation. She looked furious but fought to not let it show. Instead Maurice witnessed that all too familiar pulsating throat as the housekeeper's cheeks reddened.

"Well that's unfortunate, Mr. Leroux," she said at last. "You see, I do not have the key to the cellar."

"You do not?"

"I've never had it." She stiffened, proud to have had the last word. "It seems Mr. Wilson might have kept that key, after all. I imagine he would. Now, if you'll excuse me, I have chores to take care of."

Maurice knew the housekeeper was lying. He remembered the lone key Mrs. Cleary had kept with her when she'd shared the set with him. His intuition told him it was the key to the cellar. Why would Mrs. Cleary lie?

He had to find that cellar. He knew he could not rest nor finalise his investigation until he had visited the place where Aaron worked.

For the rest of the afternoon, Maurice pondered at the notes he'd written down in his journal along the course of his questioning.

Aside from his growing mistrust of Alfred and the deluded belief shared by Mrs. Cleary, Shannon and Ellen that the house was haunted, he only had one lead: Sophie Murphy's newly found happiness. He had observed Shannon's industrious manner yesterday. Could she have been riled by Sophie's relative ease and carefree ways? The way she had spoken of her lavish hat...

Had Shannon murdered Sophie? One temper outburst was all it would have taken for Shannon to fly into a rage and push Sophie down the stairs, or even club her. She had it in her.

Mary's behaviour also disturbed him. Maurice had never met a fifteen-year-old who behaved like a child of eight. Yet, for all of Mary's mind lapses, he was not convinced the girl invented. In fact Maurice, who in France had often been called upon to interrogate mistreated children, had felt that rather than make things up, as Mrs. Cleary accused her of doing, Mary had remembered something distressing, something so abominable that she dared not speak of it. Instead she'd diverted her unpleasant thoughts towards Willy.

What if Mary knew something? Worse. What if she had been about to reveal something that Mrs. Cleary wished to keep hidden. But what?

Something else troubled Maurice: the instant in which Mary's features had altered to resemble those of Mrs. Cleary. He could not say why, but it bothered him.

The afternoon saw him burdened by a growing disappointment. Over the course of the interviews, he felt he was no nearer to the truth about Alexandra Hall's murderer. And yet, he thought, four deaths in one year could not result from a series of accidents. Still deep in thought, and sitting at Aaron's desk, he toyed with the Aristotle bust. He wondered why there had been so much secrecy around the cellar. What had Aaron and Calista been up to prior to their deaths?

Overwhelmed by unknowns, he turned to the bookcase, ran a finger across the science volumes without a sense of where to begin. Finding one written by a certain Cuvier, he pulled it out, flicked through it, shook his head, and then returned it to its place.

Feeling increasingly frustrated, Maurice rose and left the study. He rushed downstairs. Surely he could find that cellar himself if he wished it. It would not be too difficult. While he felt certain he'd opened every door in the house and peered into every room, he might have missed one. Unless…

As Maurice pushed open the double glass doors of the entrance hall, Willy bounced along behind him. The Bolognese wagged its tail happily, and its little paws seemed to gallop, if only to keep up with Maurice's determined stride.

Oblivious to the dog's presence, Maurice paced the veranda. Perhaps there was an external door he'd not noticed earlier. If he circled the house, he was bound to discover the entrance to this mysterious cellar.

He ventured first towards the mosaic fountain. Still trotting alongside him, Willy barked for attention. Maurice smiled and picked him up. He was increasingly amused by the dog.

"And what are you up to, little one? Oh, I see. You want to take a closer look at the fountain. Here you go." He lifted Willy to his chest and stood by the crystal clear pool. Water roared overhead gushing out of the stone fish's mouth. Safe in Maurice's arms, Willy emitted a contented bark. It gazed into the pond, as though fascinated by the mosaics and their vivid portrait of sea creatures swimming in the waters.

Still holding Willy, Maurice examined his surroundings. As he had noted the day before, there was an underground set of steps but it only led to a boiler.

He resumed his stroll, scrutinising every part of the house's walls for a hidden entrance or a nearby trapdoor.

Maurice had now reached the other lateral side of the house without finding any sign of a cellar. Where was it? In his arms, Willy had settled and now rested its head in the nook of Maurice's shoulder. After a fruitless search, Maurice reached the veranda.

"*Alors, mon petit bonhomme, on fait la sieste?*" he asked, half-laughing. The dog seemed to be taking a nap against him. "Shouldn't you be with Mary? Where have you left her?"

Indeed, it was strange. Where was the young maid?

Before he had a chance to ponder over this, the glass doors opened and a sullen Mary stepped outside. In silence, she reached for Willy.

"We were just taking a walk," said Maurice, handing over the Bolognese. Mary did not answer. She cradled Willy in her arms, averting her gaze. Her eyes were swollen red. She looked as though she had been crying. Without a word, she re-entered the house.

Madeleine

AFTER dinner, Maurice took the liberty to speak with Gerard, if only to complement him on his delicious roast. While Gerard blushed and muttered thanks, Maurice noted, much to his disappointment that the cook had hazel eyes.

The discovery further depressed him. Between the housemaids' supernatural ramblings, Mary's confusing statements and the mysterious eye that he could not identify, nothing made sense.

Maurice climbed upstairs and after freshening up with the clean water Ellen had brought to his room, he took a book from Aaron's study, and returned downstairs with his journal to sit in the parlour. Relieved to find himself in more spacious surrounds where the walls did not cloy at him, he now sat by the roar of the fire.

He'd been reviewing his notes for half an hour when a slender girl with her black hair tied in a bun suddenly appeared before him. Fetching as she seemed in her maid outfit, she startled Maurice.

He recognised her as the maid who had lingered at the breakfast table on his first morning at Alexandra Hall. She had sneaked into the parlour, unnoticed, like a cat. All feline, there was a defiance in her manner. She walked as though flaunting that she went without her white bonnet, unlike the other maids.

With a daring glint in her eyes and a slight swing in her hips, she passed right by his armchair.

"Solved any mysteries today?" she asked. She began to dust the mantelpiece, though each of her movements was an act to pre-empt any sudden appearance by Mrs. Cleary.

"No. As a matter fact, I haven't." Maurice put away his journal and opened the large book on his lap.

"Well, obviously. Sitting there, idling in your comfortable chair. Hardly the manner of a proper French detective."

Maurice was astounded by her boldness.

"Do you have some work to do, Miss…?"

"Madeleine." She smiled. "Oh, I'm sorry, have we not met?" she asked, in an audacious tone.

"Miss Madeleine, no, I don't believe we've properly met."

"Well, Mr. Leroux, given you've bothered to speak with everyone in this house except for me, it is hardly surprising. Do they not teach you manners in your country?"

Maurice stammered. "I…Well, I did not think it pertinent to the case."

"Suit yourself, then. And what have you learnt today, Mr. Leroux?" Unlike all the other maids in the household, who spoke with an Irish lilt, Madeleine had a decidedly English accent but right now, she rolled the r of his surname in a flirtatious manner.

"I do not wish to discuss it. When I work on a case, I like to keep things to myself."

"That's a sensible approach," she said, turning towards him, just long enough for Maurice to ascertain that her large doe eyes were a deep green and very unlike the eye he had seen through the keyhole.

"What are you ogling at?" she asked, catching hold of his stare.

"Given you are here," said Maurice, "what can you tell me about this place? I'm beginning to think everyone believes it is either haunted or that something out of the ordinary is going on."

"Oh, you would like to know what I think. Well that's a first. Nobody ever asks my opinion. After all, I'm the new girl, right?" She lowered her voice to a whisper. "Well to be clear, let me tell you that a certain housekeeper is intoxicated out of her mind." She gave a quiet cackle.

Maurice looked disapprovingly in her direction. "That's hardly…ladylike of you…"

"But it's true, though," she whispered. "Don't be fooled by the stiff act. Oh, I've seen what she gets up to. Saw it on my first day. You just sit right there in your armchair and you'll see it too. Be ready for a surprise with that one. She even sleeps with her eyes open. I ain't joking. It's frightening to see. And…" She interrupted her cleaning performance, having just registered his previous words. "Ladylike? Did you say, ladylike? Who do you take me for? Mr. Leroux, let's talk seriously. What do I have to lose? I know they won't keep me. T'was in the terms of appointment. Rushed affair, if ever I'd seen one. Let's see, what was it…? You, young lady, will be replacing Sophie Murphy until we find somebody else," she added, superbly mimicking Mrs. Cleary's manner of speech. "Besides, what do I care? I'm only here for a couple of months, then I'll be off to London to be an actress."

Maurice lifted an eyebrow. "You wish to become an actress?"

"That surprises you? I've got a good memory, I'll have you know. I can remember entire passages from Shakespeare. I've a boyfriend in Reading who just got a job making theater sets. He promised he would take me. Better than wasting hours in a mad house. I just can't imagine Aaron Nightingale was any good in bed. The man gives me the creeps. Dead or not."

"Why do you say that?"

"What? About Mr. Nightingale?"

"Why do you say it is a mad house?"

"Oh." She brought her voice down to a tone that was close to sinister. "Wait and see."

Before he could protest, she darted near him and brushed her dress against his knee. "What are you reading, there? Let me have a look." She reached for the cover and tilted the volume so that she could appraise its title. "Did you just help yourself to any books you pleased? Quite the arrogant French, aren't you? My, *The Animal Kingdom*. You think you're quite clever." She gave him a saucy smile.

"Whatever will help me to understand the mysterious owner of this mad house," protested Maurice, crossing his legs to avoid bodily contact with Madeleine.

"I tried that trick once. On my second day here, I thought it might be nice to borrow a book. Mrs. Cleary got cross with me first thing once she knew of it. She has eyes called Shannon in the back of her head. I've been mostly well-behaved since."

She glanced again at the book's cover. "Seventh book from the right, row three," she quipped.

"What?"

"Seventh book from the right, row three of the bookcase. That's where you found it, didn't you? In Mr. Nightingale's study? That man must have been awfully boring. It didn't take me any time to remember his entire bookcase. I mean how many science books can one wish to read?"

"You remembered every book's position in that room?"

She stared back at him. "Try me."

"I'm astounded. You do have a good memory."

"Oh, you of little faith." She leaned over him, two hands on the armrests as Maurice clung to the book across his chest. Her breath was hot on his face. "I know where everything is in this house. If you want it, I can get it for you."

Maurice met her gaze. "Alright then. What's in the cellar?"

She tilted her head in a sigh. "Oh. You got me. I'm only human, after all. I've seen everything, except the cellar."

She spun about and returned to her duster, deep in thought. "Still," she said, "if there's a key, there's a way."

"I am certain there is a key," replied Maurice, more determined than ever. "But key or not, I will find a way inside."

Mrs. Cleary's night

NIGHTFALL brought disquiet to Maurice. The walls seemed to close in around him. He feared being once again locked inside his room.

Ever since Shannon had brought the fountain's noise to his attention, he thought of little else. He had mentally drawn a plan of the house and made out that the fountain lay downstairs, adjacent the wall to his right. Its sound had gone unnoticed the nights before. Why did he fixate on it now? Try as he had, he could no longer ignore the water's torrent.

Maurice pondered whether Mrs. Cleary might have deliberately given him this room so that upon suffering numerous poor nights, he might take his leave sooner. He recalled Mrs. Cleary's smug tone when she had declared that he would have long since returned to France by the time anyone was legally permitted in the cellar. She wanted him gone. But why?

The more unsettled he felt, the more clearly he heard the water. *Everything flows*, the words whirled in his mind like a never-ending rush. How could one sleep through this?

But beyond the fountain, what disturbed him was the fear of being locked in.

He decided to lay awake and speak to Mrs. Cleary once she neared his room to lock it. Despite his attempts at breathing deeply, his heart raced as he listened for the housekeeper.

It must have been about ten o'clock, when he heard her walking up the stairs. Maurice was startled by how agitated she seemed. The housekeeper stomped angrily, the timber groaning underfoot. Was she mad? To Maurice, it felt like the force of every step sent the house shaking.

He knew he had to confront her immediately. He would let her know what he thought of her imprisoning him inside his own room. Maurice leapt from his bed and reached for the door.

When he opened it, he saw Mrs. Cleary's shadow.

She stood in the far end of the stair landing, hunched, her back turned away from him. She carried a dim gas lamp that had waned. Her long-sleeved nightgown of white linen reached down to her bare feet. She wore a thin lace shawl round her shoulders. The tight bun was gone. Instead her hair fell to her shapeless hips so that strands of silver hung low, all the way down to her bony buttocks.

"Mrs. Cleary…" began Maurice. He thought he had spoken loud enough but the sounds of water deafened him.

The light in Mrs. Cleary's hand dimmed to nothing. The corridor blackened, streaked in parts by the moonlight seeping through the side window.

She was a grey shape at the top of the stairs. She threw the lamp down with force.

Maurice stepped back, still staring at her from the doorway. The lamp rolled down the stairs, tumbling down each step, until he heard the glass shatter below.

Without warning, Mrs. Cleary turned, filling Maurice with unexplained dread. She muttered in a throaty voice and he sensed her rage from afar. Maurice took another step back, stunned by the housekeeper's terrifying manner.

"Mrs. Cleary, are you alright?" he asked, his voice wavering.

The housekeeper seemed grotesque now.

"Mistake!" she spat. "A grave mistake!"

And the old woman paced towards him at a frightening speed, impelled by all the fury within her, more intent with every step that drew her near. A withered form, moving angrily in the darkness, he could make out the menacing snarl on her moonlit face as she came at him in the dark. "Made a grave, grave mistake! Grave mistake!" she hissed.

Maurice froze, unable to understand what he was seeing, unable to utter a sound.

"I told you to stay where you were! Do you not listen? " she roared. She was getting closer and the glowing moon ray distorted her features. Maurice blinked. He wondered why Mrs. Cleary's eyes appeared so bloodshot, so streaked with red.

Then just as suddenly, she came to a stop at his bedroom door, a foot from where he stood. A flash of recognition passed across her face and the threatening expression vanished. She brought a trembling hand to her temple then closed her eyes while she inhaled. When she opened them, they were still brutally red but her tone regained its polish.

"Mr. Leroux, oh my…I did not see you." She recovered her breath, pressing her hand to her chest. A glint of madness still shone in her eyes.

Maurice stared at her in disbelief.

"You must be very careful," she warned, straining to speak each word as though still out of breath. "At night, I mean. You must be ever careful. For this reason," she pushed him savagely, and with unexpected strength back into the room. "I must lock you in!"

"No! No, Mrs. Cleary, that's out of the question. I told you that I can take care of myself."

"You foolish man!" she spat. "It is everywhere. It flows everywhere like…" Her vision seemed to glaze.

Maurice held her up as she swooned.

"Madame, I think you should rest. I assure you that I can take care of myself. From now on, I will need you to leave this bedroom door unlocked every night."

She reached out and clung to his arm.

"But you don't understand. It's her," she warned.

Maurice stared wide-eyed. He held Mrs. Cleary and firmly guided her towards her room, even as she resisted.

"It's her…" she repeated. "Her and that snakelike hair…"

"Medusa?"

The housekeeper's eyes widened and Maurice shuddered at how dilated her pupils were. She nodded frantically. "Quite right, you are. Quite right. She's an evil creature."

"That's nonsense… Watch your step, now."

"…one look upon her face and one is turned to stone."

"You can't possibly believe that, Mrs. Cleary."

"But you don't understand. She was abducted! Abducted by Poseidon. Not many people know…"

"Now, Mrs. Cleary, please. You'll only frighten yourself."

"You don't understand. It's Calista! She has brought Medusa's vengeance to this house."

"No, no, that's not true. It is only a Greek myth from ancient times. It is not real. None of it is real."

They had reached Mrs. Cleary's room and Maurice stood by the door as the housekeeper entered, still in a daze.

He waited for a while before quietly retracing his steps.

As Maurice returned to his bedroom, he pondered over the nature of the housekeeper's outburst. The reddened eyes and dilated pupils did not lie. Neither did her haggard face and private mutterings.

What had Madeleine confided earlier? Was Mrs. Cleary taking medication that altered her behaviour? If that were true, it was no wonder she fabricated these visions of Medusa. Maurice thought no more of it. He drifted to sleep, this time with the door partly ajar.

The hours passed, and Maurice slept. But by a mechanism mastered only by astute detectives, his curiosity succeeded in stirring his senses at the right time, and at midnight, he opened his eyes.

Seeing nothing out of the ordinary, he was about to return to sleep when he felt a movement outside his room. He stared at the gap near the door. Stillness followed. Again, he watched and waited. Nothing.

Feeling reassured, Maurice closed his eyes.

A curious odor of sea and salt filled the room but Maurice ignored it, drawing the covers higher upon his nose.

Outside, the sounds of rushing liquid filled the nightscape and the fountain waters poured unrelenting. In the pond where the blue moonlight shone, the mosaic tiles glistened magically like tiny fish scales.

Chapter 6

The Nymph of Kassiopi

Greece, 1835

LEGENDS told of the water nymph who had bewitched Poseidon, Greek lord of the sea. Naiads of her kind lived in running waters, in the rivers, near the cascades and the creeks. Theirs was the power to give birth to the fountains and to oversee them. Korkyra was such a naiad. She was a maiden crowned with ocean flowers and gifted with breathtaking beauty. One look at her was enough to lose one's mind. Once Poseidon fell in love, he abducted her, then swept her away to an island where she might be his alone. In time, the island bore her name, and in the people's dialect, was known to all as Kerkyra.

It was a lush paradise in the Ionian Sea, a place of beauty graced with six mountain peaks, and whose rocky maquis overlooked crystal clear blue waters. Its green rolling hills burst with life, for nature and all its creatures thrived here.

Kerkyra had found itself under British protectorate since Napoleon's defeat twenty years ago. To Aaron, it seemed like the proper destination for an Englishman to inhale the Greek landscape in its natural form, well away from mystified Athens. Lately, he had grown suspicious of the new mythology surrounding the ancient capital. To hear English and French writers, the Greeks of today were the same as they had always been.

Aaron did not fancy being told how to see the Greeks. He wished to see them, with his own eyes. The raw, the dark, the savage appealed to him more than any illusion painted by those who wished to revive Hellenic culture, a culture which, to him, was long gone. He knew better than be swayed by romantic writers' nostalgia for classical dreams.

It was fortunate that Aaron spoke Greek well, for here, on the island along with her Ionian sisters, the official languages, despite British rule, remained Greek and Italian.

There was a reason Aaron had travelled to this island, which the English now called, Corfu. It was the long and captivating conversation he had had in Athens about a week ago with a fellow medical graduate.

The young man had recently returned from his appointment in Corfu's prison. Like Aaron, he enjoyed sitting on a terrace, speaking of his travels over a glass of Ouzo. A good drink could only revive his shaken morale from what he had seen in Corfu.

In the island's prison, he explained, members of the insane languished in appalling conditions alongside criminals, and many suffered terrible maladies. The young doctor then expounded on a project which the Lord High Commissioner of Corfu, Sir Howard Douglas was supervising himself – to build a new hospital so Corfu might benefit from advanced, enlightened measures readily embraced elsewhere in Europe.

"The British will use this new hospital to shelter the insane and give them better treatment than in the prisons."

"It is the least we can do," agreed Aaron.

But as riveting as the British project seemed, the young doctor soon drifted to the beauty of Corfu and its quiet village life which he claimed seemed to have been untouched, even after years of Venetian rule.

"Untouched, you say? How so?" asked Aaron, ever sceptical but hoping to find relief from an Athens overrun by visitors.

"There is, you see, a sleepy village in the north-eastern coast of Corfu. It goes by the name of Kassiopi. It is only a small community. It overlooks the prettiest beach. Clear, turquoise waters like you've never dreamt. I've seen many of these in Greece but still, there's something about that particular place. Perhaps because it seems so far away. Well in that village you see..." The young doctor's eyes had shone bright as he told Aaron a most curious story.

The details of a unique village incident poured from his lips. It sounded like a far-fetched tale. To any person other than Aaron Nightingale, the story would have seemed inconsequential, absurd even, but the young doctor noted that his table companion's eyes had lit up and that he was even compelled to write down notes in his journal.

Upon hearing the young doctor's extraordinary account, Aaron Nightingale promised himself he would not remain a moment longer in Athens. Farewell then, Acropolis, farewell Hadrian's Gate, farewell Socrates' prison, goodbye classical ruins, goodbye the newly repopulated Plaka, the ancient Turkish quarter of Athens with its snaking streets crowded with European travellers, where poverty and post-war misery thrived among eager hawkers. To the islands, then… to Kerkyra!

It wasn't long before Aaron, revived by this story, this village tale of which he believed only he could divine the full meaning, set sail, along with several British soldiers, to Corfu's port.

He was pleasantly surprised by the sight of Corfu Town. This glorious marina had apparently once been a naval power. Only Athens and Corinth had been mightier. Dominating the town were two four-hundred year strong Venetian fortresses. A charming French esplanade had been built in the short time span when Napoleon had seized the island from Venice. With its arcades, it reminded Aaron of the rue de Rivoli in Paris. Unlike Athens, here, Aaron saw no traces of an Ottoman influence, for the fortresses had long succeeded in keeping Turks at bay.

Aaron followed a local guide who promised him some means of transport and lodging in Kassiopi. As bemused as he was to discover this mode of transport consisted of several donkeys, he did not protest.

Each man was soon saddled upon a donkey. A third donkey carried Aaron's travel bags together with a day's provisions bought in the port. Eager to inform himself, Aaron purchased a copy of the official government newspaper, the *Gazzetta Uffiziale Degli Stati Uniti Delle Isole Jonie.*

Along his journey to the outskirts of Corfu Town, Aaron marvelled at the Venetian charm of the island, its serene cobblestone streets, its blooming citrus trees. He stared in wonder at the abundance of olive groves which flourished up on the hills.

Many years ago, shared the guide, long before the Venetians had encouraged the growth of olive trees, the island had been covered by vineyards and thick oak forests. Nowadays, the Corfiot wineries were of modest size. As for the ancient trees, they had long been felled for Venetian shipbuilding.

The guide continued his lively historical account, explaining how the vineyards had made way for extensive planting of olive trees, and how the Ionians were made to pay taxes to the Venetians in the form of olive oil, but Aaron was not listening. He'd grown enchanted by the idea that somewhere in the formidable Venetian Arsenal which Napoleon had looted in the last century, there might have been ancient planks of wood that were stolen pieces of Kerkyra. "And now, here we are in colonial England," whispered Aaron, his studious eye missing nothing of the foreign landscape around him.

The path began to narrow, flanked on either side by wild growth, and under the crushing summer heat, insects flew and buzzed round them. Aaron lost sight of the sea as they drew inland. The rawness of his surroundings, far from causing concern, only excited him further. Along the meandering journey from Corfu Town to Kassiopi, he reflected on his daring adventure to the Ionian island. The established English presence would make his stay comfortable at least. That part was easy. The hardest task was finding the girl which the doctor back in Athens had mentioned at length.

The girl from Kassiopi.

Aaron had not foreseen the power this girl would have on him. Already, his reason appeared to have left him. He felt inexorably pulled towards her village.

The journey seemed to never end, and Aaron forgave the unbearable stench of his donkey whose stoic endurance he almost admired. He employed this time to ponder over that astonishing tale told to him by the young doctor. The tale which he had not, at first, believed but which had driven him to drop everything and find the coastal village.

The tale about the Corfu dog that had caught rabies and which was seen wandering in the hospital courtyard. And how one of the nurses, a village woman, had run to fetch the girl. The men had readied themselves to shoot the dog despite its owner's protests. And already it showed signs of violence and was not easily contained, almost wounding one of them. Until the girl had arrived. Murmurs rose among the crowd as the dog stood still. And the young doctor from Athens had explained how, before all the men, the village girl had walked slowly towards the dog as it drooled and snarled. Then as everyone watched and believed she would be lost, she had knelt before it and healed it with her hands.

Aaron's eyes watered at the thought. Despite the heat, the hair on his skin rose and he experienced the delicious sensation of knowing something others ignored.

Aaron would seek the village doctor first. The man would be familiar with every inhabitant in the community. Then Aaron would find a way to observe this girl closely and learn everything he could about her.

He was pleasantly surprised to finally dismount in Kassiopi. The summer sun would not set for another three hours. The village lay very near the water, while inland, lush green hills and more olive groves cradled it. Overlooking the village was a stern black mountain which his guide called Pantokrator. Beyond the harbour, an expanse of balmy blue stretched as far as the eye could see, while overhead stood a mighty Byzantine fortress facing the sea. This was the serene Ionian Sea, a soothing sight for the soul. And beyond, across the ocean, the guide pointed out, you could see the mountains of Albania. It was possible to swim out to the Albanian coast, he explained, and likewise, it was not unheard to come by Albanian bandits in Corfu. Village girls were warned to stay away from the beaches but they were stubborn, he deplored.

Aaron found a small lodging near the harbour and paid his guide. The cooler afternoon brought a coastal breeze and he inhaled the odour of salt and sea.

As he strolled among villagers, one of the few Englishmen in Kassiopi, he lingered by the shimmering harbour where small colourful boats, laden with nets, were moored. Here and there, white chalk buildings dotted the coast. Olive and citrus trees spread their welcome shade over sun-heated stone streets. Blooms, in red and purple, framed the blue doors of tiny homes.

Aaron's quick glance took in the colours and manners of this innocent village. He spotted healthy looking women in black skirts and black stockings. Over billowing white blouses, they wore elegant embroidered vests with intricate flower motifs. Their dignified attire did not spare them from honest labour, for upon their heads, they carried baskets laden with vegetables and fruits.

Far up on the hillside, Aaron noticed another girl with similar attire and whose black hair was modestly covered beneath a white veil. She sat near a dozen goats, staff in hand.

What an idyllic existence, mused Aaron. One could not imagine a more peaceful village. Here, the gloom of a London winter was unimaginable. Here, the sun shone and spread life. For an instant he contemplated abandoning his life's plans and embracing this Mediterranean paradise. But he fought off this naive thought.

Led to the doctor's home, Aaron introduced himself as an English teacher from Athens. The doctor, a short plump man with a round face, heard his remarkable rabies story, and knew instantly who the Englishman described.

"She is Nikolaos' daughter."

The doctor was surprised for he met with few Englishmen. They did not venture to Kassiopi unless it was to see the beaches or the Byzantine castle. He looked sternly at Aaron.

"What are you here for?"

"I cannot hide from you. You seem to be a wise man. What if I told you this girl is unique in the world? I believe she is special."

The Corfiot began to laugh.

"For all I know, Calista Argyros is bad luck," he replied. "What do you want with her?"

Aaron's grave expression had not changed. He fixed the doctor until this one ceased laughing.

"You would have heard," began Aaron, "that since the foundation of the Greek state five years ago, there has been an astounding progress in education. Greek young girls are even learning to speak French."

"That is Athens," replied the Corfiot. "This is here. This is a British island."

"And that is why, I've come to offer the family my services to teach her English. She will learn to read and write at no charge." A gleam shone in Aaron's eye as he continued. "Corfu's High Commissioner recompenses honourable behaviour. Through her bravery, this girl has saved lives."

The old doctor had never heard of any free tutoring being gifted to Corfiots, but he presumed it was because he lived in a small village. So he did not argue. But he thought it best to warn the intrepid English teacher. He pointed a finger at Aaron.

"Her family thinks she is a witch. You come here and tell them she is special, they will laugh at you. Even the priest does not suffer her in his church."

"I will heed your warning." Aaron did not budge.

"Then God be with you. Nikolaos Argyros lives with his family in a house near the sea. Go past the harbour and follow the path along the coast. You cannot miss it. It is the house with the pink flowers, closest to the beach."

And he stared at Aaron for a long time before the Englishman disappeared round the corner.

"Who was that man?" called out his wife.

"He said he was an English teacher sent from Athens, but I've seen his eyes. He is a mad man."

"Where is he going?"

"To see Nikolaos. He wishes to meet his daughter."

"Which one?"

"Which one do you think? Only bad luck will come from this." He shook his head.

It had been a long journey, but Aaron felt no ache or tiredness as he walked past the Byzantine fortress and towards the beach. Like the donkey which had journeyed for hours, trudging an uneven path from Corfu Town to Kassiopi under scorching heat, he seemed enlivened by an unexplainable willpower. His senses were fully awakened, the moment he stepped into the tiled Argyros courtyard.

Several chickens pecked at seeds scattered on the ground while a rooster crowed, flapping its wings. Perched on the white chalk wall which bordered the courtyard, he saw a small goat, chewing with solemn nonchalance. Beside it, two cats lazed on the hot stone while a dog slumbered at the foot of the wall.

There was a stirring at the house's blue door and the goat raised its head. It dashed off the wall, and into the centre of the courtyard, where it began to leap for joy.

The house door opened and out stepped a young woman with jet black hair. She reached forth to caress the goat before looking up to meet Aaron's gaze. The goat settled instantly by her side, facing Aaron, as though protective of its mistress.

Any man on the island would have fallen under her spell. For this young girl, barely twenty, was as fresh and delicate as a nymph. Like her village counterparts, she too wore opaque stockings and a full black skirt upon which was tied an apron of brighter colours with a fringed band sewn at the hem.

Beneath her embroidered vest, a white blouse fell softly on her curves and this was made all the more fetching by the black and gold belt fastened at her tiny waist.

Coral and blue bead necklaces hung above her tanned neck, and even from afar, Aaron inhaled the scent of olive oil she had rubbed on her skin.

All this, he thought, carried the breath of youth, and a life under the sun spent near the Ionian Sea. But Aaron dismissed it all. He had had his share of whores, courtesans, mistresses, even a countess. He had lied and cheated to bed them all. This was different.

He cared nothing of what she resembled. Still, he noticed her eyes straight away. All of the villagers had sported brown or black eyes, whereas in her gaze, stirred the wild currents of the Mediterranean mingled with the black that so resembled the dark mountain towering over Kassiopi.

Those bewitching eyes would have lured thousands of men from even Helen of Troy herself, and while he saw their uniqueness, they had little effect in seducing Aaron Nightingale, nor did they leave their imprint in his mind, because in the moment in which he understood who she was, Aaron only had eyes for the way in which all the animals in the courtyard had magically gathered at the young woman's feet, leaving him wondering whether some invisible string bound them all to her, or if perhaps deep within, she bore a tremendous force that defied nature's laws and governed their every move.

Chapter 7

Thursday

IN disbelief, Maurice ran his hand across the sheets. The fabric felt moist. He rose, horrified.

Still half-asleep, a frightening vision returned to haunt him. It was the memory of his mother, her face twisted in anger.

"You filth!" she spat.

He was four. He tried in vain to hide the mess he'd caused while she came at him. Malice flashed in her eyes.

"What did I tell you, Maurice? What happens when you wet your bed?"

A dread crept through him as he remembered what she would do. Maurice's heart raced until he looked at his surroundings and realised he was in a guestroom in Alexandra Hall. He breathed a sigh of relief but it was soon overshadowed by another fear. Maurice ran his hands on top of the covers. The quilt felt damp too. So did the sides of his pillow and parts of his hair. All exposed parts of his bed had moistened wet overnight.

"Are there leaks in this house, Mrs. Cleary?" he asked at breakfast. He had decided to take breakfast in the commons dining room, the chill of winter not permitting meals on the veranda.

"Absolutely not," replied Mrs. Cleary who seemed to be miraculously composed. She looked nothing like she had the night before. Sleep and perhaps more medication had restored her. "The roof and gable are John Nightingale's pride and joy. I can't imagine there being any leaks."

"Oh."

"Why do you ask me this question?"

Maurice did not wish to alarm the housekeeper. It would be senseless to renew her fears after the efforts it took to calm her down last night. He let the matter drop. But Mrs. Cleary observed him with a keen eye.

"I warned you about this. You should have locked your door," she remarked.

"Well I suppose I shall have no other choice but to sleep with an eye open and to see for myself."

Mrs. Cleary stared at him with a look of terror in her eyes, but she kept silent.

The ornate door

UNTIL now, Maurice discarded the idea of Sophie Murphy having fallen down the stairs. But the fearful atmosphere at Alexandra Hall, and Mrs. Cleary's bizarre behaviour the night before saw him reconsider. There was a chance terror had played a part in the maid's death.

After breakfast, he examined the steps and balustrade of the grand staircase from which presumably Sophie Murphy might have fallen. As expected, he found no evidence of a violent fall: there were no signs of damage on the wooden steps or marble tiles.

Skirting the wall behind the stairs, he noted a small door which he imagined might provide access to a maintenance cabinet beneath the stairwell. The door was unlocked and the tiny cabinet empty. Finding nothing, he closed it again.

As he turned away from the stairs, Maurice's attention was drawn to a larger mahogany door near the kitchen. Carved deep into its dark wood, were large antlers, tracing the full width of the panel. Nested within the antlers were wild animal motifs: engravings of deer and bears formed a circle among birds and squirrels. How had he not seen this door on Tuesday? Maurice pondered over this omission. Perhaps due to its ornate surface, the door had appeared to him as a decorative panel and nothing more.

He worked through every key but could find none to match.

Sensing a watchful presence behind him, he turned his head. Shannon O'Sullivan stood near. She'd been observing him for some time.

"Don't even try, Mr. Leroux," she said. "I'm sure Mrs. Cleary would have spoken to you about that room."

Maurice stepped back.

"I see. So this is the cellar door. It would explain why I do not have the key for it."

Shannon nodded and smiled.

"Mrs. Cleary had her reasons. In his will, Mr. Nightingale barred us from the cellar for six months."

"Yes, I know. Eccentric, right to the end." He looked around to verify that they were alone in this part of the house. Finding no one in sight, he turned to the maid. "Miss O'Sullivan, this is so near the scene of the crime," he whispered, pointing at the door. "It would be senseless not to explore further."

"Well, we are not permitted to enter," protested Shannon.

Maurice pleaded ignorance.

"How so? Why would Mr. Nightingale choose to do this? What difference does it make if I enter it now or later?"

"We have to do what he said."

"Come now, Miss O'Sullivan, let's think about this for a moment. For what absurd reason, would he choose to do that?"

Shannon glared at him. "We should respect his wishes and on no account should we enter the cellar," she insisted, reciting this order like some rote knowledge.

Mrs. Cleary had trained Shannon well, but Maurice persisted. "I understand all that, *mademoiselle*. But surely Mr. Nightingale would make alternative arrangements today if he had some advanced notion of the extraordinary circumstances." His English surprised him. He'd worded it rather well and he was certain she'd be persuaded.

But his reasoning only brought distress to the young woman who shook her head vigorously. "I doubt it," she snarled. "You didn't know him, Mr. Leroux. He was a very organised man. If he did something, then it was for a reason. And you should learn that English people are very set in their ways."

Maurice lit a cigar, prickled by the excessive patriotism in her statement. He'd find a way to press her buttons and use that fine temper of hers to his advantage. "What do you mean by that?" he asked.

"What?"

"Set in their ways. As opposed to us French, is that what you mean?" He assumed an arrogant pose to provoke her.

Shannon waved off the smoke from his voluminous puffs without hiding her irritation. "Well… we English... and Irish," she added, "have never done away with our king William IV in the terrible manner your countrymen murdered their king."

"Well it appears now's your big chance. You should encounter less opposition now that you've got yourself a queen!" taunted Maurice.

"How dare you, sir!" Shannon's eyes filled with tears as she bore the insult for all women.

Maurice was not moved. "Listen, Miss O'Sullivan, two people were murdered in this house. I am here to find out why. And if there is anything of interest in this cellar that might advance my case, then I am determined to find it. Now give me the key!"

A spark of anger flew across Shannon's eyes. To Maurice, it seemed her red hair was suddenly set ablaze as she let out her ire. "I can't! Mrs. Cleary has it," she cried. Then, frightened by her outburst, she stammered. "You…you ought to stay out of that cellar. Bad enough there's…there's a ghost in this house. What would befall us all if Mr. Nightingale's spirit knew what you were up to?"

So then, Mrs. Cleary had lied, thought Maurice.

As he pondered on ways he might retrieve the key he'd seen her put away, a sharp sound rose from the commons area. It ushered in a heart-wrenching yelp. Maurice startled. The violent whipping renewed, growing more frantic while youthful cries rang in the corridor. The violence rose to a frightful crescendo until the screaming melted into desperate sobs.

All along, Shannon stood rigid, pressing her hand to her lips.

Maurice's face grew white. He knew what he'd heard. It was Mary's voice. Mary being beaten. "Is that Mrs. Cleary punishing Mary?" he asked in dismay. He could feel his anger rise.

"I...I don't know what you mean," replied Shannon.

"That sound we just heard, Mary's cries..."

"I can't say I heard anything. If you'll excuse me, I have work to do."

Shannon hurried away towards the parlour, her heels loud on the black and white tiles.

Maurice paced along the corridor leading to the staff area. Mary had now ceased crying but he was certain her weeping had originated from that part of the house. He peered into the commons kitchen. Finding no one, he walked across to the adjacent room, and nearly bumped into Mrs. Cleary who emerged at the same instant.

"Oh, Mr. Leroux, you frightened me!" Her voice, far from startled, was accusative and hard. Her face was flushed red. Strands of hair had escaped from her high bun. She seemed in a hurry to leave the room.

"Mrs. Cleary. What is wrong with Mary?" asked Maurice, barring her way. He knew all too well she would not admit to beating the maid, but he wished her to know he had noticed the noise. He wasn't ready to abide in silence while she struck a child so cruelly.

"Mary? What do you mean?" Her tone was dry and cutting.

"I heard her crying, *madame*. Is everything alright?"

A flicker of deceit shone in Mrs. Cleary's black eyes. She brought her hand to her temple and broke into a smile. "Oh, yes. I heard it too. Mary fell over. She's perfectly fine, now. Thank you for your concern, Mr. Leroux."

"That didn't sound to me like..."

"I assure you, she's fine," insisted the housekeeper, a flash of impatience in her voice. "Besides, she'll never finish her chores if we interrupt her," she added, insinuating that Maurice ought to leave the commons area.

"I see. Of course, *madame*." He followed the housekeeper out into the corridor. Internally, Maurice fought to not challenge her and force her to admit her cruelty.

Having reached the entrance hall, he walked outside and lit a cigarette, relieved to be out of the house. Madeleine was sweeping the veranda but she watched him from the corner of her eye.

A look of pain had darkened his face. He was reliving Mary's cries and they tormented him.

He sighed. In France as in England, it was the same. Unless one committed infanticide or aborted an unborn, one could get away with terrible crimes against a child, thought Maurice. Abandonment, malnourishment and beatings, everyone turned a blind eye. To Maurice, the thought of a child being mistreated was gut-wrenching. Hearing their pain awoke his memories. It made him feel like someone had ripped out his insides.

He turned to Madeleine as though she'd been privy to his thoughts. "Did you hear anything, *mademoiselle*? I'd be surprised if you didn't. Those shrieks could scarcely be ignored."

Madeleine clutched at her broom, barely meeting Maurice's gaze. There was a quiet look of guilt in her expression. "I was hoping this would not happen with you here," was all she said. Maurice gratefully noted that the playful manner she had sported last night had vanished.

"Mrs. Cleary beats her, doesn't she?" he asked.

Madeleine nodded, self-conscious. "She has formally adopted Mary. She is her guardian."

Maurice shook his head, more outraged than ever. "How often does this happen?" His voice vibrated in anger.

"Once a week…maybe. Sometimes more. On my first week here, she beat her frightfully with a leather thong. I tried to comfort Mary afterwards. I offered to take her with me to London when I leave. But she was unwilling to speak of it. I think she lives in her own world half the time."

"And so no one does anything about it..." Maurice was barely audible. He took another puff and stared out onto the road.

Madeleine examined him thoughtfully until a knowing light shone in her eyes.

The case of Vera Nightingale's body

IN the late afternoon, Maurice received a visit from Dr Hart. Under the supervision of the local coroner, Dr Hart had performed both autopsies and inspected the bodies of Sophie Murphy and Vera Nightingale. He was a man in his mid-sixties. His broad beard and long white hair gave him the appearance of a bespectacled lion. He'd heard from Mr. Wilson that Maurice was French and seemed more enthusiastic about meeting him than discussing the case.

He smiled, a twinkle in his eye, as he greeted Maurice. "Monsieur Leroux, jay swee enchantay," he said with the joyful mirth of someone who enjoyed practicing his French.

Maurice shook his hand. "Thank you for coming, Dr Hart."

"My pleasure. That's the extent of what I remember, I'm afraid," replied the doctor in self-derision. He laughed.

"You used to speak French?"

"Peninsular War," said Hart, proudly. "I was in Portugal and then Spain when Wellington led the British against your countrymen. I picked up a few phrases. Oh, it's a long time ago, now. Back then I was only a young lad and the sight of blood scared me. But I befriended the French prisoners. All good men."

"I might have been seven at most at the time. I've since heard we didn't treat the Spaniards very well."

"Wars are always so messy. You French had a hard time, Monsieur Leroux. Still, there's nothing like peaceful times, ay?"

"Indeed."

"And your English is marvellous. Marvellous. You put me to shame."

They moved inside the parlour where Ellen brought in some tea. She placed the platter on a low table before leaving the two men alone.

"Now, Dr Hart," said Maurice, "I've only been given a brief report of the manner in which these two unfortunate women died. I would appreciate it if you could supplement with what you know."

Dr Hart retrieved papers from a leather case.

"Yes. Where shall we start? You're absolutely right. The first victim was only twenty. Such a shame. Let's see." He studied his notes and recollected the details. "Sophie Murphy bore a severe wound to her head, a wound caused by a blunt object," he began. "If we are to assume her death was an accident, which, I am told is the official story Mr. Wilson gave her parents, then she must have hit her head upon the balustrade as she fell. She seemed otherwise to be a perfectly healthy young woman. I found no signs of trauma on her body."

"No bruises on the rest of her body?"

"That's right. And certainly not the bruises one would expect to find had she truly tumbled from the top of the stairs." He gave Maurice a complicit look. "But I'm unfortunately not at liberty to say this to her parents. On the other hand, she might have fallen straight down and then bore the full impact upon her skull. You see the skull showed signs of fracture to one side only."

Maurice reflected on this.

"Dr Hart, could you rule out that someone might have fatally struck Sophie Murphy and that she did not fall off the staircase at all?"

The doctor nodded emphatically. "It is highly possible, *monsieur*. I do not rule it out."

"Thank you. What of Miss Vera Nightingale?"

"Ah. Vera Nightingale." The doctor removed his glasses and sighed. Then he rubbed the bridge of his nose in a thoughtful fashion as though deliberating on what he might say and how to say it.

"The report I was given indicates she died of asphyxiation," reminded Maurice. "No wounds."

"Yes. The report is still valid. What I've not mentioned, and perhaps it is because I am unable to draw conclusions, is the curious condition in which I found Vera Nightingale's body." His cheerfulness had left him and he now appeared wary.

"Curious? What do you mean?" asked Maurice.

"It sounds perplexing, I know." Dr Hart gulped his tea. He took a deep breath. "I am afraid I can offer no hypothesis as to the meaning of my findings. But in the spirit of professionalism, I should share with you what I've discovered. *Mon cher* Leroux, the one thing that astounded me upon inspecting Vera

Nightingale, was the thin aqueous film which covered her entire neck and face. An unusual substance."

A knowing glint shone in Maurice's eyes, but he bit his lip. He thought back to the wet trail he had wiped off the floorboards upstairs and the moisture across his sheets. He had to remain discreet. "Where had it come from?" he asked.

The doctor shook his head gravely. "I'm unfortunately unable to explain its origin. It was colourless, of remarkable cohesiveness, slippery and…wet."

"Wet? You mean, like a liquid? A glistening liquid?" Maurice could scarcely repress the agitation in his voice.

Dr Hart almost looked frightened. "I would say so," he whispered back. "But there is more to this, Monsieur Leroux. This same film covered the membranes inside her nose. And…if you will excuse me…" He lowered his voice. "There were traces of it in her lungs also."

Maurice's eyes widened. "You believe this film played a part in Vera Nightingale's death?"

"Ah, it is most confounding. You see, Miss Vera most certainly died of lack of air," insisted Dr Hart, shaking his head. "As for the presence of that film, what it could be, and how it came to find itself on her face, let alone in her lungs, I am afraid I am much in the dark."

These last words plunged Maurice into a deep introspection. Dr Hart was quick to notice this.

"Monsieur Leroux, please don't take too much to heart. I can see this case is taking its toll upon your health. Enjoy this life. We only have one. You look so burdened."

"I'm not sleeping very well here," confided Maurice.

"Yes. I can see that," nodded the doctor. "Take care of yourself, Monsieur Leroux."

Long after Dr Hart had mounted his carriage and returned to Reading Town, Maurice remained in a daze, perplexed by the curious events in the house. When it came to Vera Nightingale's death, nothing made sense. He was left confused by the doctor's revelations.

The foreign liquid he'd found on his sheets this morning, the black and blue eye he could not match with any person inside the house, and now, this curious film on Vera Nightingale's body –

all these details puzzled Maurice. He wondered whether the maids had partly spoken true, and if there was something uncanny about Alexandra Hall.

Yet he refused to entertain the superstitions of Irish women. He could imagine the impressionable maid, Ellen, asserting that Calista's spirit roamed at night, and that her wet spectral form left a trail wherever it passed. Maurice shook his head. Such an idea was far removed from everything he knew. French enlightened society had long evolved. It no longer held such beliefs.

His ponderings drew him halfway up the grand staircase, very near Calista's portrait, just as Madeleine trotted down with a bundle of dirty linen.

"What colour are those eyes?" he asked, facing the oil painting.

"Well good evening to you, too, Mr. Leroux," replied Madeleine.

Maurice pointed to the portrait with a startling urgency.

"Take a look at them. Please. What colour are those eyes?"

Madeleine pouted. Wrinkling her nose, she leaned her body forward and squinted to better take in the delicate brush strokes.

"It's hard to make out…" she began. "But I would say…black with a little blue."

And upon her words, Maurice's jaw tensed and he fell silent. He gripped the balustrade tight, deep in thoughts.

Madeleine looked satisfied. "Yes, most certainly a blend of black and blue. A pretty lady, ain't she? So sad." She turned to Maurice and gasped. "What is the matter with you? You look like you've seen a ghost." She stared at him, slightly mocking.

Maurice inched closer to her. "I will take your offer," he whispered into her ear. "I need to get inside that cellar."

Madeleine laughed. "Is that a new trick to pull me close and kiss me?"

"I am serious. Can you fetch me the key?"

Madeleine blinked. "Are you asking me a favour, Mr. Leroux?" she teased, still rolling the r of his name.

"When can you get it?"

"Hmm… that will depend. What's in it for me?"

"What do you want?"

"I'll tell you later!" she chimed, suddenly withdrawing and dashing down the steps. Maurice looked up and saw Mrs. Cleary staring at them from atop the stairs.

How long had she stood there, he wondered. Maurice acknowledged her with a nod then stepped downstairs, affecting a casual air. As he returned to the parlour, he was quietly excited about outsmarting the housekeeper. He wondered what he would find in the cellar.

The closet

HER foreign traits, those large melancholic eyes and even the expression on her face – Calista's portrait haunted Maurice. He could not find rest, let alone sleep.

As he ran his mind through all he had witnessed and learnt, he could not escape the vision of that portrait by the grand staircase. The more Maurice pondered, the more Calista's eyes returned to haunt him. Black and blue. Yet he knew nothing of the Greek woman who had arrived in England ten years ago prior to her death. Except…

He closed his eyes, recalling Ellen's testimony. The maid had revealed how in full daylight, she had once seen a hideous face staring at her from Calista's locked bedroom. Yet when he had entered this very room on Tuesday morning, he had seen nothing out of the ordinary.

Except those stained dresses, thought Maurice. *Yes, what about those stained dresses?*

As in all households, he assumed the maids soaked clothes in a steaming tub in the washroom near the commons kitchen. For the more delicate clothing, he'd seen Mrs. Cleary bundle up linen and send it off to a laundress in Reading Town.

Why would a woman who lived in such refined surroundings choose to put away numerous stained dresses and leave them to rot in her closet? Maurice's eyes sprung open.

Because she was hiding the stain. Or perhaps…the origin of the stains. Think, Maurice. This project inside the cellar, whatever its nature, it must have caused those stains. Calista would have climbed upstairs as soon as she emerged from the cellar. If so, perhaps she regularly washed those dresses herself.

Of course, thought Maurice. Calista had been ill, unable to tend to her own laundry for weeks. Then following her death, no one had washed her clothing. The dresses had been left untouched.

There was a secret to Calista Nightingale after all.

It was not yet midnight when Maurice crept out of his room, lamp in hand. The night's chill clung to his robe as he turned the corridor and followed the stair balustrade to Calista's bedroom. In his free hand, he clutched at the large eighteenth century key. Trembling slightly, he inserted it.

Taking a deep breath, Maurice turned the key.

He stepped inside.

There was a furtive movement to his left, behind the drapes. He hefted his lantern high towards the window. Nothing moved. In the distance, he heard a crow's caw. It must have been a bird flapping its wings outside, thought Maurice. At least, there was no spirit staring out the window.

Stepping towards the bed, he was made aware of an unpleasant odour. It was strange. He recalled that the room had been perfumed with jasmine on his first visit. All around him now, were hints of the sea breeze…no, something else. Maurice often walked the long beaches of his native Normandy, and whenever the algae washed up along the shore, a strong salty tang lingered in the air.

That's what it was. As though death had clothed itself in algae, then reached out from the sea to stain this bedroom, dragging it into the ocean's depths. At first he could not explain why the scent filled him with such dread, but then, he knew. He had smelt it before. *Last night, in my room.*

What if Ellen was right? What if she and Mrs. Cleary had truly seen something?

Maurice's heartbeat quickened. No. He would not succumb to the same hysteria as the Irish housemaids. Ellen was awfully malnourished. It was no wonder she was delirious and prone to follies, no wonder she invented. As for Mrs. Cleary's visions, he now suspected they resulted from drug taking.

His light caught the coloured pieces glowing on the baroque bedside table. Maurice neared the table and flashed his lamp above it. He'd not seen the shattered porcelain figures the first time. He brought the light to each broken piece and guessed what had been a young shepherdess, then a couple of sheep, and last, a well-dressed gentleman.

Maurice recalled Shannon's concerns for the Nightingale couple. She had been persuaded that Calista resented her husband at least a year before her death. Had Aaron and Calista fought in this room?

Maurice imagined Aaron in a sudden fury, smashing the porcelain figures. But then Ellen's voice echoed in his mind. Such a nice man, Aaron was. So kind. The vision vanished.

The floorboards creaked behind him. Maurice turned, flashing his lamp onto the wall opposite the window, searching. Scattered by the lace drapes, the moonlight drew random dancing spots along the flowered wallpaper.

The timber moaned once more and Maurice knew – there was a presence here, right here, in this room. Whatever it was, it had visited him on previous nights and brought with it this smell that so resembled the ocean.

I know it is you, thought Maurice, despite his will to deny superstition. No, he would not drift into madness. He would not say her name.

His eye travelled to the tall closet by the vanity table. If he could seize one of Calista's dresses, perhaps Madeleine might deduce the origin of the stain?

Maurice flinched. Something was wrong.

He remembered closing both panels during his first visit. There was no doubt that he had shut them for he had been horrified by the stench of the soiled fabric.

Now, as he approached, he could see that one of the doors was ajar. Maurice felt a chill down his spine.

"Calista…" he whispered.

It was foolish to expect her to respond but he believed that by calling out her name, he could show her that he knew who she was. He could acknowledge her presence.

Maurice trembled.

"Calista, is that you?"

Right before his eyes, the left closet door slowly opened. Maurice blinked. How was this possible? Had he lost his mind? But he knew the answer was there, all along. Why did he not choose to accept it? Perhaps Aaron Nightingale had died, not of the grief that followed his wife's death, but of a similar cause as Sophie Murphy and his sister, Vera. Perhaps a supernatural force played a part in all three deaths…

Calista was here. He felt it, though a shadow of doubt clouded his mind.

He raised his waning lamp, peering into the gloom. The dim light flickered over the hanging fabric, causing a shimmer of silks and taffetas, in red, blue, and black. Maurice breathed fast. He could see nothing.

Until the other closet door swung open on its own. It made a malignant creaking noise. In that instant, all Maurice's doubts vanished.

He stepped back, shaking with fright. He flung himself outside, fumbled for the key, and closed the door. Behind him, he heard both closet panels slam shut. There was a heavy thud inside the bedroom, and then the floorboards groaned as though something moved towards the door just as he locked it. A shadow of himself, Maurice fled to his room.

Chapter 8

Friday

MAURICE could hear singing outside his room. Lulled by the soothing voice, he rose from his sleep. Dark images of algae, the beach on a starless night, and the murky ocean – they faded from his mind. His eyes blinked open and daylight brought him back to Alexandra Hall. He lay there, recalling what he had seen in Calista's room. He reached out a hand and felt for the water glass he usually placed on the bedside table. Finding nothing, Maurice lifted his head.

The near empty glass sat near the table's edge. Water had collected in pools across the table and the rug was sodden with it.

A jolt saw him spring to his feet. Clad in his nightrobe, he pushed his feet into his shoes and threw open the bedroom door. He found Madeleine humming a melody as she polished each of the staircase banisters.

"Were you in my room this morning, *mademoiselle*?" asked Maurice.

Madeleine looked amused. "Why, Mr. Leroux. Who do you take me for?"

"I... My water glass. It was moved. Somebody...somebody came into my room last night. Was it you, *mademoiselle*?"

Madeleine erupted into light laughter. "Had I visited your room, you certainly would have known," she said cheekily.

"*Mademoiselle*, it is not funny. You see, I usually place my water glass in the middle of the bedside table. When I woke up this morning, it stood much nearer to the edge. Did you perhaps see someone else enter my bedroom earlier today?"

"No one's come within an earshot of your room. The others are downstairs having breakfast. Besides, how would you know you did not move the glass yourself? Perhaps you felt for it in your sleep, drank, then clumsily put it back," said Madeleine with a shrug.

Maurice did not insist. Madeleine was right. He was being ridiculous. He must have moved the glass himself. Feeling newly doubtful, he returned to his bedroom.

Leaning across the wash basin, Maurice poured water from the pitcher onto his face then stared into the mirror above the porcelain bowl. The sinister encounter in Calista's room flashed in his mind. He met his wild, haggard eyes. *Now you listen to me, Maurice*, he thought, addressing his reflection. *Keep your wits about you. Tout va bien.* All is well, he repeated, as he wiped his face with the towel. He would not let himself be haunted. He had to remain level-headed.

As he buttoned up his vest, his eye fell on the desk. An uneasy feeling swept over him. Someone had touched his journal. His writing implements lay in a disorderly fashion. Ink spots ran on the lacquered surface beside the journal. More ink blotted the page in front of him. Barely breathing, Maurice picked up the journal and turned to the previous page. He gasped. In a hideous script, with no care for spacing or form, a single word was written.

OVEE

Recovering from his stupor, Maurice fled the room and raced downstairs. As he entered the commons kitchen, he found Shannon and Ellen. Shannon sat at the head of the table, where the housekeeper normally ate.

"Where is Mrs. Cleary?" he asked.

Shannon shot Ellen a dark look as though she wished her to keep quiet. "She is not awake yet," she said. "Would you like some tea, Mr. Leroux?"

Maurice made no answer. He steadied himself, placing a hand against the wall. Silence hung above the wooden table where the maids were having breakfast. The only sound was the crackling of the hearth fire, casting its warmth throughout the tiled room.

"Mr. Leroux, you look awfully tired today," noted Ellen in a sweet voice. She'd ceased eating and stared at him.

Shannon glowered. It was unlike the young Ellen to speak up so rashly but Mrs. Cleary's absence seemed to give the girl confidence. Shannon studied Maurice. He had as yet not answered her offer for tea. He seemed stunned, almost shaken. A knowing glint passed through her eyes.

"We are all afraid, with many ways of hiding it," she whispered, still gazing up at the Frenchman. Despite her unexpected gentleness, her tone had a distinct, I-told-you-so quality.

Maurice smiled thinly. He couldn't bring himself to reveal the dread he felt. "Miss O'Sullivan, where is Mrs. Cleary?" he asked again.

"The truth is, she is ill. You must understand that the past two months have been a trial for her, what with Mr. Nightingale passing away and then..."

"She saw it," blurted Ellen.

"Ellen, please be quiet." Shannon turned apologetically to Maurice. "Pay no mind, Inspector Leroux. Like I said, Mrs. Cleary is not well."

"What were you saying, Ellen?" asked Maurice, ignoring Shannon's protests. "What did Mrs. Cleary see?"

Ellen hesitated. She averted her gaze from Shannon's scornful face. "She saw the ghost. It was early this morning, around six. Mary was still asleep. I took Willy out for a pee and saw Mrs. Cleary through the glass doors."

"Ellen, be quiet!" cut in Shannon as she slapped a hand on the table.

Maurice ignored her. "Go on," he urged Ellen.

"She was acting… strange, like she was afraid and seemed about to swoon. So I ran back inside and I saw her trembling and clutching the stairs. She looked awful."

"She was just ill," dismissed Shannon.

"No!" cried Ellen. "She told me she saw Calista's ghost. Then she collapsed on the stairs and did not move. I thought she was passed out but Gerard came out of the kitchen to see how she was and she told him she would be retiring for the rest of the day."

"I see," replied Maurice.

"She's resting now," explained Shannon after lapsing into silence. "I think we'll get along just fine without her. We've got plenty of work to get through before Sunday. You finish cleaning up, Ellen, and we'll be on our way."

Ellen promptly obeyed.

"May I ask you something, Miss O'Sullivan?" asked Maurice who still lingered by the doorway.

"What is it?"

"This scar, on your hand, how did you get it?"

Shannon blushed.

"It's not so bad. It's a long story. Willy bit me."

Maurice frowned. "Willy? Mary's little dog? You find me surprised. It looks like he wouldn't harm a fly."

"I don't know what came over him that day. But it's been years. He's been harmless ever since. There's nothing to worry about now."

Maurice reflected on Willy's unusual behaviour.

"What about the scars I see on Mary's neck and arms?" he asked, watching Shannon's reaction.

Her eyes had widened. "I don't know what you mean," came her evasive reply.

"Very well." Maurice sighed. Shannon was too fearful to speak against the housekeeper. He returned to the purpose of his visit. "Miss O'Sullivan, have you ever heard of the name, Ovee?" he asked, feeling his pulse quicken.

Shannon looked confused though the earlier tension in her voice was gone. "No. No, I don't think so."

Maurice nodded. He'd have to ask Mrs. Cleary later.

He left the room. As he neared the kitchen, he glimpsed Madeleine, helping Gerard tend to the stove. She'd rolled up her sleeves and bore stains up to her elbows. Both were laughing, and even Gerard sported a rare grin as he applied black lead to the cast iron surfaces.

Catching sight of Maurice, Madeleine whispered something to the cook then darted to the French doors. She poked her head out.

"Now is the right time," she whispered. "I can fetch that key for you."

"How will you manage?"

"Oh, I have my ways," she smiled. "Shannon's found herself a new role as housekeeper. She'll be keeping us busy all day. But don't worry. This afternoon, I plan to sneak into Mrs. Cleary's bedroom. I'll find that key. If she awakes and surprises me, I'll say I was looking for next week's grocery list."

"Didn't you tell me earlier this week she sleeps with her eyes open? What if she sees you?"

"No fuss, Mr. Leroux. It'll be fun. You'll have that key by your bedside tonight."

The cellar

MAURICE felt anxious all day. He feared that Mrs. Cleary might awake before Madeleine had the chance to fetch the cellar key. It was around eight o'clock when he climbed upstairs just as Madeleine furtively emerged from his bedroom. She nodded, then walked past him.

"Done," she whispered. "Shannon caught me leaving Mrs. Cleary's room. I told her I had come in to pick up soiled linen and didn't find any."

"Thank you, Madeleine."

As Madeleine dashed downstairs, Maurice entered his bedroom and closed the door. He found a copper key by the bedside and slid it into his pocket.

He waited for hours. When he was certain the household had retired, he rose and left his bedroom. It was a humid night and the moist air had clouded all the windows of Alexandra Hall.

Clad in his woollen nightrobe, Maurice carried a small lamp which he would light once he was through the cellar door. The faint moonlight from the high windows illuminated his path down the staircase. In place of leather shoes, he'd worn his slippers to muffle the sound of his footsteps. He hoped this might also allay suspicion should he be discovered roaming the house at night.

As he reached the ornate cellar door on the first floor, he glimpsed a slithering shadow behind him, towards the stairwell. Maurice faced the stairs, blinking into the gloom. An undisturbed stillness greeted him. He waited, peering into the dark with his pulse racing. What if Mrs. Cleary had awakened? What if she followed him inside the cellar and saw what he was up to? What would he do? He stood by the door for a few more minutes. The silence held and nothing stirred.

Breathing a sigh, Maurice turned to the cellar door. He inserted the key with care and disengaged the lock. Holding his breath, he pushed. Much to his relief, the hinges did not creak. He lit his small lamp and stepped inside.

A narrow stone passage lay before him, unlit, and of such height, he was forced to crouch as he advanced. He reached a set of stone steps and began to descend. He wondered how Aaron Nightingale would have fared going down these stairs. According to portraits, the Englishman stood much taller than him.

The steps continued deeper than Maurice could have guessed and after a few seconds, a tight feeling gripped his chest. In this narrow stairwell, closed in, and cast in darkness, a familiar fear stirred. His memories resurfaced, uninvited.

Years ago, Therese, in one of her many fits of cruelty, would lock him inside the pantry.

Maurice pressed a hand against the cold wall by his side and paused to catch his breath. Even now, the walls rang with the echoes of her threats. "Don't ever think you'll leave, Maurice. You'll never come out! Never!"

He remembered the nasty tone of her voice in the kitchen while his five-year-old self was locked in the wooden cabinet. There was clamouring at the door as he banged his fists against it. Out of breath, he whimpered, begging her to let him out.

He would press his eye against the pantry door's keyhole, and see a terrifying figure in a shapeless green dress. This woman could not have been his mother, for what mother inhabited such a loveless angular frame, what mother uttered words with such spite, or walked with those menacing, erratic movements.

Maurice never knew what Therese would do next. Like a famished crone who feasted on little children, her face would surge before him, twisted and cruel. She was unpredictable. Her rage, nursed by ale and poverty, was overshadowed by more than one mean bone, and by the spite she held against all men.

And now Therese stood there, facing the kitchen table with her back turned towards him. In her hand, she held a white chicken by its legs. Maurice saw her pick up a knife. The blade swiped the air, sparking a violent flutter of wings and flying white down. Therese held the dead bird and plucked its feathers. "I know you are watching, Maurice," she warned. "Don't let me catch you."

Even now, her voice echoed in the passage, ringing in his ears. Maurice paused halfway down to the cellar. He shut his eyes, letting the wave of horror pass through him. He told himself he was no longer in the pantry. He was in Alexandra Hall, faraway in England. He swept aside the horrid vision of his mother's face and continued his descent.

Before long, the steps ended. Beneath his feet, he felt the uneven ground. It was not tiled. It seemed worn and ancient, a relic of some old cottage, perhaps centuries old. He shone his small lamp across.

A vaulted chamber of astounding proportions existed directly beneath the house. It was much larger than Maurice had suspected. He advanced, slowly at first, using his lamp to peer into this vast, humid cavern. The floor was bare, dirty and mottled with stains. The unpainted walls glistened with lichen and moss.

The main piece of furniture was a large wooden bench on which rested a medical leather bag, metal implements and mysterious vials that had gathered dust.

Behind this large table, against the wall, there towered a medieval medicine cabinet with dozens of tiny drawers. The gleam of golden letters on each compartment illuminated this monstrous piece of furniture that seemed to belong not here, in the English countryside, but in an oriental palace in some faraway land. That it had found itself here was remarkable.

Unable to see any further through the darkness, Maurice shone his lamp to his left. Glass formations of various shapes and sizes crowded the numerous shelves across the left side wall but he could not discern what these were or what they contained. Seeing a small stool with a five-member candlestick, he worked with his own matches to light each candle. A brighter light soon filled the chamber.

As he raised it high, it revealed a ghastly spectacle. There were rows and rows of shelves to his left, and stacked upon these, was the work of a mad man. Grotesque pieces of flesh, limbs, bone and all manner of creatures floated in sealed jars of various sizes and shapes. Maurice shuddered. In one of the jars, the dark, swollen digits of a severed hand floated in a greenish liquid.

What evil had taken place here?

Maurice retreated to the large table. He caught the glint of sharp implements which he'd not seen earlier. He pulled at the drawers, hoping to find work records, or maybe some written material. Instead he found a revolver. Maurice stared at the weapon.

"What is all this, Aaron? What were you doing?" he whispered.

He shone the candlestick to the right. Stacked against the far right wall, in uneven fashion, were numerous large wooden and metal boxes and trunks. Some were draped in sheets of calico and other wrapping material that had been discarded. Maurice neared the boxes.

From their labelling, he learnt the mysterious origins of each parcel: Congo, Rhodesia, Gambia, Senegal, and the Gold Coast. There were boxes from as far away as Peking and Macau.

What had been inside those boxes?

He returned to the oriental cabinet, suddenly inspired. If he were to find written records, perhaps they might be stored in one of its larger compartments. He tugged at each brass knob, half-way down the cabinet. The first two drawers were filled with towels and medical tin dishes. The third drawer was locked. Maurice applied force and tore it open. The hinge snapped, revealing a pile of worn leather journals. One of these was dated from 1840 to 1847. His heart beating fast, Maurice buried this booklet beneath his robe, fastening his belt tight to keep the journal in place.

As he lifted his eyes, he grew conscious of the broken latch on one of the medieval cabinet's tiny doors. He tugged on it to see it open. Medicine pills. Maurice opened another compartment, then several others. They all contained pills, but while most compartments were neatly organised, reflecting Aaron's concern for order, others were in disarray, almost as though someone had rummaged through the cabinet.

Returning to the drawer with the broken latch, Maurice took note of the drug's label. Moved by instinct, he seized one of the pills and slid it into his pocket.

It was time to leave. He had no wish to remain down here. Maurice raised the candlestick and waved it to find the staircase. To his surprise, the light seemed to reflect upon a surface on the far right. Intrigued, Maurice crept closer.

And then something strange happened. Maurice froze. His light had shone upon a plant.

A plant? Here?

Maurice inspected the tall green shoots hovering over pebbles. They waved, as though… He tried to reach the plant which bore an uncanny resemblance to algae. A hard surface obstructed his hand.

Maurice stood back. *It was algae.* It seemed to live behind some sort of window.

He ran his hand across, attempting to feel behind the glass. But the structure seemed to never end. The plant he had seen was enclosed behind a set of glass panels joined together by a wooden frame.

The entire structure stood three feet from the ground and its glass panels reached up to his chin. Maurice calculated that it was over eight feet across. Inside this curious glass container, he could make out eerie rocky formations and thin plants immersed in a liquid. How much had Aaron spent on this odd piece of furniture? Whatever it was, it would have cost a hefty sum.

A sudden rattling noise resonated in the chamber.

Maurice whipped his head round. He blew out the candlestick and stared out, with only his small lamp still lit. The sound repeated itself.

"Who's there?" he asked.

There it was again. It came from the back of the cellar.

Seizing the lamp he'd left on the stool earlier, he swept it to his right, searching.

The far wall was blackened by a large shape. Maurice gasped. There it was! A shadow moved behind the mound of boxes. Now it shifted across. The movement was swift and now the shadow had disappeared.

"Calista?" Her name had shot out of his lips. His entire being fought this idea, but he could no longer suppress what he felt.

"Calista, are you there?" he repeated. His own words made no sense to him, yet he wished for an answer.

And there was one. A violence shook the trunks. The boxes rattled with such force that two of them tumbled down with a crash. Maurice advanced, drawn to the noise despite his mounting dread. He wished to know. Was she there? Was she doing this?

The rummaging redoubled. Pieces of wood, and dust flew above the stacks.

The cellar went dark.

The light! The light in his hand had waned. Maurice worked frantically to revive it, but something hard hit him, and he flinched. He gripped his shoulder. Before he could make sense of it, another metallic object – this time a broken latch – was flung at him. He doubled over in pain, his hand clasped over his burning eye.

The light returned. Maurice looked up, stunned by what now flew in his direction. It was too late to dodge it. The small cage struck him so violently that he cried out.

"Why?" he yelled. "Why are you doing this?"

Maurice blinked. The blow to his temple had almost knocked him senseless. Blood trickled from a gash near his eye, blurring his vision. And yet, he could swear that something was there, right there, among the trunks.

He shone his light across the distant shape, his head throbbing. He gasped. A shrouded and crouched form sat among the trunk stacks. It seemed to observe him. Its slow movements were odd, otherworldly.

"Calista? Is that you?"

As though it understood his words, the draped figure rose tall, then taller still, its shroud lifting and billowing in the dark. Maurice stepped back. The fabric danced, uncanny, furious.

Maurice ran. Fear choked him as he made for the staircase. Daring a glimpse, he saw the ghostly shape rush from the trunks and towards the stairs. It came for him… He thought no more and raced up into the narrow corridor where the past clung to him. Therese's voice rang in his ear, but still he ran, up the stairs, towards the ornate door, and out of the cellar. Was she close? Was she after him? He did not know. He dared not look. He slammed the door shut and locked it fast, horrified that he might have witnessed the rage of a Greek peasant girl risen from the dead.

No sooner returned to his bedroom, Maurice bolted the door. Tonight, he would rather feel closed in than meet with a remnant. He sought for his cigar case and lit up with trembling fingers, still eyeing the door. He was terrified Calista's spirit might fly in.

There was no denying it any longer. She was real.

Chapter 9

Calista

Corfu, 1836

"WHEN Calista was born, her grandmother fell ill and died. That's how her family suspected. Here, we have a belief. People can hurt you with only a look. We call this, *kako mati.* It is like they have placed a curse on you. With *kako mati,* anything can happen, usually something bad. You might fall ill or lose property, or even die. Here, we say that those with blue eyes can easily give you the evil eye. At first we did not believe Calista had anything to do with it but her older brother also fell ill and died when she was six months old. You see, Calista was born with blue eyes."

Aaron could not believe the nonsense pouring out of the villager's mouth but as always, and as he had done for months, he allowed Calista's uncle to speak animatedly about his family. It was mid-afternoon and the two men were leading a donkey to the harbour where Calista and her father waited with the fishing boat. Aaron's grasp of Greek was much improved now, and through conversation with villagers, he was astounded by these superstitious people.

"My brother tried everything," explained Sakis. "He took her into town. He saw a priest about *vaskania.* The priest made a special prayer and he spat on her three times. It came to nothing. When Calista was ten, her best friend, another girl from the village, fell ill and died."

Coincidences, thought Aaron. Nothing more.

"You see, everyone in the village," continued Sakis, "we all wear *mati* to protect us."

"What is that?"

"It is like magic. We wear a charm that looks like an eye. Or else we keep garlic around the house."

Aaron recalled that when he had begun teaching Calista, her mother, Nectaria, had wrapped a piece of garlic in a thin cloth and given it to him. "*Skorda*," she had said. "To protect you."

He mentioned this to Sakis.

"I always carry garlic," replied Calista's uncle. "But most of us wear blue beads or glass necklaces."

"And if you wear these beads, nothing will happen to you?"

"Yes. You should be safe."

"Splendid. As it turns out, ever since I arrived in Corfu, over five months ago now, I have spent hours teaching your niece to speak and write in English, yet so far, I've not had a spell of misfortune."

Sakis appeared concerned. He said nothing. He scowled and turned his attention to the donkey. He tugged hard at the stubborn animal who had dug in its hooves and refused to descend the sandy slope towards the beach. "Perhaps… perhaps she has cursed you already and you do not know," muttered Sakis.

Aaron laughed. "If I must be cursed, so be it. Nikolaos doesn't seem to like me much, anyhow."

"My brother thinks it is British foolishness to teach her anything. She's just a girl," replied Sakis who was now out of breath. "And what is wrong with you?" he barked at the donkey. "Impossible animal." He brandished his stick and whacked the animal's flanks. The donkey shook its head but stood its ground.

"It does not seem to want to budge," observed Aaron, a keen spark in his eyes.

Sakis redoubled his efforts but the donkey was proudly anchored to the ground.

"Stay here," ordered Aaron. He walked towards the harbour.

Aaron reached the boat where Calista had been helping her father sort out the fishing spoils of the morning. They hoped to load the donkey and carry the fisherman's catch home where her mother would prepare it.

As he greeted Nikolaos, Aaron could not help but glimpse Calista's longing eyes.

Aaron had much experience with duping women. Over the years, he'd learnt to uncover what pleased each one of them, and to peer into their heart's desire. He sensed when a woman was in love with him and in the last months, he had deployed all his art to captivate Calista. It almost touched him how easily the girl from Kassiopi was won. But he bided his time, conscious of the prize she represented. He understood full well what he had witnessed so far.

He turned to her deliberately. "Alas, it seems we are faced with a difficulty. The donkey does not wish to come."

Calista smiled. She spoke to Nikolaos in their Greek dialect. Her father scowled as he answered.

Aaron sought only one thing. It was his new source of pleasure – to find occasions where Calista might employ her gift. As she did so, he would witness once more what others in the village frowned upon but which so stirred his passions, that each time, he trembled a little more with delight.

And now was such an opportunity. Aaron was determined to not let the moment slip. He addressed Nikolaos, knowing Calista would already agree.

"We tried everything. It will not obey. Please, give Calista a moment with it."

"A good whack with the stick and it will move," protested Nikolaos. What good farmer doesn't know this? I'll show Sakis how it is done."

Aaron stood in front of him.

"You would strike an animal when no force is needed?" he asked, in perfect Greek.

Calista was moved. She stared lovingly at Aaron, the man who understood everything about her.

Nikolaos looked furious but he relented. To waste further time would only spoil the fish. He turned to his boat and waved them away. "Just bring the donkey, here."

Calista was suddenly enlivened. Her eyes shone bright. She spun around and fled to the spot where her uncle waited.

Aaron knew what would transpire and it was no surprise to anyone when it did.

Calista approached the donkey. She reached a hand to its forehead and whispered to it. The donkey shut its eyes in a docile fashion. There was an exchange between them as the animal meekly lowered its head.

She began to stroke it, and once it was lulled, she stepped back down the slope. Facing the donkey again, she held out her hand, as though she wished it to follow.

It was instant. Without hesitation, the animal moved towards her, taking eager steps until it reached the boats. Before long, it stood at the ready before Nikolaos.

Aaron looked upon the girl triumphantly. She was smiling back at him and he knew at once that it was more than love. Calista adored him for he had been the first to encourage her talents when all in the village shunned her for it.

"That, Sakis," he whispered to the girl's uncle, "that is what we call animal magnetism."

Sakis shook his head. He didn't understand the term. He shot Calista's teacher a resentful glare.

"And now, you are happy, English man? You are happy with yourself? Do you think it's funny?"

"You should not be afraid of something which is perfectly natural," replied Aaron icily.

"The villagers, here, do not think like you. There are people in Kassiopi who are fearful of her presence."

Aaron pondered over those words.

Flowers of Kerkyra

UNLIKE England, Corfu was always green. There was the green of the olive trees, the green of the tall cypresses, the green of figs and oaks, and year round, colourful wild flowers dotted the island. One could observe the passing of time with the changing blossoms.

Aaron had arrived on the island during the late summer of 1835. Before he knew it, it was October, and the pink cyclamens were in bloom. In February the mimosas and cherry trees were spraying pinks, yellows and whites across the village. March awakened the purple and lilacs of the orchids, and these thrived well into the summer. More than a year had passed and it was autumn all over again.

Aaron had filled his time well. Not content with his regular English lessons and his successful courtship of Calista, he'd occasionally sneaked into Albania with English officers, for sport and game. Few people knew that in 1809, Lord Byron had explored Albania on horseback. Aaron had been just as keen to set foot in this fascinating landscape. He found the Albanian locals so unlike the demonic portraits that had been spread of them among the Ionians.

Aaron was now well-known in Kassiopi. Over time he had even made friends with a Venetian descendant. He'd rented a large wing in the man's decrepit mansion, up on the hill, a little inland from the beach. His new apartments were more spacious than the lodging by the harbour, and their seclusion more to Aaron's liking.

On this November day, Aaron stared broodily at his swarthy reflection in the mirror. He'd absorbed so much of the sun's rays on this island, that he seemed unrecognisable. I might even pass for an Albanian, he thought. Kneeling over a ceramic basin, he splashed water over his face.

Tonight, he would win. Upon his arrival in Kassiopi, he'd not guessed what he was capable of. Back then it all seemed out of reach. Then when the village doctor had come to him yesterday and blurted out the scandalous situation, Aaron knew it was just a matter of time.

An hour later, when Aaron stepped inside Nikolaos' home, a dinner guest of the Argyroses for the first time in over a year, he was surprised by their welcome.

He was greeted with kindness and respect, not just for having taught Calista wonderfully over the past months, but because a tragedy had struck, and on account of this calamity, Aaron had not seen Calista for weeks.

It was a curse, had bemoaned the village doctor as he'd shook his head. Aaron suspected everyone in the village might have learnt of the violent event by now, even if no one spoke of it in public. There were likely whispers in every home in Kassiopi. The word, *bandits*, was on everyone's lips.

Aaron sat himself down at his hosts' table. He could still hear the rhythmic murmur of the waves outside. He let himself be soothed by its gentle breath, his keen eye studying the home where Calista had grown up and where he'd been invited for a meal at last.

It was a simple tiled home with an arched ceiling, built in thick white-washed stone. Beside him, bordering the hearth, was a stone ledge where pink geraniums were arranged in blue vases. Candles glowed within tiny alcoves along the walls. More candles were lit along the mantelpiece, while a larger one presided in the middle of the table.

Nikolaos sat beside him as Nectaria brought an earthenware dish of stewed beef and diced potatoes.

Aaron cleared his throat.

"You physician has shared some distressing news about Calista," he began, a look of concern painted upon his face. "May I ask when this attack took place?" His manner was almost priestly. Privately though, he reflected on the tastiness of the *sofrito* dish; the beef, swimming in a zesty garlic sauce, made his mouth water with each bite.

A weighty silence followed his question. The couple looked upon each other and then Nikolaos made a brief motion with his hand to let his wife know they had no choice but to speak.

"Six weeks ago," admitted Nectaria, her voice lowered, for she spoke in shame. She poured Aaron a glass of homemade wine.

Despite the seriousness of the subject, Aaron could not suppress a feeling of triumph. Part of him enjoyed seeing the couple trying to please him. It was his reward for all the time he'd striven to pass as an English professor. With the villagers' scorn upon them, the Argyroses were desperate.

"We must think of Calista's safety," said Aaron, his face more solemn than ever.

"It is the right thing to do," replied Nectaria.

Nikolaos nodded. But he seemed conflicted.

"Do we know who they were?" asked Aaron.

"No one does. The police think they might be Albanian bandits. But now the harm is done. Calista refuses to remain alone. She is afraid to go outside. She fears for her life here. Who are we to trust? Who in the village hates her? We don't know. We do not know anything. But the harm is done."

"What does the priest say?" asked Aaron, savouring his meat.

"The priest…" grunted Nikolaos. "He has recommended that Calista be married. But what are we to do if no one will take her? Death follows her, Mr. Nightingale. Now she has brought us shame."

"The men who raped her knew what they were doing," said Nectaria. She was near tears.

There was a long pause as Nikolaos rubbed his wife's arm to comfort her.

Aaron took a deep breath. "In what curious position you seem to have found yourselves," he said at last. He drank his wine.

"I don't know what to do," pleaded Nikolaos. "The British, they have suggested Calista be taken to the asylum. At least there, she would be safe."

Aaron raised an eyebrow.

"To an asylum? I do not understand," he asked coldly.

"In the past," explained Nikolaos, "it was tradition to send the mad and those who are ill of mind to the monasteries. But not Calista. The monks do not want her. She is bad luck. You see now how hard it is for us."

"But…Calista's not mad," protested Aaron.

Nikolaos and Nectaria exchanged a quiet look.

Nikolaos suddenly grasped Aaron's arm.

"What am I to do, Mr. Nightingale? What am I to do with her? You tell me."

Aaron reflected on what he knew. "To send Calista to that prison now, is unwise," he said. "Who knows what ill treatment she might receive? It is too dangerous."

The couple looked confused. Nectaria brought a hand to her mouth and fought back tears.

"If you send Calista away now, she would remain one year in a prison," explained Aaron. He sighed, as though this truth burdened him. "Let me make this clear. Firstly, it is not my opinion that Calista is a lunatic. I find this difficult to believe. But to employ the term psychopath, you must know that for now, in the United States of the Ionian Islands, as in all of Greece, psychopaths and criminals are housed together in the same prison. Do you understand what this means? What if she is carrying a child?"

"She cannot stay here!" cried Nikolaos, revealing his true feelings at last. He seemed more alarmed at the thought of a bastard Albanian child than for his daughter's safety.

Aaron seized on this. He drew on all he remembered from his encounter with the doctor in Athens. "It would be wiser," he said, "if she were sent away only once the new British asylum opens its doors. Then she might benefit from proper hospital care and be treated with respect. In the meantime, if it turns out she is carrying a child, at least it will be born in your home, in a better place."

A look of utter contempt drew itself on Nikolaos' face.

"Could she not go to the new asylum, now?" pleaded Nectaria.

"I'm afraid not. It is not yet operating." Aaron looked gravely at both parents. "It might not open until another year."

Nectaria looked weary, conscious of the village status to which Calista had lowered her. "What will we do?" she cried.

"She cannot remain in this house," muttered Nikolaos under his breath. He could barely face Aaron.

Aaron saw what he had suspected all along. Nikolaos would be dishonoured for as long as his soiled daughter remained under his roof. His honour would not permit the young woman to remain in the village, let alone in his home.

"Perhaps I may be of some help," said Aaron.

That was all it had taken. Nikolaos and Nectaria had looked at him as though a great burden had been lifted off their shoulders. And if, for weeks later, Calista remained secluded inside her home, Aaron pressed on with plans for their departure.

The day came when Calista stood outside the very courtyard where Aaron had first set eyes upon her. Nectaria embraced her daughter by the gate. As for Nikolaos, he stood on the threshold of his home as though he feared Calista might run back inside.

Aaron waited near the donkeys. He noted the regret in Nectaria's eyes. He glimpsed the weathered hands she brushed against her daughter's face, watched her smile and whisper the last Greek words Calista would hear.

But as he looked past her, and past Calista, his attention caught onto a flurry of red and rust feathers. For the rooster paced wildly around the courtyard, fluttering its wings as though in anger. And it was not just the rooster. The courtyard had acquired a menacing atmosphere. All the animals that had gathered there seemed restless, and to Aaron it appeared the goat had never bleated as loud, nor had the cats ever emitted such high-pitched cries.

Aaron's hand tightened around the donkey's harness. He had a fleeting presentiment. It came as a warning, as though nature bore a secret message and he had been summoned to listen. But then Calista drew away from her mother, dispelling his doubts. She glanced at him, flowers in her hair, oblivious to how they would wilt on the long journey.

"Come," he said, reaching out to her.

A timid smile drew itself on her lips as she welcomed her new life.

"I will take good care of you, Calista," whispered Aaron. As he spoke, he helped her up on the saddle. His firm grip took her by surprise and he felt her tremble at the memory of her tragic ordeal. When she looked upon him again, her gaze was one of stolen innocence.

"Mr. Nightingale, you have saved me," she whispered back.

"I will soon be your husband, Calista. Please, call me Aaron."

He noted the blue beads around her neck and as a man of science, he felt it his duty to speak up. So he slipped a hand under the necklace.

"Where we are going, my dear, you'll have no need for these superstitious baubles. But wear them, if you like. It changes nothing."

Chapter 10

Saturday

MAURICE was disheartened. The journal found in Aaron's cabinet contained only bookkeeping records.

Shannon had not overstated Aaron's orderly streak. He had devised a register for all medications in his oriental cabinet. It allowed him to efficiently identify products on which he ran low and have these restocked as required. Each month, he would jot down the date and the number of pills left for each medical product at that time.

As thorough as it seemed, the journal told Maurice nothing of what he wished to discover. He had no choice. He would need to re-enter the cellar to retrieve the remaining documents. He would have to do this soon, then return the cellar key before Mrs. Cleary awoke. He dreaded her awakening at any moment. If the housekeeper discovered her key missing, she might question the maids, and Shannon would no doubt suspect what Madeleine had been up to in the housekeeper's bedroom. Maurice had no wish to jeopardise Madeleine's references.

The cellar door lay in the busy corridor nearest to the kitchen and grand staircase. The maids and the cook often circulated past. It was a huge gamble. Visiting the cellar in full daylight meant there was a high chance someone might see him. Maurice reflected on the maids' daily tasks, thinking back to all he had observed over the week.

There was a slim period during the afternoon when the corridor was certain to be clear. It was the thirty minutes, just before dinner, when Gerard busied himself in the kitchen while the maids were either in the washing room or upstairs. He only hoped Mrs. Cleary would remain asleep during that time. He would take that risk.

John Nightingale was calling in to Alexandra Hall after lunch and Maurice hoped Aaron's brother might know the meaning of the cryptic word left in his journal, *Ovee.*

Jarred by his frightening experience in the cellar, he wandered outside to stretch his legs in the garden. He pondered over the uncanny incidents he had so far witnessed since his arrival. Had he encountered Calista's spirit in the cellar or was someone in the house playing tricks on him?

He saw things with a different eye since last night. The living took on a surreal aspect, with every line on their skin more salient, every trait more pronounced. Lost in thought, his footsteps drew him in the direction of Calista's grave.

As he neared the herb garden, he glimpsed a movement behind the hedgerow. With caution, Maurice approached, wary of another encounter with the axe-wielding groundsman. He peered slowly behind the foliage. Alfred's menacing figure surged from behind the leafy wall.

Maurice shrank back, his pulse racing.

"Alfred?"

"Inspector Leroux."

The gardener remained near the hedge as though he did not wish to be seen. He held a small parcel in his hands. "Inspector Leroux. I thought I might have a word with you, sir."

His tone surprised Maurice.

"Certainly."

Maurice eased past the hedgerow and the two men were soon out of view.

Alfred stared at Maurice for a few seconds.

"That's a nasty bruise on your eye, sir."

"Ah, yes. I was a little clumsy last night. Nothing I'm proud of."

"My, and your temple. You got yourself in a fine shape."

"I'm afraid it comes with the job."

Alfred nodded. Then his gaze darkened. "I hear from the young Ellen that Mrs. Cleary isn't well," he began.

"Yes, that's right. I'm afraid she's ill."

"Well she won't know what I'm up to then."

"What do you mean?"

"See, I meant to tell Miss Vera something before she died."

"I see. Is that why you entered the house? The day Shannon asked you to leave?"

Alfred nodded.

"See, Miss Sophie and I…we… We had something going on. I thought she was keen on me. She'd send me love notes and leave them in the garden. She was a sweet girl. I never touched her though. I swear it. I'd take the carriage and drive her to town often and we had a fine time together."

"Did Mrs. Cleary know of this?"

"She didn't much like it. Kept a sharp eye on Sophie. She's got eyes everywhere."

"Why didn't you tell me this before?" asked Maurice.

Alfred glowered back at him.

"My heart wasn't in it," he answered at last. "A few weeks before she died, Sophie let me know she was planning to leave me, see. She was off to London. I was sour for weeks. I hadn't seen it coming."

Maurice eyed Alfred suspiciously. In past cases, he'd often found that jilted lovers committed violent crimes. He wondered if the gardener might have murdered Sophie after all. *Un crime passionnel?*

Alfred interrupted his thoughts.

"Like I said, I was sour about it. I kept to myself for weeks. But the night after Sophie died, Mrs. Cleary tossed away some old things for me to burn."

Maurice eyed the paper envelope Alfred held in one hand.

"Now I normally don't pry into people's things, see, but I recognised some of Sophie's things," said the groundsman. "And I wanted to see if there was anything for safekeeping." He opened the parcel. "I found those." He held out burnt letters to Maurice. They were charred, save for the dated letterheads.

Maurice held the letters up close. "Did Mrs. Cleary write these?"

"No sir, this ain't Mrs. Cleary's writing. It's Sophie's writing. The main thing is, you can see the letters are addressed to a Louise March."

Maurice flinched. Shannon had once alluded to an argument in which Sophie had called Mrs. Cleary, Louise. Why would Sophie choose to write to her own housekeeper? There was only one possibility…

Maurice cleared his throat, conscious of not revealing what he knew. "I see. Judging from the date, they were written a few weeks before Sophie died."

"Do you know who Louise March is, sir?" asked Alfred. "I guess she never got her letters."

"Yes, I'm afraid so. Leave it with me, Alfred. I am sure we can find out who Louise March is." A glint shone in Maurice's eye. "Thank you for coming forward. Not a word about these. I appreciate your discretion."

"Oh, I ain't speaking of this with anyone, sir. See, I'm the type that says nothing, and before you know it, I have people speak on my behalf. Happens all the time."

Maurice understood that Alfred had once gone to jail unfairly.

"Why didn't you speak to Miss Vera about these letters?"

"I tried. But Shannon got in my way. I would have told Miss Vera, but the lady died. And I'm not keen on John Nightingale knowing I was sweet on one of the maids."

"Yes, I understand. Thank you, Alfred."

"Have a good day, Inspector."

After slipping the letters inside his vest, Maurice made his way back to the house. His heart beat fast. He had a growing presentiment about Mrs. Cleary. He would have to confirm it later.

As he neared the front veranda, he saw John Nightingale alighting from his coach. Maurice waited for him by the entrance. While not as dandy as the portraits he had seen of Aaron, John nevertheless cut a dashing figure, even in his late forties. He was well-heeled and his suit was expensive.

"Inspector Leroux," he called out as the two men found each other by the colonnades. "I'm pleased to finally meet you. I've heard only good things about you. And how was your journey from…from…where is it again?"

"Normandy. I'm from Normandy. Delighted." Maurice shook John's hand.

"Normandy, of course! What a week! Should we move into the parlour? It's like a Russian winter out here."

Maurice sensed that the Englishman's exuberance was a mere attempt to hide his nervousness. As the two men stepped inside the house and towards the parlour, they continued to exchange civilities.

Maurice was quick to note that Shannon, who until then had been avidly peering out from the entrance hall, found the perfect moment, in full view of John Nightingale, for ordering Madeleine to bring out a platter of sandwiches.

Maurice had no sooner settled by the chimney, than he was burdened by the house's cloying atmosphere. The walls oppressed him. He was haunted by his encounter in the cellar, the mysterious scrawl in his journal, and the notion that someone, whoever it was, had entered his room multiple times as he slept.

He eyed the imposing portraits hanging upon the parlour walls. All these faces, how demonic they seemed now, as they stared down at him. He no longer felt at ease in Alexandra Hall. A lingering evil clung to the house. He was suddenly seized by an urge to flee to his room, pack his bags, and travel far away from Alexandra Hall.

He now understood why Mrs. Cleary's nerves were so shot, or why Ellen remained a pitiful waif despite Gerard's hearty meals. It was not the famine she had known in past years which kept her thin. It was fear. Fear, ruined her appetite.

John Nightingale drew him out of his dark thoughts.

"Why, Mr. Leroux, you look like you've had no rest."

"That might be true, yes."

"Well that's not good. Not good at all. And where is the ever chirpy Mrs. Cleary?" He pronounced the word chirpy to convey that it was entirely unlike Mrs. Cleary.

Maurice attempted to smile.

"I'm afraid she is unwell. She took to bed early yesterday and hasn't been seen since."

And I hope she stays asleep for a while, thought Maurice as he anticipated his visit to the cellar.

"Oh. Well that's unfortunate. I was hoping to speak with her about terms of appointment."

"The shock of the last months, I suppose," lied Maurice.

"I was told she's rarely ill. Solid nerves. The only time was after my sister-in-law passed away. Mrs. Cleary doted on Calista. In one of his letters, Aaron told me she was inconsolable and kept to her room for days."

"Speaking of your brother, tell me, Mr. Nightingale, do you think it not peculiar he would amend his will to ensure you wouldn't be permitted here for another six months? I remain sincerely baffled by this. It is a rather odd number, isn't it? I mean why six months? Are you not concerned about this?"

Though he fought to conceal his anxiety, Maurice's mind raced. For a man as organised as Aaron to suddenly adjust his will moments before his death, puzzled him. What had he been hiding?

"Honestly, I am not," said John. "My brother was quite the eccentric. Vera and I remained in the dark about his business. What I do know, is that he had marvellous taste in women."

Maurice reflected.

"Did he ever mention something about Ovee?"

John shook his head. "I'm sorry, did you say, Ovee?"

"Yes, does it remind you of anything?"

"No. I've never heard of that. What is it?"

"I was hoping you might know."

"I can't say that I do."

Maurice was disappointed.

John stood, seemingly aloof. He faced an antique cabinet and opened the front panels.

"Now, I believe…" he said, searching for something. "Mind you, I've not been to Alexandra Hall since the wedding. Now where was it? Aha! I knew he had some!"

He pulled out a tray of crystal glasses then helped himself out of a decanter of brandy.

Madeleine had since breezed in, carrying a tray of fresh brioche buns filled with salmon and cream cheese. She placed the tray on the coffee table. Before leaving, she eyed Maurice insistently as though to enquire if he had finished with the cellar key. She seemed anxious to return it.

"You seem to know this place quite well, Mr. Nightingale," observed Maurice. Glancing back at Madeleine, he quietly shook his head and mouthed a 'no'.

The maid walked out just as John sat back down.

"Call me John, please. Yes. Yes, you might say so. I helped build it, you see. It was a challenge to say the least. Aaron and his ideas." He leaned forward. "Now Mr. Leroux, how is your investigation progressing? Are you as dumbfounded as we all are? I myself have given up. I wish only to believe that my sister fell, just like the poor maid. No point delving into it. Nature takes its course as Aaron would say. I'm far too tired to grieve all over again. Bless her, she didn't have much of a life, my sister. There's a point where marriage is an altogether forgotten prospect. And when you've not married, well… It's a man's world out there. If you ask me, she is in a happier place, now."

"This investigation is not progressing much, I'm afraid," lied Maurice, concealing his secret visit to the cellar. "I feel I've only been scratching at the surface. I'm beginning to think that…"

Say it. You think Vera's death defies the laws of nature. You think Calista killed her. Say it!

No. He wasn't ready. He still had to ascertain what Aaron had been working on in the cellar. "Mr. Nightingale, I wanted to ask you what you knew of your brother's work. According to Mrs. Cleary, he was involved in quite an important project with his wife. Right up to his own death. Did you ever go in his cellar?"

John drank another mouthful of brandy. He emitted a sigh and reclined in his armchair. "And here I was hoping you'd ask me about the house's architecture. Blasted Aaron, even when he's no longer among us, he still manages to attract all the attention."

"I'm sorry," said Maurice, detecting the envy in John's voice.

"Don't be. I'm only joking." John's face turned grave. "I've never been down in that cellar. It was out of bounds for professional reasons."

"Tell me more about your brother."

"What would you like to know?"

"Anything. Your memories of his personality. Who he was as a man. What he did. Surely you must know something."

John reflected. "As a child, Aaron was easily fascinated. Never knew anyone so enthused by how things worked, so entirely obsessed with ideas. He wouldn't leave it alone."

"We all have our obsessions. Why was his any different?" asked Maurice.

"Yes, that's quite the truth, isn't it? But Aaron was frighteningly intense. I still have a letter he sent me while he attended medical lectures in France. He carried on about a book he'd read. *Franken… Franken* something…"

"*Frankenstein*?"

"That's the one. He was utterly enthralled by the idea… And he would not leave it alone for months. And long before that, when we were children, if something caught his imagination, he'd be unstoppable. What else? He'd try to teach our dogs some tricks. Poor creatures. He'd pester them, alright…"

"I see," said Maurice, recalling the medical cabinet and the disturbing jars in the cellar. "He was a doctor, I understand?"

"You could call it that," replied John. "And you know, I'd always known he'd become one. I just could not guess what sort of doctor. For a man of science, you see, he had this enormous faith in the mystical. It bordered on professional heresy. And it worsened over the years. Ever heard of *animal magnetism*?"

Maurice shook his head. "I don't know. Vaguely. I think we had an Austrian in France once who was an expert on the subject. Or was he German? I don't remember."

"Precisely. His name was Mesmer. Aaron read everything about him, about this *animal magnetism*. And then… he never let it go. He believed in the inner powers within each one of us. Anyway, I digress. Forgive me. But you get a sense of things, don't you? Aaron and his interests."

Maurice began to wonder whether John knew more of Aaron's work than he chose to say. "And over the years, then, what did he get up to, your brother? What was he working on?"

"Well, I'm afraid that when he graduated, I was no longer privy to his activities. If there's one thing I learnt over the years it's that there was no use prying into Aaron's business. He'd be more than generous, he'd come to my aid, and as a brother he was as supportive as they come, but if he ever dealt with the devil, then I sure wouldn't know it. Manner of speaking of course." He interrupted himself and stared grimly at the walls.

"Mr. Nightingale, why was your brother so secretive about this cellar? Doesn't it seem suspicious to you? I mean why go to such pains to hide what is in it?"

"I do not know." There was a new tremor in John's voice. Maurice wondered whether John feared what he might eventually discover about his brother. It seemed he deliberately shunned the truth.

"Surely you must recall something of it," insisted Maurice. "Anything. A man with such strong obsessions permits certain words and ideas to slip out of his lips at times."

John thought for a moment. "The only thing I do remember is that when we built this house, Aaron was adamant that the fountain be connected to the cellar."

"The fountain outside?"

"Yes. You see, there is a system of pipes running down the fountain and into the cellar. That, I remember. Is anything the matter?"

"No, nothing. Nothing at all. Please continue."

"It was Aaron's vision; inexplicable to me, of course. But in the grand scheme of things, I'm only the engineer and Aaron was the eldest so there was no point arguing. We ordered that gorgeous custom made fountain from Italy. And once he'd moved in, Aaron wanted the water pump to operate at all times. That stone fish you see leaping above the fountain has always had water pouring out of its mouth for as long as I remember." He laughed nervously. "I admit, there's nothing ingenious about it. After all, for centuries, numerous French chateaux have possessed similar fixtures in their gardens. But it took a certain know-how."

"I fail to understand, Mr. Nightingale. As an engineer, is it not pertinent of you to ask questions? Why do you think Aaron wished it done that way?"

John looked piqued. "Isn't it curious how one can feel proud of one's achievements and yet have not a clue what they've been used for? That's a dangerous idea, right there." He gave a half-smile.

"It sounds to me like you didn't want to know," cut in Maurice.

"Well, what would you have me do? Interrogate my own brother? For Pete's sake, it was only a fountain." John had dropped the easy going façade. He now seemed irritated. "I always suspected he had it built for Calista," he said at last. "She loved the ocean. I'm sure that pretty tiled work reminded her of her home in Greece."

Maurice sensed John's guilt. "Aaron was certainly a visionary," he said, hoping to uncover more.

"Oh, yes. When he wasn't hiring stray cats to buy their loyalty, he also liked to surround himself with great minds. Always did. You know, he invited a notable scientist at his wedding in the year after he returned from Greece. And blasted, she was a clever woman. I forget her name. Aaron was all over her, manner of speaking of course. He didn't remain a moment with his new wife. And the two discussed something for hours over cake and champagne."

"What were they talking about? It might give us a hint about his work."

"Well, funny you ask. Their conversation actually began about the fountain and... it digressed. But I remember Aaron questioning her about some device, a contraption of some kind."

"What device?"

"I'm sorry, it escapes me. I dismissed it as some *Frankenstein* fancy of his and at the time, I had taken on the role of entertaining the guests. But he did take her down there."

"Where?"

"In the cellar. They excused themselves for half an hour."

"Who was this woman?"

"I honestly cannot remember. But like you, she was French. She'd just returned from a long stay in the Mediterranean. I'm sorry, you'll have to ask Mrs. Cleary. She remembers names, that one."

"Your brother had many secrets, Mr. Nightingale," said Maurice darkly. "I'll be honest with you. It would not surprise me if the deaths in this house are linked to him."

John nodded. "You know that's just the thing about Aaron. Here you are, believing you are investigating two sudden deaths but you're beginning to understand that Aaron, himself, is his own mystery waiting to be solved. Is that not the case, Mr. Leroux? Do you not see what this house is? I've learnt over the years that possessions are a reflection of their owner. But knowing Aaron, he didn't just fashion Alexandra Hall as his trophy home, it's likely much more than that. Look at these portraits. Better still, at all the animals. You must learn to interpret them a little more. I've tried and I can't. Anyway, maybe you'll soon be able to answer this question for me: with a brilliant mind such as his, why did my brother kill himself?"

Maurice was taken aback. "What do you mean? He killed himself?"

"A family secret. No one knows of it and no one is to know. The coroner found traces of poison in Aaron's body."

"I did not know this," was all Maurice could reply. His mind raced. He had fixated on the notion that whoever had caused Sophie and Vera's deaths, might have also killed Aaron. But poison was in no way the work of a ghost. "How do we know someone did not poison your brother?" he asked, eyeing John with suspicion.

"I know what you are implying by this, Inspector Leroux, but you are misled. My brother took that poison himself. He knew he was dying. He had the time to change his will, right before expiring. He'd locked himself in his bedroom the whole time. There was no one with him when Mrs. Cleary summoned a locksmith to force open the door."

"I see." Maurice fell silent.

"Alas, if only you could see." John appeared to drown his fear in another mouthful of brandy.

Maurice remembered the cellar and peeked sideways at the clock. Gerard would soon be preparing dinner. It might be the only time he could re-enter the underground chamber, unseen. Already a chill worked down his spine at the thought of descending that narrow stairwell.

"Is there anything else you might know about Aaron's work, Mr. Nightingale? I find it impossible to rule out that whatever occupied your brother may be related to these deaths. And, I suppose now, to his own."

John seemed to recollect something. "Aaron would often ask me to collect things for him from London over the years." He paused. He looked grim and stared down at his empty crystal glass.

"What kind of things?"

"Well. Let's see..." John stood and poured himself another brandy. "Are you sure you don't want one, Mr. Leroux?"

Maurice saw exactly what had driven John up to now, and why he remained so evasive. It was guilt. The Nightingales' instinct for preserving their reputation was undeniable. "I don't like alcohol," he replied.

"Why, Inspector, that's unheard of for a Frenchman. Why is that?"

Maurice waved away the question. "It...disagrees with me," he mumbled.

"Suit yourself." John replaced the liquor into the cabinet and swirled his glass before sitting back down. "Look around you. All those faces. You can see his obsession can't you? He'd see something and he just had to have it. It didn't matter if he had something of the kind already, he desired it in another colour or another shape. He was a collector of things. And when those things bored him, he looked elsewhere. Aaron liked to import exotic shipments."

Maurice thought back to the numerous stacked boxes in the cellar. "How did you help your brother?"

"I helped supervise the shipments. I signed with my name because he was very clever that way. And in that period there were packages by the dozen."

"You mean, all those masks, the ivory tusks, the antique books in the library, the Abyssinian artefacts? The scimitars in the rooms upstairs?"

"Those? God, no. I mean illegal shipments. Consignments that needed to somehow evade customs unless of course someone bribed custom officials. If you'd forced open a box, who knows, you might have found a dead African's teeth or perhaps a skull, and I'm afraid that would only be the start. But to be quite frank, Maurice, I still have no idea what Aaron was up to. I'm sure it was harmless in the scheme of things. It's not like Aaron murdered anyone."

Maurice reflected on those words. Something John had said bothered him. He couldn't quite place it.

"Perhaps they were gifts," suggested John, catching Maurice's frown.

He was filling the silence now, thought Maurice. It was the guilt again.

"I recall that on three occasions," continued John, "a shipment arrived with some mysterious lettering. It was a small package. If my memory is correct, there were three of those over the years. Each time, Aaron assured me they were for Calista."

"Do you know what it might have contained?" asked Maurice, attempting to hide his agitation. He had just looked at the clock and was running out of time.

"No. I really can't say. It was a fragile consignment. We had to be especially careful transporting it from the ship to here. And we had to do so in a timely fashion."

"You never looked inside it, yet you seem to vividly recall that particular package. Why is that?"

"Well, it was Aaron who behaved strangely those times. He sent me letters daily. He was anxious to find out if it had arrived. I was to bring it to Alexandra Hall the minute I learnt of its arrival. That's Aaron for you. I was his little page boy." John swallowed the last of his brandy and stared at a portrait on the wall. "My God, those are frightening."

"One more thing, Mr. Nightingale," began Maurice.

"What would you like to know?"

"Did your brother ever speak about his wife? I mean, Calista. Did he ever… I mean, did he confide in you about anything?"

"How do you mean? About her illness?"

"No. I mean. Just in general… about their marriage. Did they…argue often? Did he say anything at all?"

"Only that she was cursed."

John blurted out the words before biting his lip. He stared silently at Maurice who had gone pale. Taking a deep breath, John revised what he had said.

"She could not have children. That's what I meant."

Return to the cellar

JOHN Nightingale was content to linger in the parlour with another drink in hand while awaiting dinner. Maurice excused himself. He quietly crept towards the empty corridor by the staircase. Aside from echoes of female voices in the commons, not a soul stirred. The maids tended to their chores and would likely not intercept him. He glimpsed Gerard's busy silhouette through the French doors of the kitchen, then looked at his watch. He had exactly half an hour.

The presence he had seen last night, on his first visit to the cellar, filled him with fear. Would Calista's spirit reveal itself once more? He dreaded another encounter.

Lamp in hand, Maurice leaned quietly against the cellar door and worked at the lock. A flurry of white hair dashed across the checkered tiles. Before he knew it, Willy bounced at his feet, more playful than ever, its tiny pink tongue searching for his hands. As the dog gave a sharp bark, Maurice felt a jolt of panic. He lowered himself to Willy.

"Hush, you!" He pressed a finger to his lips and shook his head. Willy made joyful leaps to lick Maurice's hand. "No. No more playing for today," whispered Maurice. He gestured frantically towards the commons. "Go," he ordered gently. "Go find Mary."

The dog hesitated. It looked up at Maurice, wagging its woolly tail and panting loudly.

"Go find Mary," encouraged Maurice. To his relief, Willy darted out to the washing room.

Without a second to lose, Maurice tore open the cellar door and rushed inside. He ceased thinking. He all but ran through the dark passage and down the stairs. As always, the confined spaces tormented him, but he fought off the sensation. He focused on the steps, paying no attention to the cloying walls or memories. He could hear his own frightened breath down the passage and the clatter of the lamp as it shook with each step.

Maurice had reached the chamber. He paused, hands on his knees, to recover from his manic race. As he looked down, he noted how wet the ground seemed. While the chamber was a humid place, more so than the rest of the house, this was not what he remembered. The floor's surface glistened under the lamp's glow. He shone the light across. Moisture, which had been absent on his first visit, now ran across the floor, all the way to the disturbed boxes. Feeling a chill inch down his spine, Maurice neared the trunks, fearing the worse.

Nothing stirred. The presence that had so frightened him last night was nowhere in sight. Relieved, he rearranged the empty trunks, peering behind them in passing. Nothing. Maurice shone the lamp around the cellar, weary of seeing a rising shadow. Again, nothing.

Nothing except... His eyes were drawn to the table, then to Aaron's medical case. They caught the shape of several metal objects that should not have been there. Maurice raised his lamp, in disbelief.

The missing spoons from the kitchen cabinet. Seven of them. Maurice was certain they were not present yesterday. *Someone had placed them on the table overnight.*

Had Mrs. Cleary been right all along? Had Calista's ghost taken spoons from the kitchen and now returned them? But why? And how? He recalled that several spoons had been found near Vera's body. Whoever had taken these had likely used them to cause Vera's fall, even if she had later died of suffocation. Maurice was wary. In the event Calista had never taken those objects, then who had? And who had entered the cellar after him?

He was running out of time. Upstairs, the corridor by the cellar would only remain clear for a few minutes. Maurice turned to the oriental cabinet and pulled open the third drawer. All of Aaron's work was recorded here. At least, he hoped. Retrieving the remaining two large leather-bound journals, Maurice secured them under his coat.

A sly creaking sound rose from the stairwell behind him. Maurice whipped his head round. He had left the door to the cellar unlocked. He hoped Willy had not lured any of the maids to it. His pulse raced as he wondered what he'd heard. Was it Mrs. Cleary? He drew nearer to the stairs and waited. After a few minutes, he shone his lamp within, but there was no one there.

He was about to return upstairs, when he remembered the pipes John had described, and which linked the fountain to the cellar. Curious, Maurice neared the unusual glass furniture he had bumped into the night before, and which he knew to be nearest the fountain outside. The water-filled case was larger than he remembered: ten feet in length and three feet wide. Maurice flashed his lamp around it and searched across the back wall. At last, he found it. Above, jutting out from the stone wall and immersed into the water, were two steel pipes.

Maurice stared at those pipes, more and more confused. He only hoped the journals would reveal all.

Mrs. Cleary Sleeps

JOHN stayed for dinner, a little perplexed that Mrs. Cleary was still confined to her room. Eager to curry favour with a potential employer, Shannon, who had steadfastly waited on the entire meal, used that opportunity to assure him they were managing quite well in Mrs. Cleary's absence. John downed his seventh drink before announcing he was taking his leave. He promised he would return early in the next week to speak with the housekeeper.

Maurice accompanied him to the entrance hall, worried that in his drunken state, the Englishman might fall and hurt himself. As they stood by the glass doors, John leaned against the wall to steady himself. He seemed to remember something. He turned abruptly to the detective.

"Jeannette Power," he slurred.

"Pardon?"

"The name of that French woman, the scientist… the one who came to Aaron's wedding. She's married to an Irishman. That's why I couldn't remember her last name. I forgot it wasn't French."

"I see. Is this woman still in England?"

"No, she's long returned to her native France." John teetered onto the veranda. "Well, best of luck with your investigation, Inspector. Hopefully by next month, you'll all still be alive."

There was, in John's last words, a dark humour reflecting an unsettled mind. The Englishman had lost three members of his family in the space of barely a year.

Maurice watched him totter along the path toward the awaiting coach, then closed the doors.

He longed to read Aaron's journals but he had to find Madeleine and give her the cellar key.

As he passed the commons, he could not help overhear an agitated conversation between the maids.

"We have to help. She is still ill," insisted Shannon. "I just came by her room with a tisane but she was sound asleep."

"How would you know for sure?" asked Ellen.

"I waved my hand across her eyes," insisted Shannon.

"She's an addict, no doubt," volunteered Madeleine.

"Mind your manners," warned Shannon in a senior tone.

Madeleine pressed her tongue against her cheek, stifling an urge to speak her mind with a less diplomatic tone. "I'm only saying that she's taken those pills again," she said.

"She needs her rest," snapped Shannon. "This month has been difficult for all of us. You, miss, were not here all year, so you have not a clue what she's been through since Mrs. Nightingale passed away."

The maids fell silent just as Maurice walked past.

He managed a nod towards Madeleine and hid himself into the kitchen to wait for her. She came in afterward, armed with a broom as though to sweep the kitchen floor.

"What are those pills you mentioned?" questioned Maurice, keeping his voice low.

Madeleine kept her eyes on her broom and whispered back. "You can't miss them. They were by her bed when I entered the room. She's been taking them for as long as I've been here. At this rate, they'll only make her terrors worse." She turned to him. "Mr. Leroux, did you go down there?"

Maurice nodded.

"And what did you see?" She studied the recent wounds on his face.

"I am not sure yet."

Sensing his reserve, Madeleine did not insist. "I'm afraid I can't return the key this evening," she said. "Shannon has given us more chores. She's been watching me closely all day. Knowing her, she'll report anything odd to Mrs. Cleary. You must do it yourself. Do it while Mrs. Cleary is still asleep. Slip it in the hidden right pocket of her black dress. It is hanging on the chair by the bed. Be quick about it." Madeleine resumed her sweeping, actress all the way.

Maurice left the kitchen. He climbed the stairs to Mrs. Cleary's room. The door was slightly ajar. He slipped in.

The sound of Mrs. Cleary's restful breathing rose like a murmur. Her face was turned towards the door. Beneath the bulge of her white bonnet, were loose tuffs of black and grey, framing a creased forehead. Her lips were perpetually pinched, even in sleep. Her eyes were wide open.

Maurice shuddered. He expected the housekeeper to startle awake but Shannon was right. Mrs. Cleary was fast asleep.

By the dim glow of a candle on the bedside table, Maurice quickly saw that Mrs. Cleary's room, while Spartan, was nowhere near as tidy as he had imagined it. By the bedside table nearest the housekeeper's face, he glimpsed the pills Madeleine had described. There was a tiny jar that for an instant seemed familiar. It lay opened, upon its side, its contents, half-spilled. The little yellow capsules had rolled, their fall averted by the coils of a silver necklace bearing a large Christian cross.

Maurice sought for the chair. His gaze fell on an oak table of Napoleonic style by the window. Upon it, were writing implements and sheets of paper. A crystal vase, filled with brown wilted flowers, held tainted water that lent the air an oaky odour. Finding the chair, Maurice approached. He had not noticed the shawl laying upon the floor, and his foot found itself entangled between it and the rug. Wary of tripping, he gripped the bed post. There was a thud. Maurice froze.

He stared at Mrs. Cleary. Her light snoring had diminished. He watched her eyes. They remained transfixed, staring ahead. Was she still asleep? He waited. Mrs. Cleary's breathing steadied.

Maurice held his breath. He reached for the chair and felt the black fabric, seeking the hidden slit. There was a slight rustling of taffeta but Mrs. Cleary did not stir. Finding the opening at last, Maurice pushed the cellar key into the skirt pocket.

He was not ready to leave. Not just yet. With cautious steps, he neared the bedside table, keeping his gaze on Mrs. Cleary. Her uncanny black eyes still watched him. The eeriness of those pupils was frightening.

Maurice listened until he felt reassured by Mrs. Cleary's regular breathing. He picked up one of the scattered pills by the tipped jar. Retrieving a small pellet from his own pocket, he inspected both gelatine capsules. Maurice frowned as he realised he was staring at identical capsules.

Astonished by his find, and what it meant, Maurice felt his pulse race. He returned the tiny pellet into his pocket and stared one last time at Mrs. Cleary's eyes. Had they moved? He was unsure.

Without a sound, he hastened to the door.

Maurice was sweating as he re-entered his bedroom.

He felt glad he had never thought to return Aaron's bookkeeping journal. He flipped through its pages, knowing precisely the product name he was looking for. He'd remembered its label from the compartment with the broken latch and he knew its pills were the same as those on Mrs. Cleary's bedside.

It took him an hour to pierce through Aaron's tiny handwriting, but he found the corresponding entry for the drug. The last time Aaron had accounted for this medicine was at the start of August, right before his death.

Maurice caught the generous figure in the last entry and knew something was wrong. With the cellar sealed and abandoned since Aaron's death in August, there should have been a near full amount of those pills remaining. Yet from what he had glimpsed, only a quarter of this amount remained in the cabinet.

Had Mrs. Cleary used up the rest? If so, she must have secretly entered the cellar. Perhaps she had even draped herself in a calico sheet to frighten and injure him… Maurice's thoughts raced.

What if someone in the house had surprised Mrs. Cleary entering the cellar and helping herself to these drugs? Sophie Murphy, perhaps? He remembered the blazing row Shannon had recounted, and Sophie's strange words: "*You won't get away with it, Louise.*" Shannon believed she had misheard. But after seeing the letters the gardener had given him, Maurice knew Shannon had heard correctly.

To employ John's own words, Mrs. Cleary was just another one of Aaron's hired stray cats. And stray cats possessed secrets. As for Sophie, she had known Jane Cleary's real name and so she must have been familiar with the housekeeper's secret past.

Maurice thought back to Shannon's other statement: "*She gloated about having come upon some money.*"

Ellen had stressed the same: *"An expensive one, sir. Shannon even said she was surprised Sophie could afford that sort of hat."*

Had Sophie blackmailed Mrs. Cleary? It would account for the maid's unexpected good fortune, and those letters Alfred had found addressed to Louise March. Sophie must have hatched that scheme upon witnessing the housekeeper enter the cellar. Why threaten Louise March over a small misdeed, when she had much more to gain from terrorising her over a darker secret?

Maurice sighed. It had taken him days but he had at last found some answers. If Mrs. Cleary had been taunted by Sophie, she could not have gone to the police without risking exposure of her true identity. She would have had to rid herself of Sophie.

I've got you, thought Maurice. All the pieces fell into place.

But what about Vera Nightingale?

Maurice was disheartened. There was no chance of Mrs. Cleary murdering Vera, for the housekeeper had gone to London at the time.

Or had she?

After reflecting upon this, Maurice sat at his desk. His pen ran furiously across a sheet of paper.

Mr. Wilson,

I bring to your attention the unsettling contents of Aaron Nightingale's cellar.

I have two of his medical journals in my possession. Perhaps they will elucidate what has taken place in this chamber, and what it may mean for your other client, his brother.

Time, however, is short, and I must speak to you in person.

I may have made a discovery relating to Sophie Murphy's murder. I ask you to promptly launch an investigation. I need to know all you can find on a certain, Louise March.

Now with regards to Miss Nightingale's death, it appears that Mrs. Cleary had an alibi. Two staff members have sworn that she took the carriage herself the day before and travelled to London to prepare her upcoming immigration to Australia. If this were true, she would have visited the Colonial Land and Emigration Commission. I entreat you to call upon the commissioner to ascertain whether this was the case.

Inspector Leroux

On a separate letter addressed to the Reading Town police station, Maurice penned the following,

This is Inspector Leroux investigating the murder of Sophie Murphy and Vera Nightingale at the behest of John Nightingale. I believe I have a suspect. Please send armed men immediately to Alexandra Hall. Occupants may be in danger.

There was quiet rap at his door. Maurice rushed to open it, convinced it was Madeleine.

Before he could reach it, the door swung open, making way for the dark folds of a long black dress. Mrs. Cleary's gaunt frame advanced towards him.

He startled, noting how composed and well-rested she seemed while only an hour ago, she had been fast asleep.

"Good evening, Mr. Leroux." She feigned light-heartedness but her voice bore an icy quality.

"Mrs. Cleary, I did not expect you."

"Who did you expect?" Her eye travelled to his desk. With a casual hand, Maurice shifted his journal so that it covered the letter he'd just penned.

"No one, Mrs. Cleary. It is rather late. I will be retiring very soon," he said, hoping his voice revealed nothing.

"I thought I might pay you a courtesy visit to apologise for my absence these last two days." As she spoke, Mrs. Cleary edged closer to the desk. She cast a keen eye on the documents in front of her. Maurice breathed a sigh of relief. The parcel Alfred had given him lay underneath his coat on the table. She would not see it.

"No harm done," he chirped. "I understand you have been ill. Are you… feeling better, Mrs. Cleary?"

To Maurice's horror, she gave a sly smile. It was an uncanny row of teeth. "I've never felt better," she said, almost sweetly.

Maurice waited, feeling his discomfort rise. He expected Mrs. Cleary to leave, but she stared at him, her gaze more intense. "Aren't you forgetting something, Mr. Leroux?"

Maurice felt a coldness spread across his scalp. He suppressed a desire to shrink back.

"I…I don't know what you mean."

"I thought you might have letters you'd wish to send out. The delivery boy is usually in early on Sundays. I could hand them over to him for you." There was in her tone, a lick of menace, something unsaid that made the blood rush to Maurice's cheeks. He wondered if she had seen him creep in her room. Had she truly been asleep? What had she seen with those staring eyes?

Despite his galloping heartbeat, he straightened, adopting a neutral expression. "No, there'll be nothing to send out," he replied. "Thank you for asking, Mrs. Cleary."

The housekeeper gave an austere nod.

"Well, goodnight. I must see to it that the girls have completed all their chores."

Maurice felt his pulse return to normal. Had Mrs. Cleary intuited that she was now his primary suspect in the death of Sophie Murphy? He brushed the thought aside. There was nothing he had done or said which would give that away. He was overly anxious, that was all.

Having regained his calm, he folded his letters and sealed them in envelopes.

He had just finished writing out the addresses when another tap at the door alarmed him.

Through the keyhole, he glimpsed Madeleine's silhouette.

"Come in," he whispered as he opened the door.

Madeleine quietly slinked in.

"She's up Maurice. I saw her walk into the commons. I don't know why she would think of roaming around at ten o'clock at night. Did you do it?" she asked nervously.

"Yes. I returned the key," began Maurice. "But in the process, I might have discovered something. I'm afraid it's not good. I need you to be wary of Mrs. Cleary. I cannot say anything further."

Madeleine stared at him in mute astonishment. "You think she might be a murderer?" she whispered.

Maurice hesitated. "Perhaps. I can't talk about it."

Madeleine fixed him, a look of enquiry in her eyes.

"You have been a great help, Madeleine," said Maurice still speaking in a hushed tone, "but I'm afraid that's all I can reveal for now. I'll find out soon enough. In the meantime, avoid Mrs. Cleary as much as you can. Better still, can you absent yourselves from Alexandra Hall tomorrow? All of you."

"Tomorrow?"

"No one should remain alone with her until John Nightingale returns next week." Maurice actually counted on the police's presence more than anything.

"Well, we could ask Alfred to drive us somewhere… It's Sunday tomorrow. I'll ask Shannon if we could all go to the markets and then sleep at her aunt's until Monday. She lives in Reading Town."

"Perfect. Now, something else." He blushed. "Have you…time at your disposal early tomorrow morning? Or perhaps tonight? I… I'm in need of your help."

"What do you have in mind, Mr. Leroux?"

"You said you had a solid memory. It might serve this investigation. I need you to search through Aaron Nightingale's scientific journals. There are too many volumes in his study. I'm afraid I'll have no time to do it myself and I feel I can…trust you."

"What will you get up to while I'm in his study?"

Maurice smiled. "I've discovered Aaron's personal journals in the cellar. There's quite a lot to get through. I was hoping to read them while you peruse the bookshelves. Please, I need you to look up anything you can find on this woman." He seized a pencil from his desk and scribbled the name, *Jeannette Power* on a sheet of paper. "Here, take this. All I know is she was a scientist and that Aaron was keen to speak with her."

Madeleine's eyes glowed with excitement but there was caution in her voice. "A woman? Really? What kind of scientist?

There's an awful number of books in that study. It's like looking for a shell in the ocean. Really, Mr. Leroux."

"I can't be certain but I have a feeling that her work relates to...water. Can you look for that? Anything you can. You see, I saw something in the cellar. Whatever it is, it seems to have been extremely important to Aaron Nightingale."

Madeleine studied the name thoughtfully. "If I recall, Mr. Nightingale owned many books on sea life," she replied. "Do you think this woman might have been a marine scientist?"

Maurice gazed at Madeleine with renewed respect. "Whatever she was or did, John spoke of her this afternoon. He said Aaron took her down to the cellar on his wedding day. If that is true, she is key to Aaron's secret projects. Start as soon as you can but don't let Mrs. Cleary see you. I'll be here if you need anything."

"Why Mr. Leroux, this is quite an adventure. Of course, I'll help you. Whoever thought Frenchmen were fun, huh?"

"Fun? Is that what it looks like? I'm terrified, Madeleine. Everything about this house is wrong."

"Now, don't you start, as well! I've seen the same look in Mrs. Cleary's eyes. Are you quite sure you are not going as crazy as she is?"

"Well if she is crazy, then we must be ever careful around her. Now hurry."

Madeleine opened the door, peering out to verify that all was clear.

"Be careful, Madeleine," said Maurice as she slipped out of the room.

When the maid had left, Maurice pulled out the journals from under his vest.

"*À nous deux, maintenant*," he whispered as though Aaron had suddenly become his lifelong adversary.

It would take him hours to read each journal, and to piece together years of secrets. But whatever Aaron Nightingale had been involved in all these years, Maurice had an unsettling feeling that Calista had been wronged.

Chapter 11

Mr. and Mrs. Nightingale

Alexandra Hall, 1840-1845

"Man acts upon everything that surrounds him with an animistic force: doctors do not know it.

Floods of rays escape from him at all times: they have discovered nothing of the kind.

— Jules Denis, Baron du Potet

FOR a while now, Calista no longer tasted the joys of simple pleasures. Marooned in the Berkshire countryside, and rather friendless, she had once gained cheer from occasionally treating the maids, and having tea in Mrs. Cleary's company. Lately all her pastimes had left her with a lingering emptiness.

It wasn't that she had become bored of reading Greek philosophy and tending to her garden roses. It wasn't that she had grown accustomed to Aaron's kisses or his firm touch. By the same token, the intensity and the quiet manner in which he admired her every move continued to thrill her, as it had, when she had first set eyes on Aaron Nightingale back in Kerkyra.

But it was true that since leaving her village in Kerkyra, and upon having lived three years in Alexandra Hall, watching her husband disappear in his cellar at long intervals, she soon sensed that Aaron had grown impatient. It seemed her husband withheld something from her, and the very act of not revealing it fed his resentment.

Whatever the cause, or mechanism for Aaron's disquiet, Calista succumbed to the trap which those lacking self-assurance tend to fall into. She began to feel ashamed, suspecting that Aaron might have regretted bringing her, a stained woman, all the way to England.

This tension came to an abrupt head one day, on a rare occasion in which Aaron broke their solitude by inviting an old medical friend to dinner. It was a standout event for Calista.

Her English had much improved and by remaining quiet most of the time, speaking few words, she believed none could ever guess at her background or her modest origins.

Calista's eyes shimmered the moment she donned her new dark blue crinoline dress. She had chosen this one over the crimson or black gown, because she loved the way it showed off her shoulders, and the stunning effect the colour had on her eyes.

In her village, the blue had been reviled. Here, it often sparked compliments.

Sophie chirped with delight as she laced up Calista's perfectly shaped corset and groomed her mistress' long black hair. Attired in the latest London fashion, Calista could have passed for a Welsh brunette, all traces of her Greek traits wiped away.

Calista remained withdrawn for the entire meal, playing the accommodating hostess on occasions, but for the most part, letting her English husband drive discussions to avoid any attention on herself that might prove unseemly. She hoped Aaron would be pleased, and then perhaps this dinner would prove to be a new pattern in their lives, and one day, they might even take a coach into London. It wasn't that Calista disliked Alexandra Hall but part of her felt estranged from the rest of the world.

The tone was set soon after Shannon had delivered the Yorkshire pudding to the table. Aaron's elegant guest spoke up and addressed his host with the following words: "I would be doing you a disservice, my friend, if I did not alert you to your reputation among our fellow graduates."

"Pray, tell. I am so much of a pariah, these days, it would not disturb me in the least." Aaron reached to his right for Calista's hand. "My sister, Vera, knows I am immune to hearsay. No gossip has ever stopped me before."

"As a student, you were known for dabbling in animal magnetism, a tenet whose theories have long been disputed if not disproven. It made you downright unpopular. Am I right?"

"Is that where discussions lead you when you visit the clubs these days? Raymond, this is old news. It's hardly a scandal."

"Oh, but it is, and it pains me to hear it. Several of my colleagues are convinced you've given up medical practice on account of past disagreements with leading physicians in this country."

"Hardly. I've given up medical practice because I've other means to make a living. And to assuage your curiosity, I never intended to become a practicing doctor. There are more glorious pursuits in this world."

"Such as?"

Aaron reached for his wine glass.

His friend mirrored the gesture.

A cold, and almost chilly exchange issued between the two men as they drank.

"A wonderful wine," conceded Raymond. "Well of course, you're a well-travelled gentleman, my friend, and your lifestyle is your affair, after all. But I'll be honest with you, there is debate among some of us that you might even possess your own laboratory."

"My, it would seem I am the talk of town."

"Some of us have long suspected that you've buried yourself here, far from London, on the sole pretext of one day proving that animal magnetism is real."

Calista's heart began to pound inexplicably in her chest. She stared at their guest, seemingly passive but her eyes widened.

Aaron had paused, taking in the accusation. Calista took a deep breath and watched the tension in her husband's jaw.

"What if I am?" he replied.

"Come now," said Raymond, "you are a student no longer. Leave it alone. We both know Mesmer was a charlatan. There is no such thing as a magnetic fluid inhabiting either you or me, nor can it be credited for any healing effect on other beings."

"Funny you should say that, Raymond. There is work being carried out as we speak, in France, about its validity in the power of suggestion."

"It will all fall apart, as Mesmer's theories eventually did."

"Wrong. I have read Simon Mialle's treatise, have you?"

"Never heard of it and most certainly will not bother."

"You should. He detailed cases of magnetic healing through the application of animal magnetism for the period between 1774 and 1826. All cures. Every single of one of them. Each of the cases outlined the disease that was treated and the animal magnetic procedure that was applied, followed by the results. And these results spoke for themselves. This is hardly the work of charlatans. But Raymond, before you give way to hearsay and laugh away my ludicrous ideas with your medical colleagues, let me remind you of another case in 1829. It begs to be heard. An adherent of Mesmer, Dr Pierre Jean Chapelain, assisted surgeon Jules Cloquet in a cancerous breast operation performed on a sixty-four-year-old woman. Her name was Madame Plantin. Not an easy operation, and one which could have had tragic effects. Chapelain used the power of suggestion to mesmerise Madame Plantin who reached a state of near-sleep where she was, in all appearance, at rest, with no discernible changes in pulse or respiration, yet capable of conversing during the entire twelve minutes of the operation. Let me finish. Her wound was closed and dressed. Madame Plantin was left in this state for two days. Dr. Chapelain rose her from her mesmerised state after which she continued to feel no pain and had no recollection of what had transpired. Now, Raymond, what do you call this? If not evidence for the effectiveness of animal magnetism?"

"An accomplice, without a doubt. The entire operation was a farce."

"Like you, there were numerous attempts to discredit Mr. Cloquet. But he asserted that everything was true despite being ridiculed in the *London Medical Gazette* and the *Nottingham Journal*."

"An assertion of conspiracy! So what do you suggest, Aaron? Do you sincerely believe that by waving your hands, you can change a staff to a writhing snake?"

Aaron's old-fashioned biblical name was often the subject of derision. "Spare me the mockery. The scientific basis is perfectly clear. Similar procedures have been replicated in America."

"Scientific basis? I am astounded, Aaron." Raymond shook his head while attempting to finish the meat on his plate.

"What you persist in ignoring is that I am far from alone. Hear this. For almost three years now, the Baron du Potet, a French mesmerist, has conducted promising work at the North London hospital. While physicians have directed their studies on applying animal magnetism to the practice of pain free surgery, du Potet has evolved it to the art of magnetic healing."

"Magnetic healing? For goodness' sake. I don't wish to offend you, Aaron, but all this seems a little fanciful to me. I consider myself a man of science. If I cannot see it, it does not exist."

"Have it your way, Raymond. Call me a madman, but know this: du Potet has successfully healed an epileptic girl. You ought to read the letter in the Lancet from a couple of years ago. Better still, I'll lend you a copy of his *Introduction to the Study of Animal Magnetism*, it might even open your eyes."

Raymond had ceased eating.

"My dear colleague," he said, "might you not agree there is a significant leap between allaying pain and healing a patient? You seem to place enormous faith in this du Potet. My friend, return to London. Leave this place. Isolation corrupts the mind. Listen to yourself. Do you realise what you are saying?"

Aaron straightened. His recent excitement had given way to a grave expression.

"I have travelled the world, Raymond. The incredible things I have witnessed in India are contrary to what the medical sciences would have us believe. Du Potet only scratches the surface of true potential. I, for one, hold the unshakeable belief that certain individuals, more than the rest, have in them something of this magnetic quality. Without a doubt. I believe this force can heal. It can redress imbalances in others and, yes, it can lead other beings into different states of awareness."

"Like Jesus? Forgive me, Aaron. And I say this as your friend, but I fear many of us remain dubious about these Mesmerism fancies. If you want the rumours to cease, you are going to have to prove all of this."

A cold smile drew itself on Aaron's face.

"That is exactly my intention," he replied.

"Oh, really? What are you planning to do? Hire a mesmerist and conduct vivisections on willing patients? You'll hardly find any volunteers. All the best of luck with that."

At Raymond's signal, Shannon brought over the wine and refilled his glass. Calista sat on the edge of her seat, her eyes riveted on the trickling red liquid. With each drop, she felt a growing sense of dread.

Aaron reached for her hand and brought it to his lips. His palm was moist.

"I'm sorry we have bored you, my darling. Mr. Rogers, here, does not believe in an extraordinary phenomenon that has fascinated me all of my life. It unsettles him, you see. Often, so-called wise men remain anchored to their prejudices, and in this, they may as well be fools."

Calista smiled despite a wary premonition that chilled her spine. She had felt the heat of her husband's kiss on her skin. She had known instantly that Aaron's cool charm belied the seething rage she sensed now, coursing through him like an electric fire. She turned nervously to their guest. "And how was your dinner, Mr. Rogers? I hope you enjoyed it."

"Oh, wonderful, madam. I've not had the pleasure of venison in months. My compliments to your cook. And you, my lady, you've been such a charming hostess. It's a wonder you've not thrown me out for lecturing your husband. I must say, I deeply admire your patience. That is the way of the world in the medical field, I'm afraid. We find ourselves constantly at each other's throats and we seem to exist only to disagree." Then before Calista could respond, he turned abruptly to Aaron, "But I insist that being away from London has muddled your head. I've wondered how you can possibly fare so far from everything. This house is still a long way from Reading. Does Mrs. Nightingale not feel lonely?"

Calista was heartened by Raymond's words. She'd never had the courage to voice how she felt to Aaron. Perhaps Aaron would also be swayed. Mrs. Cleary had fondly spoken of London and Calista already imagined Regent's Park, the river Thames, the elegant boutiques and coffee shops. There was a world to see out there. It wasn't sunny Kerkyra, but it was something. She turned to her husband, awaiting his response. But Aaron's faraway expression had blackened.

"There are means to bring the best of all we need to Alexandra Hall. Everything, anything at all can be purchased and transported here," replied Aaron darkly. He seemed miles away, barely looking into Raymond's eyes as he spoke.

The latter tilted his head, suddenly aware of Aaron's changed mood. He set his wine glass on the table.

"I meant it, you know," insisted Raymond. "If you can find a method to prove your far-fetched theories, then all the best to you. But tell me, do you have a mesmerist in mind? Another Frenchman, perhaps?"

Aaron did not reply to this ultimate provocation. He glanced at Calista, who stiffened, before meeting her husband's gaze with her own penetrating blue and black eyes.

"I have better than a mesmerist," said Aaron.

And he grasped her hand tighter than he ever had.

Lost Souls of Alexandra Hall

IT had begun with dogs then later, cats. Aaron would encourage her to caress the animal and bond with it. For the first few days, it grew accustomed to the cellar. This would take a week and then the subject, as Aaron liked to call them, would attach itself to her and begin to obey all her orders.

It was her favourite period. She loved them and they loved her. But what she loved most, was the enchantment it seemed to have on Aaron. When he saw her interact with the animals, he fell once more under her spell, and she glimpsed the wonderment in his eyes. It reminded her of how he used to stare at her in Kerkyra. It reassured her that all was well between them. As the days passed, Aaron was continually impressed by her abilities, her animal magnetism, as he called it. It made her feel useful. It made her feel loved for who she was.

In the early days, he also taught her how to use a stethoscope. With the dog or fox, lying down strapped on a table, she would press the end of this wooden tubular contraption and listen for the animal's heartbeats.

She learnt to recognise when the animal was unsettled or when it was calm, just by listening to the ebb and flow of its breathing and the pulsing beats deep within its chest.

"If the subject is in distress," advised Aaron, "then you must take over."

Aaron had designed what he called his pain free experiments. It began as a period of soothing where Calista caressed the animal and monitored its heartbeat. She would record the number of beats per minute. Aaron prepared the instruments and washed his hands in a basin.

The first time the candlelight reflected on the metal implements, Calista had almost swooned. As Aaron laid out various surgical contraptions from his opened leather case, she felt herself grow weak.

She had lost all courage. "What are you going to do?" she had asked in disbelief.

"You can do this, Calista. Do not fail me," had replied Aaron. He shot her such a stern expression that she felt a nasty jolt in her chest. From that moment, she asked few questions.

And in his journal, Aaron would describe the nature of each experiment. He undertook the minor operations first, those he deemed would inflict less pain and were unlikely to harm the animals. Then, over the months, if the animal remained alive, he performed more advanced vivisections – removal of a paw, an ear, the kidney, or else an entire limb.

The method was simple. Soothe, operate, monitor and soothe again.

"I can't do this," she cried out, the first time he brandished the knife over a yelping Labrador puppy.

"Calista, you must trust in your capacity to diminish its pain. Everything rests upon you and your magnetic force."

Calista shook her head violently.

"No, no, Aaron. I cannot do this. I can barely look. Don't make me look."

"Shut it out. Look away if you must. Focus on its heartbeat. Raise your arm, like this, if you find it is in distress and you wish me to pause. Then it is up to you to soothe it. If you do not apply yourself properly to calm it, it will feel pain, Calista."

Calista flinched away, trembling. "I don't know what you mean."

"Calista, my darling. We've spoken about this. I do not possess your abilities. But this dog," he said, pointing to the puppy strapped upon its side, "has utmost faith in you. Use it. You must caress it and speak to it like you always have, continue to hold its attention until it focuses only on your voice, until it falls into a trance and begins to lose sensation and feels no pain. Do you understand?"

Calista had not been convinced. But she'd tried. To her great relief, the minor operation was completed smoothly, with the puppy's expressive eyes fixed upon her face. It yelped a little when the knife was inserted but she worked her magic, covering its groans with her soothing voice until it quietened. Calista was astounded. It had barely registered the pain. Its breathing remained steady and the heartbeat had not changed. She had dressed the wound and watched the puppy settle upon its paws, a little shaken but without noticeable distress.

This very first experiment revived her faith in her husband. Perhaps Aaron was right and the subjects would never feel pain. What point was there in being afraid? After all, it was up to her, wasn't it?

Aaron worked only on minor vivisections in the first years. On each occasion, the subject was bundled up in a blanket then released and returned to the countryside or in a farm. Calista had not known what to expect but over time she felt saddened, realising that she would not see them again. Each subject began to represent an impending loss. It was her silent wound. For to bond with it so deeply and to impress on it her magnetic force, she made herself vulnerable to letting it go.

Over the years, for each operation, Aaron made corresponding notes in his journals describing his methods and whether or not the results were significant in demonstrating the effect of animal magnetism. The first indication of success was an observed stability in the subject's pulse over the entire operation, with no significant variation. The second measure of success was whether the animal stabilised after the operation – whether it ate normally, ignoring its sutures, or showed signs of stress and pain.

Aaron had been pleased with the results of the minor operations. He had written that so far, animal magnetism had proved effective in producing pain free operations.

He had devised a naming convention for the subjects. D1 was for the first dog subject. D2, applied to the second dog, and so on and so forth... He employed F, for fox and then later, C, for cat. Calista conceded it was easier to refer to the subject by an initial, rather than a name. Though it lacked warmth.

Things worsened in the following years.

The first kidney vivisection did not go as planned. Calista stared in dismay as blood spilled from the wound, staining her red dress. The cat shrieked and she lost its attention. Pressing her own ear on that damned wooden tube, she had noted the cat's galloping heartbeat. Her nerves were shot. She shook throughout the entire operation. As for the cat, it shrieked until it lost consciousness.

But over time, the couple made progress. Certainly, animals succumbed to their wounds following the procedures, and most of them eventually died, but it appeared to Aaron they felt no pain.

"We need to work harder, Calista," he would say. "Stronger results, would require the creature to stay alive. The subject needs to be oblivious to what it has undergone. For days afterwards, it must go on living, feeling no pain."

But despite all her efforts, the animals kept dying soon after. Dispirited, Calista would lay them inside an old wooden trunk and Aaron would bolt it shut then ask Alfred, who ignored everything, to burn the trunk.

On the day following an operation that went awfully astray, Calista was staring expressionless at the remains of a fox on the operating table. She was hunched forward and stunned by what she had witnessed. Aaron wiped the blood off his hands and threw away the cloth in anger.

"Something is not working as it should," he grunted. "The creature knows too much. It knows in itself that something is wrong and it behaves accordingly."

Calista ran a trembling hand over her forehead. She wrapped the dismembered fox in a hemp cloth and laid it into a trunk which the gardener would later burn.

Aaron sat by his desk, brooding over the flaws in his experiment. “They are too intelligent. They know what they have endured, even if they are soothed. We will need to make use of a stupid creature. Or else, I will have to stun the subject…”

Aaron soon settled on the idea of drugging his subjects, employing various pills and medicinal concoctions he had studied during a past trip to Nanking and Peking. He experimented with various combinations and in the first instance, where he had once been curious to see if the animal would live, he now grew fascinated by another idea.

“What if it were made to be more aggressive?”

Calista’s vision blurred. They had strained themselves all week and she had so far witnessed the death of two dogs.

“You wish them to be more aggressive?” she asked in disbelief.

“Think of it, Calista. If in the first instance, the subject were to be rendered anxious or aggressive, if it were agitated, then we could measure the degree to which the animal magnetism succeeds in returning it to a calmer state. Think of it. In what extreme state must a subject find itself before you fail to soothe it?”

“But it will attack us…”

“Calista, will you cease fretting? We will strap it down, like we always do.”

Aaron set about to order and catalogue various medicinal capsules and tablets.

I am astounded to discover that, for minor operations at least, a rise in aggressive behaviour does not lead to any significant tempering of the effect of animal magnetism. The subject heals steadily and does not feel pain.

When Calista had read Aaron’s stunning conclusion, she felt herself grow numb. Could he not see that with subjects in an aggressive state, she was more and more afraid to enter the cellar? Could he not see she was exhausted with each attempt to becalm the animals? They would often scratch and bite and to maintain them in a calm state, robbed her of her own inner peace. Over time, these violent exchanges had seeded in her a feeling she had never experienced before – a simmering rage that she fought to suppress.

These days, Aaron's interest in her powers no longer made Calista proud. She had noted the rise in his arrogance. He snapped at her more often. He would grow impatient if she needed to rest or if she averted her eyes from the operating table. But more upsetting, was the cruel light glowing in Aaron's eyes when he handled the subjects. Where in past years, she and Aaron would simply burn the dead, now Aaron wished to keep a severed part of the animal in a sealed jar, like a relic. Calista never questioned her husband but she felt the disquiet grow within her. There were now dozens of these trophies upon the shelves. Every day, the underground chamber acquired a nightmarish quality.

When Aaron began to experiment with stronger drugs, Calista somehow found the strength within her to continue.

On a tin tray, she would crush the contents of several drug pellets and blend this powder into the animals' food. One day, she called Aaron.

"It's gone. I've only just released the fox, and already, the food has disappeared before it could get to it."

They looked everywhere and in the end, Calista was forced to setup another bowl of crushed biscuits where she had stirred in the powdered tablet.

In the evening of the same day, Aaron heard Willy had bitten Shannon. It had demonstrated aggressive behaviour all afternoon.

Soon afterwards, Aaron examined Shannon's hand and dressed it. Calista had locked herself in her room and told everyone she was not having supper.

"I understand Mrs. Nightingale's distress. I've had Willy tied up in the gardener's shed. We shall have to put it down," said Mrs. Cleary after dinner.

"You will do no such thing," said Aaron.

"I beg your pardon Mr. Nightingale, we cannot have Mary's dog running around like it did, and biting every living soul. Mary was quite upset about it. And Shannon is lucky she still has her hand. That dog might have had rabies, have you thought of it?"

Aaron had thought of it. He took Mrs. Cleary aside. "Now there's no reason to put down that dog. I can assure you it does not have rabies. Besides, I know how attached Mary is to it. Let me examine it tomorrow and if it seems normal, as I'm certain it will be, we'll untie it and return it to the little Mary."

But Mrs. Cleary was adamant that the dog should be put down as soon as possible.

"Suppose I tell you, Mrs. Cleary that it was my fault. Willy has somehow found itself in the cellar and taken some tablets which it should not have."

"Well I…how on earth did it find itself in the cellar?"

It was a valid question.

The following day, Willy looked quite sheepish. It had returned to normal and Mary was grateful to be reunited with her favourite companion.

Calista and Aaron looked in vain for the means by which Willy had crept inside the cellar. "There must be a hidden passage abutting this chamber. It can't be far. Willy must have followed it and then crept out of a hole in the cellar wall. Wherever it is, we must seal it."

But they had not found it.

"I shall make sure Mary does not let Willy roam around, don't worry," said Aaron.

And so the months followed and the gruesome operations grew more complex and dangerous. Now Aaron had control over two variables: the degree of aggression in his subject and the nature of the operation. Dozens of animals died.

After every procedure, Calista collapsed on a stool, shaking uncontrollably, her hands dripping in blood. Then she would weep, unable to look at the subject. Beside her, in a state of shock, and still strapped to the operating table, the animal groaned. Often it manifested such violence that Aaron would muzzle it.

"*It is my belief that Calista is exhausted,*" wrote Aaron. "*I may even conjecture that the animals we have so far handled exhibit much too strong a will. They are, as I suspected, far too intelligent to let themselves be influenced. They remain fully conscious of their pain.*"

And that's when Aaron had the fabulous idea of using the least intelligent animal he could think of.

For, if a wise Greek man which Aaron admired had himself spoken of it as so, it must indeed be stupid.

And Aaron set about sending letters and enquiring about what measures might be needed to have this creature sent to England. Not a simple endeavour, but he was ready to pay, as always.

"*All along, a part of me,*" he wrote "*has longed to come face to face with such a creature though I had not imagined it would be for this purpose. But if it must be now, then I welcome it at last. And I deliberately do not name it, nor describe it, for I believe if anyone should come upon my notes and attempt to plagiarise my procedures, I wish for it to be difficult, if not impossible for them to do so.*"

Those acts were frequent in the scientific world. Even Jeannette Power had discovered her work plagiarised by another Frenchman.

Aaron remembered this scandal, along with what Mrs. Power had warned of the creature.

"You must feed it well, for it will try to eat you."

"Are you telling me that it eats flesh, Mrs. Power?"

"Oh, yes. It will eat human flesh. You must make the conditions of its home just right."

They had spoken so passionately on this subject, that in Aaron's memory, the conversation had even eclipsed his own wedding day. He replayed her advice in his head and was pleased with what he had learnt.

The Nightingales had now toiled in the cellar for five years.

The winter snow had not yet melted in Berkshire, when the infant Ovee arrived.

And when she saw it, Calista knew she would never be the same again.

Chapter 12

Sunday

HORRIFIED by the ghastly details he had read, Maurice heaved a sigh and ground the last of his cigar into the ashtray. It had taken four painful hours, and on numerous occasions, he had fought against his desire to hurl Aaron's journal across the room. Only a tenacious will to discover the Nightingales' secret had kept him reading. As the clock struck midnight, he read the name, Ovee, for the first time. It was the name he had seen scrawled on his notes on Friday morning.

From 1845, Aaron only mentioned Ovee subjects.

The name leapt at Maurice from every page. What creature had Aaron brought to his home? Maurice had never heard of any animal called Ovee.

And why would Calista's ghost write that name in his journal?

Maurice could scarcely remain awake. His heart ached with exhaustion. Aaron's journal slipped to the floor.

It was shortly after Maurice had fallen asleep, when the latch on his bedroom door shifted.

When the door had fully opened, a perceptible chill settled in the room, rushing in from an open window in the corridor. Along with this draft, came this otherness, a discernible odour of sea and salt, as though the ocean itself had come to pay Maurice a visit.

When the first rays of daylight shone upon Maurice's face, calling him awake hours later, his first desire was to run water from the pitcher onto his burning arms and wrists. Seeing them, those circular welts, not knowing what they were and where they had come from, he was horrified.

Staggering to the small table by the bed, he grabbed at the water pitcher and filled the porcelain basin. He plunged his arms deep, emitting a sigh of relief.

Images flashed in his mind as he pieced together last night's nightmare. Therese had caught him, just as she always had, time and time again. He'd felt her seize his arms. Her favorite game was to threaten him with the guillotine, instilling in him such a terror he thought he would die.

Therese liked nothing better than to scream obscenities at condemned Parisians on their way to the guillotine. But it was not enough. Her need to avenge herself on every male even if he was but a boy, had twisted her into the home tyrant she was.

In Maurice's dream, it was her hands that had cruelly gripped and wrung his skin. He had wrestled in vain but found no escape.

Maurice drew out his arms from the basin, feeling the cold water rush down his reddened skin. He returned to the bed and saw that the sheets were streaked with a familiar glistening liquid.

Was it her? Calista? Had she found him as he slept? If that were true, why was she doing this?

It could only be despair for the cruel work she had been forced to conduct in the cellar. That was it. Her soul could never rest. But what if he was wrong? What if her wish was to torment him?

Frantic knocking drew him out of his thoughts.

He dressed in haste and opened the door, still barefoot.

"Madeleine. You were right." His voice vibrated with excitement. "Ms Jeannette Power must have been an expert in ocean creatures. I sat up last night reading Aaron's medical notes. He referred to her several times." Maurice could not bring himself to reveal the rest. It was too distressing.

Madeleine slinked inside the room. She wore no apron today, and the emerald of her Sunday dress brought out her eyes. "Do I have news for you," she burst out. She seemed eager to speak at last. "Jeanette Power is not only an expert, Mr. Leroux." She brandished a volume whose title Maurice made out as *The Magazine of Natural History*. She flicked through its pages. "The woman you asked me to search for yesterday is a bona fide inventor. She was living in Sicily at the time this magazine was published. But here's what I've learnt. She was here, in England, in April 1837."

"The year when Aaron and Calista married."

"Jeannette Power," continued Madeleine, "is known among reputed scientists for her study of ocean creatures in Sicily. Isn't it astonishing? I spent forever last night reading her articles. And look, read this passage. It's extraordinary! See, here. She invented a form of cage to study ocean creatures. It's called the Power cage. I've never heard of anything so incredible."

Maurice leaned over the bed where Madeleine had laid out the volume. He ran an eye over the article.

"Excellent find, Madeleine! This means much more than you think. You see, I'm convinced I saw one of those cages."

Madeleine looked doubtful. "Where did you see it?"

"In the cellar. But it was made entirely of glass."

"Well, this doesn't make any sense. Mrs. Power invented these cages to be immersed into the sea. Why would Aaron Nightingale wish to place his cage in the cellar?"

"To hide it, I suppose. The Power cage I saw may not be immersed in water, but it is filled with water, Madeleine. You see, that's the brilliance. I did not realise it at first, but I'm certain of it now."

"I do not understand."

"Aaron had long known of Mrs. Power's expertise. He invited her to confirm the proper workings of his underground Power cage. But long before that, he had already built the fountain… My guess is the fountain water flows into the Power cage. Now, it's only a hunch. I remember what Shannon O'Sullivan said when I interrogated her. She said Aaron wished the fountain to be continually turned on. It must have been for that reason. The Power cage likely depends on water with certain conditions. I'm not an expert on the subject matter, but I see no other reason why this fountain mattered so much to Aaron."

"But why would he own a Power cage? He was a doctor for Pete's sake, not a marine biologist."

Maurice lit up a cigar and drew deeply. Now the room filled with smoke as he paced, wondering what to reveal to the house maid. "I read something about this last night," he confided at last. "Aaron imported several unnamed creatures in the last two years.

My suspicion is they were a species of animals that dwelled in the sea."

"What sort of creatures are they?"

"If only I could answer that, Madeleine. To us, earthlings, the ocean remains a daunting mystery. For all I know, it is a dark abyss, a realm as unknown as the world of the dead." Maurice shuddered at the thought.

Madeleine's eyes shone.

"Well, this is terribly exciting. I don't even wish to go to the markets anymore."

"No, no, you must go."

She looked disappointed. "I suppose I must fetch the girls now and get going. Alfred said he would take us to town at ten-thirty. We are due to return on Monday morning. I wish you luck in your investigation. Well…good bye."

Maurice saw Madeleine to the door, but she suddenly turned, her cheeks flushed red. "We got all carried away with the Power cage and I almost forgot to tell you. I didn't just explore Aaron's books, as you asked me. I was good. I searched his drawers. On my first day here, when I was dusting, I saw Vera Nightingale search everywhere in Aaron's study. I think she was looking for this." She handed him a tiny antique key. "I found it wedged at the back of the second drawer."

Maurice noted the curious engraving on the ornate bow. He wondered where he had seen the same insignia before. Was it in Calista's room? He couldn't say.

"I looked everywhere in the study," said Madeleine, "but I found no document box or casket for this key. There has to be one, though. I'm sure it's somewhere in the house. Perhaps you might have a better idea, Mr. Leroux. Who knows what Aaron was hiding?" She winked.

"Well done, Madeleine," said Maurice. He felt a tinge of emotion that surprised him. "I suppose…I must say goodbye, for now at least. And…take care of yourself."

Before he could finish, Madeleine had raised herself to his height and laid a kiss on his cheek.

"You must come see me on the stage some time," she suggested. "When this is all over, I mean."

She did not wait for his answer. She slipped outside without looking back.

Maurice wiped the smile off his face. He dropped the key into his pocket, promising himself he would hunt for its casket once he had finished Aaron's journal.

He waited a few minutes after Madeleine had left, then buttoned up his vest and headed for Aaron's study.

Aaron's Secrets

THERE were countless volumes on marine life. All the mysteries of the sea unfolded before his eyes. Dark, monstrous, and forbidding. Yet as much as he rifled through these scientific pages, Maurice could find no references to an Ovee.

Had this creature actually existed?

Maurice had closed the door to the study, but he could hear the maids' vibrant voices as they prepared to leave for Reading Town. Willy's playful barks brought a smile to his face. They would all be gone soon. Mrs. Cleary would not like it. She hated losing control.

Maurice's thoughts drifted back to Ovee. There was much he still did not understand.

It must have been for a reason if Calista's spirit had written this name in his journal. Why Ovee? What did she want Maurice to know?

Maurice opened Aaron's journal. He had abandoned it since last night as he was too sickened by its contents. But he had no choice. He had to continue reading, however painful. It was the only way he might discover what had happened to Ovee. Perhaps it would finally shed light on why Calista haunted Alexandra Hall.

He picked up from where he left off.

Aaron eschewed all descriptions of Ovee. He had done so to ensure no one could replicate his grotesque research. Yet several passages caught Maurice's attention.

It is a creature of enormous appetites, and with such a short lifespan, less than 18 months, it must live at an accelerated rate.

Ovee One is more clever than expected. Within the first week, it approached Calista readily and presented its head to her. As for me, if I near, it retreats, and even now, it does not reach out.

Like a dog, it knows boredom. It seeks to pry and to wrest objects from our hands. It attempts to flee.

It is mischievous like a child. The first time we carried it to the operating table to ascertain the best means to restrain its movements, it evaded our grasp. It climbed upon the far end of the table, seized my writing implements and smeared ink all over the desk.

In later notes, Aaron mentioned failed experiments.

Calista's attempts are in vain. Ovee One continues to feel pain. Animal magnetism seems to have no effect during operations.

But I am not deterred.

Despite my reduction of the drug dosage, Ovee One has become more revengeful and more aggressive. In this, it will only attack me and is ever bonded to Calista.

And further down the page,

Ovee One has died. Calista wept for weeks.

Maurice flicked through the journal. A new shipment. Over the course of 1846, Aaron reached a breakthrough. Minor operations on Ovee Two were recorded as successful and painless. Then suddenly, as the year progressed, the experiments began to fail. Like its predecessor, Ovee Two began to show signs of aggression, despite receiving smaller drug doses. It, too, died soon after.

Over the Christmas period, there were no experiments. Only the following lines,

Calista is greatly distraught.

But the surprise is mine. Despite the emotional distress which these premature losses have occasioned, I observed a stronger bond between Calista and this species than has existed with any other.

And then this epiphany, which Aaron had sheepishly written at the foot of the page,

Aristotle was deeply wrong. So shall I continue?

Perplexed, Maurice's eye fell on the ceramic bust on Aaron's desk. Returning to the journal, he saw that in the spring of 1847, the Nightingales had suspended all work to give Calista time to recover from past losses.

Then in May 1847, Aaron had scribed an unsettling entry.

Science has made enormous progress. I have, in my desk drawers, several phials of this ether which renders operations painless.

Today begins a new endeavour. For what is the use of employing animal magnetism as an anaesthetic when ether now makes this readily achievable?

From today, I shall design experiments aimed at creating trauma in the subject.

In disbelief, Maurice read on. In August 1847, a new shipment had arrived. Ovee Three. It had cost Aaron a fortune, for the creature had been born only two weeks before being ushered to London by private cargo.

John had supervised the shipping. In his notes, Aaron even spoke of the champagne he had drunk with his brother in celebration. Confused, John had accepted, though he was ignorant to what Aaron toasted.

When Aaron finally summoned Calista to return to work, she had lost much weight. She seemed overcome by an unabated darkness. But to Aaron's astonishment, she soon fell in love. Ovee Three became her world.

Calista has never felt the same way towards a subject as she has now. The effect Ovee Three has on her has been beyond my imagining.

With this new subject, I aim to prove trauma can be undone, physical harmony can be restored, and that the means to achieve all this, is animal magnetism.

Maurice's heart lurched in his chest. Upon this ominous statement, Aaron's folly descended into cruelty.

Maurice flicked through pages, eager to discard the passages that followed. For three months, the young Ovee Three had endured unimaginable experiments – forced medication, burning, amputation of limbs, electrical charges – all aimed at inflicting pain and imbalance, in the belief Calista's magnetic powers would restore it to wellbeing.

Poor Calista. The terror she had suffered. Torn between her duty to Aaron and her love of Ovee, no wonder she had fallen ill in the winter. Anyone's spirit would be broken by such savagery. But to be forced to partake in such vile acts… It explained her anger. Was this why she was returned in spirit form? Did she mourn Ovee Three? Was she doomed to roam Alexandra Hall, fettered by the memory of all she had seen?

Maurice skipped to the end of the journal. There was no mention of Ovee Three's death but he guessed it must have died too.

The last page had been ripped out and only its jagged outline remained. Within the inner folds of the journal's leather jacket, was a sealed envelope stamped with a Penny Black. Maurice tore open this letter. It was dated on the first week of August 1848, only a few days before Aaron's death, and most odd of all, it was addressed to Vera Nightingale.

Dear Vera,

What is done, is done. I have forgiven you.
Lay your mind at rest, for you are lucky. Mary could have ruined everything for all of us. However, all is well.

Aaron

Forgiven? For what? Why would Aaron place a stamp on this envelope only to take his own life without posting it? It made no sense.

Maurice re-read the letter until he knew it by heart. He tried to understand what Aaron meant about Mary. In his 1845 journal entries, Aaron had described how her little dog had broken into the basement and ingested medication that rendered it aggressive. Maurice thought back to Shannon's scar. Willy must have shocked the entire household.

Perhaps Mary ranted about the dog's behaviour long afterwards. As Maurice had discovered while questioning her, she was fixated on this event and the cellar. Was this what Aaron meant by, *ruin everything*?

Downstairs, the clock struck ten. Footsteps sounded in the corridor. He wondered if Mrs. Cleary might stride in to enquire why he had not come to breakfast. Maurice hastily put away the journal. The footsteps faded away.

He worked for another half an hour, perusing the scientific volumes Madeleine had found about Jeannette Power. He read all he could about the mysterious Power cage.

It now became clear why Aaron had insisted on linking the fountain to the Power cage. He needed oxygen inside the cage. For Ovee!

John Nightingale believed the fountain was a gift, a means to soothe Calista's homesick heart, and satisfy her longing for the ocean. But he was wrong. Aaron had built it for his own selfish reasons.

"The fountain was only a front, a disguise," murmured Maurice. Aaron could order the boiler be fed with coal at all times. To everyone's eyes, the steam pump governed the fountain's water flow. They ignored its other purpose: it blew air into the Power cage. Aaron had employed the fountain to conceal his underground secret. It was no wonder nobody was ever invited to witness its beauty. Such a pity. Shannon had been right all along.

Aaron had researched this well, going as far as questioning Mrs. Jeannette Power on his own wedding day!

Maurice felt a knot in his throat as he retraced the sequence of events. Well before wedding Calista in April 1837, Aaron had spared no efforts to link the Power cage with the fountain during Alexandra Hall's construction. It was only in 1845, eight years after they were married, that Aaron and Calista began experimenting on Ovee One.

Aaron's long term designs awed Maurice. It was no longer a question of *what* Aaron had done, however cruel, but rather, how *early* he had planned it. It drew such a malignant portrait of Aaron Nightingale that Maurice stood. He began to pace, seized with dread, yet unable to pinpoint the true nature of his fear.

At last, he glimpsed it. The curious void in Alexandra Hall's decor. The absence of Calista Nightingale's touch everywhere inside this home. She'd had no voice. Had she only ever been an instrument of Aaron's scheming and nothing more? Had Aaron loved Calista at all? No. He loved only her gift, and the use he could make of it to further his own ambitions.

Maurice thought of the stamped yet unposted letter to Vera and he was now certain Aaron had not taken his own life. Why would he? He did not love Calista. Only his own obsession had ever driven him.

A distinct rumbling stirred in his stomach and he could no longer ignore his hunger pangs. Peering through the study window, he saw the swaying of the trees. Blustery weather swept through the valley and grey clouds cast the estate in near darkness. Dressed in their Sunday best, their hair braided down their backs, the four maids of Alexandra Hall stepped towards Alfred's awaiting coach.

Shannon, Ellen, followed by Madeleine had mounted the carriage, but as it came to Mary's turn to climb aboard, a raven silhouette sprung up the path. Maurice recognised Mrs. Cleary. The wind's might came alive through her black dress. The housekeeper was fast by the roadside and she held Mary back with a vile grip. Maurice felt a twist to his heart. He watched the young maid shake her head in protest then bury her face in her hands.

As the coach made its way to Reading, Mrs. Cleary dragged a sobbing Mary back to the house.

Now only the delivery coach waited along the muddy road.

Colours and shapes, all illusion

Maurice suddenly regretted sending the maids away. The house felt eerily empty.

In the kitchen, he found Gerard O'Malley, arranging a plate of roast beef and butter sandwiches. After reading of Aaron's dark work, the sight of cold meat was not as pleasant as it would otherwise have been, but Maurice resigned himself, wary of collapsing.

"Why do I go to such trouble, eh?" asked Gerard. "Nobody tells me anything. Now, who is going to eat all of that? All the girls have gone to Reading Town." He turned to Maurice as though to confide in him. "All of them except Mary, I should say. Poor thing wasn't allowed to go to town." Then shaking his head, "That's Mrs. Cleary, right there for you. If you ask me, she's looking a bit unhinged today. Puts on those grand airs, but you dig a little deeper past the surface, and that's what you get."

Maurice eyed Gerard sharply but kept his thoughts to himself.

"Mind you," said Gerard, "they say women know best how to raise a child so I'd hate to say anything."

Maurice nodded coldly. He picked up a roast beef and gherkin sandwich from the platter.

"You'll tell me what you think of those," chirped Gerard. "Mrs. Nightingale used to love them at first. Another thing about women is their stubborn dislike of a good roast and steak. Mrs. Nightingale didn't much like the sight of meat over the years."

Maurice nearly choked. He coughed, then ran his tongue across his cheek in an attempt to swallow each bite without chewing the meat.

"Would you like some water, Mr. Leroux?"

"No, I'm alright," said Maurice, raising a hand to ease the cook. "I was a little hungry and forgot to chew."

"You should try the corned-beef sandwich. Less chewing. Corned-beef, Mrs. Nightingale could still eat," said Gerard. "She'd often ask for them sandwiches to be sent upstairs when she was too tired to come down. Poor woman. She'd work so hard. I'd prepare a plate and hoist it up."

Maurice eyed the hallway nervously then peeked at his watch.

"Where is Mrs. Cleary now?" he asked.

"She said she was off to the gardener's shed. Something about burning leaves and fallen trees, and composting kitchen waste. I wasn't paying much attention. The less I hear of her these days, the better I feel."

"Splendid, thank you. Gerard, what did you mean by 'hoist it up?' Would you not bring the sandwiches upstairs to Mrs. Nightingale, yourself?"

"Oh, no. I am never permitted upstairs. No need to, though. Mrs. Nightingale's room is the one with the dumbwaiter, see. We didn't have one initially, but Mr. John Nightingale made it for her. Simple steel plate that we hoist up and down a shaft with some pulleys."

Maurice stared. He recalled no dumbwaiter inside Calista's bedroom.

"A clever thing, really," continued Gerard, "considering it was a last minute modification. Or so I'm told. Do you want me to show you? It's near the commons kitchen. We don't use it now, of course, so the plate is stuck down there. Hasn't been up since she passed. Might not work any longer."

"No, no, I'm a little busy right now. Thank you for the sandwiches, Gerard. They were fabulous."

"Nice to be appreciated. Thank you, Mr. Leroux. Have yourself a good afternoon."

Maurice glanced nervously at his watch before stepping out of the kitchen and into the entrance hall.

There was no sign of the housekeeper. He pushed open the glass doors. An icy gust unsettled the leaves at his feet, and stirred the poplar trees. Feeling the chill, Maurice hurried down to the road where the delivery boy waited, his boots drenched in mud. Coming as close as he could to the young man, he slipped the first letter into his hand.

"Please deliver this urgently to Mr. Wilson at Waileys Brothers in London. Once he receives it, he will need to come to Alexandra Hall in person, right away. As for this one," he said, presenting the letter addressed to the police, "you must deliver it in person in Reading Town. Be discreet. And make haste."

The young man tilted his head.

"As you wish, sir. I should be getting on pretty soon, now. Just waiting on one last order from Mrs. Cleary."

"Mrs. Cleary? Really…" Maurice looked at his watch. "It's a little late for house orders…"

"I thought so too. She said she'd forgotten a few things and would return with a list. She's been a bit sick, you know. Hasn't had time to get organised."

Maurice nodded, a frown upon his face. "Of course, yes. Well, good afternoon to you." He retraced his steps along the path to the house. As he reached the grand staircase, a figure suddenly sprung up in front of him.

Maurice reeled back, jerked from his thoughts.

"I'm going to retire for the rest of the afternoon, sir," said the cook. "Mrs. Cleary's kindly allowed me to leave an hour earlier."

Maurice tried to control the iciness in his voice. "How kind of her."

"Blasted woman's never given me an hour off since I've worked here. I'd best run off before she changes her mind."

"That's a sensible idea."

"I thought I'd let you know I've left a roast dish for your supper, Mr. Leroux. There's potatoes and butternut pumpkins there, too. I made some gravy." He looked pleased with himself.

"Thank you kindly, Gerard."

"Well if there's nothing else, sir, I'll see you on Monday. Mary and Mrs. Cleary are the only persons here."

"Have a good afternoon," answered Maurice.

For a heartbeat, he felt wary of Gerard's last words, then he heard the familiar trundle of the coach in the distance and knew the driver was now on his way to Reading Town. The police would soon be here; three hours at most.

As he climbed the steps, Maurice slipped a hand in his pocket. He felt the cold metal of the antique key Madeleine had given him. He studied its contours, as though its shape might inspire the matching casket in his memory.

The house's new emptiness weighted upon him, but he hoped his plan would work. Yet as he passed Calista's portrait, a fear swept through him. He wondered what Mrs. Cleary was up to now. Aside from that moment when she'd wrestled Mary away from the carriage, he'd not seen her all day…

And where was Mary?

He was about to return downstairs to find the girl, when his eye settled on a door at the far end of the second floor. Of course. He knew now where he'd seen the casket the first time. Maurice dashed to his room to fetch the house keys then headed to Aaron's bedroom.

As he opened Aaron's door, he thought he heard shuffling footsteps behind him, but when he spun around, there was no one in sight. He pushed open the door.

Maurice walked to the large leather trunk and lifted its lid. There it was— the medieval casket he'd admired earlier in the week. It bore the same insignia as on the key. Maurice picked up the small box. He inserted the tiny key, holding his breath. The casket was old and he wondered how it held together, but the lock yielded easily as though it had been used a number of times in the past year. What was Aaron hiding in there? He'd gone through such effort to hide this key…

There was a dozen unopened envelopes, bundled together by a hemp string. They were all well-travelled, worn, stained, and obviously from far away. They had all been addressed to Calista Argyros. Maurice stared in disbelief. Cyrillic letters flashed before his eyes as he tried to make out the names of the senders. No. It couldn't be. Calista's parents had written to their daughter over numerous years. Maurice felt his heart lurch in his chest at the thought of Aaron isolating his wife from her own family. The Argyroses had wished to reach out to her but never could.

Was there no end to Aaron's cruelty?

In disgust, Maurice was about to replace the letters when his eye caught a lone envelope, resting at the bottom of the casket. The stationary looked expensive.

It was addressed to Vera Nightingale.

Finding the envelope already opened, he drew out the letter.

The handwriting bore a style he'd not seen in the rest of Aaron's journal. The script was awkward, erratic, as though the sender had penned it in haste.

It was written by Calista Nightingale.

Dear Miss Vera,

Forgive me for writing to you but I have no one else. I need to speak with you before it is too late and before there are no witnesses to the things I have seen.

I feel you are a good woman. It saddens me we are not friends. In my village, women gathered often and spoke of their troubles. Ever since my marriage, I have had no one and it is with a troubled heart that I am writing to you.

If only you knew your brother as I know him. I say this now because it has been too painful to hide and now everything I have kept inside, flows out of me and to keep it in, will only hurt me.

Miss Vera, you must think me foolish to write to you of such things. You know nothing of me, nor I of you. This letter will surprise you and you will not believe what I have to say. I fear you may even detest me for speaking ill of your brother. If so, then I am doomed. For I cannot live like this.

If you had only seen the things I have seen. There is in Alexandra Hall a horrible place where unspeakable things are done to the most fragile creatures. The light of the sun does not reach here. I spend hours in a room where no one goes, do you understand?

There have been countless animals. Even young black slaves taken from illegal ships. I cannot say more. Your brother believes he is going to prove that animal magnetism is real. But I am exhausted and I no longer believe in his work. I only see the cruelty and the madness. I wish for it to stop.

If it does not cease, if no one will stop it, then I feel that only χάος will result. Do you know this word, Miss Vera? Chaos. You think it is the same in my language and in yours? You are wrong. Because in Greek, it means the abyss and into this dark world, all things are sunk. What Aaron has done is so wrong.

What could be worse, Miss Vera? What could be worse? I know of one other thing. I believed he loved me. But I was wrong. He has tricked me. He has tricked the people in my village. I am forever wronged and it hurts so much.

There is in Alexandra Hall a stain that can never be washed away. I beg of you, I cannot remain here. Please. I must return to my village. I cry every night. I try to forget the horrible things he has made me do but I cannot.

I understand if you do not wish to see me but I beg you, please come as soon as you can to Alexandra Hall. Please have pity on another woman so far from home.

Maurice read it again, horrified by its revelations. He seized the letter and threw the casket back into the trunk.

As he left Aaron's room, thoughts rang in his mind. He recalled what Mrs. Cleary had confided earlier in the week: Vera had received a letter from Calista and rushed to her while she lay ill for several days.

This was the very letter. The date did not lie. It was Calista's plea for help. How, then, had it come into Aaron's possession? How could it have been hidden in his locked casket?

Maurice's throat tightened as he understood. Vera must have betrayed Calista. She had revealed all to her brother and handed the letter to him.

And now the pieces fell into place. For Maurice recalled Aaron's own unsent letter to Vera, months later, right before he died.

I have forgiven you.

Lay your mind at rest, for you are lucky. Mary could have ruined everything for all of us. However, all is well.

He knew, now, what Aaron meant. Mary had seen something.

Maurice's thoughts raced. Upon interviewing Mary this week, he had grown convinced that she knew something and refused to speak of it. The maid had giggled at the thought of Vera's death. Had she not also made a statement? He had ruled it out, and never recorded it in his notes. What was it?

"I think Miss Vera was smothered with a pillow. It would make perfect sense, don't you think?"

Mary implied that Vera's smothering to death was befitting… or perhaps, deserving?

He had dismissed Mary's words as evidence of feeble-mindedness, but what if it wasn't? He could still hear Mrs. Cleary, warning him about Mary. *She confuses everything. She is untrustworthy.*

No, thought Maurice. Mary had done more than confuse everything. She had disguised the truth about Vera.

There was only one way to find out for sure.

Where was Mary?

He bolted down the stairs, then looked for the girl in the commons kitchen, the scullery then the washing room. She was not there. Maurice cocked an ear for Willy's barks. Nothing. He pushed open the French doors. No sign of Mary or Mrs. Cleary in the kitchen.

Maurice returned to the entrance hall and peered out from the glass doors. There was no one outside. Turning to the parlour, he felt a jolt of surprise.

Mary sat there all along. She faced away from him, her brown hair cresting over the velvet divan. As he approached, he heard the young woman soothing herself while coddling Willy.

It was unusual for Mary or any of the housemaids to be seated in the parlour. Maurice sensed this oddity but he brushed it aside, determined to question the young maid.

He crouched in front of her with a smile.

"There you are, Mary. It's lovely to see you. I have been thinking," he said.

She looked up, her eyes widening with fright.

"It's ok, Mary. Would you like to know what I think? I think you are cleverer than you let out. I truly believe that. I think you know things about the people in this house, and that I should have listened to you from the start."

Mary blinked. A new light shone in her eyes as she studied him with curiosity.

Maurice took note of the fresh bruises along her neck and arms. He cursed Mrs. Cleary internally. "Here, Mary, I would really like to show you something."

He removed his vest and undid the collar of his shirt. He pushed aside the fabric to reveal the large scar on his shoulder where Therese had once burnt him.

Mary's lip parted in surprise.

Maurice replaced his collar. "It no longer hurts. Just remember that. I've never shown this scar to anyone. You are the first one to see it." He buttoned up his vest. "Sometimes," he said, "other grown-ups do not help even when you wish they would come to your aid. And it is hard to be all alone. I know it, because it is what I've lived." He stared into her eyes. "Mary, I think you are a very brave girl. Braver than you think. More brave than anyone in this house. And I know you saw something that you have kept hidden." He paused. "Do you think you can help me, Mary?"

Mary sat in silence. Her lips trembled.

"I need to know about the night Calista died," whispered Maurice.

The maid shook her head. "I didn't see anything," she moaned.

"It's perfectly fine. In fact, you don't have to tell me what you saw. No one will ever know what you saw. You only have to say, yes, or no. That's all."

Mary blinked. She seemed to reflect upon his words.

"Only yes or no, Mary. That is all you have to say. Do you think you can do that?"

Mary nodded.

Maurice heaved a sigh.

"Did…Miss Vera kill Calista Nightingale?"

His pulse quickened. Mary had cast her eyes down to the floor.

"Just yes or no, Mary."

"Yes."

"Thank you." Maurice stood. "Does Mrs. Cleary know what you saw, Mary?" If Mrs. Cleary knew Vera had killed her beloved Calista, then she would have wished to avenge her… Maurice held his breath. He watched Mary carefully.

A nod. Mary lifted her head, still nodding. "When I told her, she warned me not to speak of it. She…" Mary froze, unable to say anything further.

"What's wrong, Mary?"

Up to this moment, Willy had sat beside the maid. Now he leapt up on its hind legs and barked at Maurice, fierce and loud.

Mary's eyes widened. All the while, her mouth remained agape and Maurice thought she was choking.

Then he understood. The dog had not barked at *him*. Maurice took a step back.

He turned.

A violent blow struck him on the back of the skull. He collapsed to his knees; his head, a mindless cage, his vision blurred. Willy's barks rose up, more furious than before, as Mary's screams filled the parlour.

Maurice crawled to the nearby table, his limbs still shook from the pain. As he gasped, wrestling against the blackness, another sharp blow to the head felled him.

Images flashed before him as he drifted in and out of consciousness. He sensed the floor rub against his body. He was being dragged to the entrance hall. Mary's screaming had not ceased. He had a vision of a key inserted into the cellar door, then he saw the ornate door swing open. The dark folds of a long dress swished above him and a sinister voice rose over Willy's frantic barks.

"Dear, dear, Mr. Wilson, do you wish to know what I've learnt? She's a mad, mad woman, that one," mimicked the voice, intimating that his letter to Mr. Wilson had been opened and its contents read. "Can't have that, can we? Snooping in my private business. But no more, Mr. Leroux, no more."

A firm grip seized his collar and he felt his body slide across the checkered tiles.

Then followed a repeated thud, as his heels banged across the stairs and a grip pulled his inanimate body into the underground chamber he dreaded.

Chapter 13

The Woman from Kassiopi

Alexandra Hall, January 1848

CALISTA lay on her bed, her head propped up on three lush pillows. Occasionally her body shook, seized with a bout of coughing. The physician would not arrive for a couple of days. She felt her pulse fade. The days succeeded one another, and while Vera had come, Calista remembered only pain from the cold look her sister-in-law had given her upon arriving at Alexandra Hall.

"I came as soon as I could," began Vera as she took in the beauty of the room with a prick of envy. Responding to Calista's invitation to sit, Vera found a cushioned armchair and sat beside the bed, already irked by the woman who had bewitched her brother and turned her own life upside down.

"My dear Vera, I am so glad you came." Calista spoke from the heart but her voice was weak. In truth, her breath was laboured, crushed by a long illness which Aaron attributed to the foul air of the cellar.

"I suppose one must do one's duty," responded Vera, absent-mindedly. She removed her gloves.

"Did you read all my letter, Miss Vera?" came Calista's anxious voice. The look of alarm in her tired eyes reflected the distress of not finding any sympathy from the woman she had long awaited.

"I certainly have," sniffed Vera. "I understand you are quite ill, my dear. I have spoken to Aaron."

"What...what... did you tell him?"

"Do not trouble yourself. My brother is most understanding of your condition."

"Please, you must believe me. I can tell you everything."

"I think you must rest," said Vera, eyeing her coldly.

Beneath the covers, Calista shuddered. Her skin already so pale, had grown ashen with fear.

Vera examined Calista's tired face. At thirty-three, the Greek woman remained as beautiful as she had looked upon her first arrival at Alexandra Hall, her thick hair, still long and dark, even in illness. As for Vera, she had withered. It was alarming how envy could devour one's insides. If she had never married, it was Calista's fault. Aaron could hardly help the man he was. Nor the brother he never was.

"My brother has vaguely spoken of your research in the cellar. He admits, he ought not have worked you so hard. He has expressed his wish that you rest, now."

"But, I must tell you..." Calista's voice trailed. She gazed at the tea she had finished a moment ago. She wondered what she had drunk. Her mind clouded.

Vera's keen eye ran across the rose wallpaper where blooming rose bushes, in pink and salmon, neighboured leafy green foliage. Overhead, she took note of the golden motifs along the cornices. Each corner of the room depicted an elaborate bouquet of flowers and— as odd as it seemed, here in the country – shells. In the centre of this heavenly ceiling, was an oval alcove with a gilded frame that might have belonged in some Greek palace. The alcove's artwork evoked floating clouds against a celestial blue sky. If Calista had stared above, she might have imagined her Greek homeland. Vera sighed, overwhelmed with disgust.

"What an ungrateful girl. Now, what am I going to do with you?"

Calista's Secret

SEATED on a chaise longue, Vera had not budged. The clock

downstairs struck midnight. She lifted her head, suddenly realising that she had travelled to Alexandra Hall almost a week ago. Thanks to Aaron's advice, a dosage of herbs in Calista's tea had done wonders. She certainly slept better. The days had passed, uninterrupted, and given Vera had spent many hours by Calista's bedside, she had done much thinking.

She'd handed over Calista's letter to Aaron. He had read it, not said a word, and then locked himself up in his study.

"Don't shut me out, Aaron," Vera had warned, by the door.

He had let her in. He bore the same weak reluctance as when they were children and she had invited him to kiss her. They both knew how that had turned out.

She'd longed for more, and for years, her hopes were fulfilled: Aaron had belonged to no one else. And then, without warning, he'd left for Athens. Now, as she stood alone with him in his study, he stared hungrily at her, and they both knew he had shunned her long enough. His mask had fallen.

"What is she alluding to, Aaron?" she'd asked, much later, as she re-arranged her dress, and coiled her hair back into its bun.

"I thought she understood. But perhaps I have been mistaken."

"Well whatever it is, she is going to bring you down."

"Of course not. She is ill and exhausted. Naturally, she is prone to writing foolish things. Once again, you alarm yourself over nothing."

"Over nothing? Aaron, your wife is accusing you of being a monster. Did you not read the letter?"

"I don't want to speak of it, Vera."

"Well confront her! Tell her what you think! Set it straight."

Aaron had turned his body away. He avoided her gaze.

"She is your wife after all," insisted Vera as though she spoke of a nuisance.

"She has called upon you. I understand she longs for another woman on whose shoulder she might cry. So be it. Be her confidante. Let me know what is on her mind. Now, leave me alone. I need to think."

Vera had replayed the conversation and she was unsure what she detested most: being drawn into the wild accusations of her sister-in-law, or the maddening secrecy of her brother. He would push her away once again, when all along, she had warned him. Calista did not belong here. It had been foolish from the start. That witch would invent any story to bring down the Nightingales.

Vera had thought long enough. Almost a week had passed, and she was tired of wondering. She had grown too curious. This time, she had deliberately not drugged Calista.

It was now past midnight. Aaron would have gone to bed. The house had fallen quiet. Calista was wide awake. Much to Vera's distaste, she looked like a princess, swimming in blue silk sheets.

"I am ready to speak now, Miss Vera. I can tell you everything."

"Begin, then," said Vera. She clutched at her shawl and glanced apprehensively at her sister-in-law.

"Last year, while Aaron was away on a short trip to London, I received a letter," began Calista. "You can't imagine how happy I was. It was the first letter I'd ever received since leaving my village. At first, I was pleased. I was going to tell Aaron all about it. But then…" Her brow darkened as she recollected her thoughts. "It was written by my uncle Sakis, in Greek. He told me my parents were well. They did not know that he was writing this. He said he had learnt something terrible."

"What is this to do with Aaron?" interrupted Vera.

"Please. I will tell you. Sakis told me that Aaron had wished to marry me for months since arriving in Kerkyra."

"Well, you should count yourself lucky, I suppose."

Calista stared up to the lofty ceiling. Vera's curt voice only brought pain, but Calista trusted that if her sister-in-law heard everything, she would understand. So she fought back tears and resumed her story.

"I should have known, but I was too in love with him." Calista closed her tearful eyes.

"You should have known what?" insisted Vera.

"All these years," said Calista, shaking frightfully, "I believed Aaron was my saviour. I believed he had rescued me from a terrible life. You see, one night, two men abducted me. My father said I had brought shame to the village and that my family would not regain its honour until I had left his home. They wished to send me away. They wished to send me to an asylum."

Vera stared. She took in every word.

"It was Aaron who offered to marry me when no one would. All this time, I was so grateful. I loved him. I would have done anything for him. What I did not know..." Calista's throat tightened. She could not suppress her tears. "It was Aaron all along," she cried. "Sakis found out Aaron had hired two local men to hurt me..." Her words grew indistinguishable. Calista let out a painful cry. Years of quiet torment were unleashed from her soul as the village girl wept. She held down her emotions no longer; she grieved the judgements she had endured since her birth, her dishonour, her parents' rejection, the cruel illusion she had suffered at the hands of Aaron, and worse, the shame of not having known better.

Vera had now turned to stone. Her mouth twitched, repulsed by Calista's sobs.

She knew not what to think of Aaron. But it cost her dearly to judge her brother, even if it meant showing her support to another woman. So she said nothing.

Vera looked upon the bed, attempting to find the right words as Calista gasped for breath and wiped her tears. "Well," said Vera. Then she applied herself, sweetening her voice as much as she could. "You must tell me more, my dear. You must tell me everything. In the letter you sent me, you said Aaron is not the brother I know. What did you mean by that?"

For the next hour, Vera listened, dumbfounded, while the woman she deemed to be a cunning liar poured out her heart and recollected the horrors she had lived in the cellar for years.

"Everyone in the house would have heard those poor animals scream, but they pretended they did not. They would have seen me take the dogs and the cats, down there, and never see them return. But what could they say? Aaron was master of the house. I tried to confide in Mrs. Cleary. I took her aside one day. I was crying and she tried to comfort me. I told her what I was forced to do down there. What we did... but I don't think she understood."

Calista left nothing out, so relieved was she to find a friendly ear and to finally name the cage that was her home. She did not hesitate, even at the part where she had to explain the extent of her uncanny abilities, knowing full well Vera would not comprehend them. It did not matter. Oh, at last, she had found someone to save her from Aaron. And for being a woman, Calista had long ago intuited that Vera must not approve of Aaron's ways. For what woman approves of a selfish man? Reassured in her belief, Calista told all and relief rushed through her at the end of every sentence.

And then a deadly silence fell upon the room. Calista waited. She hoped Vera would overcome her deep reserve and bridge the gap between the two women. She hoped Vera would walk to her bed and take her sister-in-law gently in her arms. God knows, she needed it.

As Calista gazed in hope at her sister-in-law, Vera grew aware of the repulsion filling her own chest, a burning sensation that surged from deep within and rose to her throat, choking her.

She stood slowly, overwhelmed by a deep urge to vomit. She began to pace the room, not knowing precisely what it was she felt. Her confused thoughts swirled in her mind. At last, she turned towards the bed and stood there, studying Calista.

Calista's eyes widened. Behind Vera, the door handle had shifted. A limb, which Calista recognised, slid into the room, seeking. Calista froze, horrified that Vera might also see it.

"Ovee..." she whispered, unheard and out of breath.

For a heartbeat, Calista's attention was drawn to the flurry of movement by the door, until she stared back at her sister-in-law, and gasped. A malignant light had taken hold of Vera. Her gaze was hardened.

For in the instant she had learnt of Aaron's extraordinary endeavor, and the various wrongs in which her brother found himself implicated, Vera was swept by a storm of frightful emotions. And now a violence animated her face and it was this which Calista saw as she trembled in her bed.

Calista's eyes searched for Ovee across the room, but the shadow she had glimpsed earlier was nowhere to be seen. Vera moved closer until her outrage shot from her lips.

"You cunning bitch!"

"But... it is all true, Vera..."

"Is this why you had me come? To fill me with lies? So I might listen to your inventions? All lies. You wretched creature.

It was not enough you ensnared my brother. Now, you invent stories about him like a low-class cur."

Calista stared in shock as Vera edged upon the bed, towering above her. There was a movement at the drapes. She attempted to scream, but her breath failed her and only a hoarse whisper escaped her lips.

Vera reached for the larger pillow.

"Ove…" Calista fought to call out its name but the pillow came fast over her face, and her voice was muffled. Realising that no air came, and upon sensing Vera's intentions, a bolt of fear ran through Calista's body.

Blinded and breathless, Calista could not see that Vera's face had changed. Rage deformed that face, and her lips were twisted into a demonic mask. And as Vera clamped down the pillow, vengeful words burst from her lips.

"You lying, lying bitch! You shan't get away. How dare you tell lies about Aaron! How dare you come into our home and wreck it for us. He should have been mine. Now, you will keep your mouth shut."

Calista's flailing arms waved about aimlessly until the last of her strength waned. Then all was still.

Behind Vera, a small dog had found the door ajar and it sprung towards the bed, filling the room with its barking.

Vera's face smoothed over. She lifted the pillow and saw what lay beneath. It was astounding that not a moment ago, the reason for her rage still lived. Vera stepped back, quietly relieved. It was such a liberating feeling. The weight of years lifted from her shoulders.

Captivated by the look of death on Calista, she barely heard Mary scold Willy by the door.

"Willy! Get back now! Let Mrs. Nightingale sleep! You naughty dog."

Vera startled. She caught a glimpse of her face by the mirror. Her bun had collapsed from its tight coil and sweat trickled down her forehead.

She recomposed herself. Smoothing the sheets, to make it look like Calista slept, she re-arranged the pillow before staring one last time at Calista's closed eyes.

Then she spun round, sped towards the door and seized Mary who had remained frozen outside.

"What were you doing, snooping inside this bedroom, miss?" Vera hissed, still panting.

"I'm, I'm sorry, Miss Vera. I was going to ask Mrs. Nightingale if she wished me to bring her another tea. I wasn't doing anything bad."

"She's asleep."

"Oh, yes. I saw. I mean, I know she is sleeping."

Still wary, Vera studied the young maid. She recognised her. It was that simpleton Mrs. Cleary had told her about. Vera smiled.

"You may return to your quarters. You are not to disturb Mrs. Nightingale until the morrow."

"Yes, Miss Vera. I won't."

Satisfied, Vera closed the door behind her.

She failed to notice the glistening trail Ovee had smeared along the floorboards upon entering the room.

As Mary hastened down the stairs, holding Willy in her tiny arms, Vera returned to her room, still astounded by Calista's claims.

Alexandra Hall was plunged into silence. Beneath the celestial sky, where the roses and peonies bloomed on the wallpaper, Ovee extended a limb from behind the drapes. Reaching out, slowly, in dread, it felt Calista's cold hand. Crawling along her arm, it tasted every pore on Calista's skin. Entangled, firm, intense, it sensed every nerve impulse of Calista's last moments. And then suddenly, it let it go.

An indistinct shape, hideous, of changing colours and gradients, rose up on the bed to face the lifeless Calista. Two lidless eyes found her sweet face. An endless second followed as Ovee took in what it saw.

Then came a wide sweep as the creature flung its limbs about, and in its rage, the tiny porcelain figures by the bedside, were smashed to pieces.

Chapter 14

Monday

MAURICE's eyes snapped open. A flood of memories came rushing back. Aaron's mistreatment of Ovee, Vera's murder of Calista, Calista's angry spirit… Aaron had used his wife for her extraordinary gift. He'd never loved her. Taken from her village, far from her home island, she'd lived with a man who wronged her daily.

Maurice felt the hard surface beneath him. He tried, but could not move his legs or arms. They felt heavy. He blinked, trying to piece together the last moments before he had blacked out. He remembered being dragged down into the cellar. Mrs. Cleary had spoken to him. In his semi-conscious state, he'd imagined it was Therese. Mrs. Cleary sounded just like his mother and somehow, the housekeeper had found the strength to lift him up. She'd hoisted him on some kind of table.

Strewn atop the wooden panel, he had felt her work at his limbs. She had found some concoction from that oriental cabinet and forced it down his throat. He saw her hideous features above him and heard her words, "You stay right here, Mr. Leroux. I have to attend to Mary. She'll raise the devil with her screaming." Then she was gone and he passed out again.

Maurice attempted once more to free his limbs but he felt a tightness round his wrists and ankles. He seemed to be stretched out and tied. A deadening fear crept through him as he understood. There was only one place where he could be. He looked around in fright. She had known about Aaron's laboratory. She had found a way to strap him down in the manner Aaron had dealt with those poor creatures. To his right, towering above him, was the medicine cabinet with its gilded handles. And to the left, he distinguished the greenish gleam of dozens of sealed jars.

Maurice worked at the left strap. He had to inch his way out of them. There was no telling what she would do once she returned. It was her. It had been her all along. Mrs. Cleary, whose real name was Louise March, had known of the presence of drugs in Aaron's laboratory. When Calista's spirit had begun haunting Alexandra Hall, the distraught Louise had lost her mind. Disobeying Aaron's wishes, she had entered the cellar. By trial and error, she had begun to use the capsules.

She'd fallen into such erratic behaviour, it had scared Gerard. Then Sophie Murphy caught her entering the cellar door. Sophie had known of the housekeeper's secret past and made the grave mistake of blackmailing Louise March.

The left strap had loosened. Maurice pulled out his hand, his fingers were torn and twisted as he tried to remove them.

She was not done. Now that she knew he suspected her, she would return to kill him. He had to free himself and get to Aaron's gun. It was his only hope.

It was easy for her to kill. She had fatally clubbed Sophie then dragged her dead body to the stair landing to make it look like a fall had caused the maid's death.

The cellar door slammed open. Louise March's heels clattered down the steps.

Maurice wrenched at his right hand, tearing skin. He reached forth to untie the straps around his ankles.

The glow of a candlestick swept through the chamber.

She was here, in the cellar.

Maurice leapt to his feet, hiding behind the table.

"Maurice," she called out. Her voice almost sounded sweet as she dragged out the last syllable of his name.

The last time he'd heard his name spoken this way was… Maurice shuddered. Still weakened by the drug she'd forced upon him, he crouched down the side of the table and tugged clumsily at its drawers. He'd seen the gun there on his first visit. He just hoped Aaron kept it loaded.

"Maurice..."

He saw her tall silhouette edge towards the trunks. She shone her candlestick on the deserted operating table, then across. The candlelight found Maurice just as his hand felt the empty drawer. The gun was gone.

She grinned.

"Too late, Maurice." She banged the candlestick on top of the table. "I thought it prudent to get rid of Aaron's toy when I tied you up. You wouldn't want to hurt anyone now, would you?"

She glided past the table. She seemed to be carrying something heavy in one hand.

Maurice blinked, horrified by her appearance. Her eyes were black marbles where a vicious light blazed. She wore an old nightgown, her long grey hair loosened down her back. The thin fabric barely concealed the jutting bones of her hips.

There was a devilish grin on her face as she brandished the axe. "I hear you French enjoy a good blade."

And then she drew near and he saw the furious red of her eyes and the familiar dilated pupils.

Gasping, breathless, Maurice scrambled to his feet, and all but slammed into the oriental cabinet. The axe swung past, cleaving into lacquered wood, narrowly missing his shoulder. Pills poured out of compartments, scattering across the floor.

Maurice lunged blindly towards the trunks. He weaved through the high stacks, his head throbbing, his legs, cotton under his weight. And in his foggy mind, it was not Mrs. Cleary or Louise who, axe in hand, chased him. It was no other than Therese, the woman he dreaded most. Therese, drunk and revengeful, returning from her work shift, more hateful of her little boy every day.

"I know you are here," chanted Louise. She chuckled. "Come out, boy, I've got some scones for you to eat."

Heart pounding, he moved deeper behind the stacks of trunks, holding his breath, praying to himself in the way he would pray as a boy. To disappear. To dissolve into vapour. Why could he not disappear?

"Big mistake you made in coming here. You ought to have remained in France. Why did you come here? Well that's too bad,

Mr. Leroux. We'll just have to tell Mr. Wilson the ghost scared your little heart and that you ran off."

She gave a deep throated cackle and moved among the trunks. She could not see him but Maurice knew it was just a matter of time.

He huddled behind a stack of sea chests, just opposite the candlestick which had remained on the operating table. He eyed the top most chest, promising himself he would throw one at her once she drew closer.

"Well, well, well, Maurice." She was searching for him, peering behind every stack nearer to the stone staircase. Her voice echoed in the underground.

"I know what we'll do with you. We'll light a bonfire on your bones and forget you were ever here. Nothing will stop me, Maurice. I've given up so much already. I've saved years for my new life in Australia. You think you could come here and ruin it all? Sophie tried that too. The little tart thought she'd eat up my savings."

"She didn't deserve what you did to her."

Upon hearing Maurice's voice, Louise whipped her head round to the left and retraced her course.

"Wrong. She got what she deserved. You don't understand, do you? Of course not. You've never in your life grovelled for a living. That's all I do. Well, no more. I won't put up with being anyone's servant any longer. I'll settle in my Queensland home while the crows pick at your bones."

It was his best chance. She was closer…

"You'll be right at home with the convicts, Louise."

Louise's nostrils flared at the mention of her real name.

"Foolish Frenchman."

It was now or never. Maurice erupted from his hiding spot. Seizing the highest most sea chest, he lifted it and hurled it with all his might. Louise screamed. She spun just in time, smashing against a tower of boxes. The thrown chest tumbled past the operating table and skidded across the floor.

"You missed!" she hissed.

The blood drained from Maurice's face. It was his last chase and he'd failed. Slack-jawed, he stepped back, horrified by the demonic expression on Louise's face. But he had to know. The words shot out of his mouth: “What then, Louise? You’ll just kill me, like you murdered Aaron and Vera?”

Louise’s upper lip curled.

“You imbecile! I never killed them. Never!”

Maurice hurled himself towards the light, knocking over a stack of trunks. He rose to his feet and tried to run to the stairs but skidded on the wet floor.

Her laughter rose up behind him.

“Well that’s too bad, Mr. Leroux. I shan’t miss you this time.” She hefted up the axe above him.

Maurice gave a pitiful cry. Already he’d closed his eyes, his arms raised above him. He expected the full force of the blade. He waited for the pain to surge through him like fire, but nothing came. Instead Louise March tottered back, wide-eyed. She opened her mouth but no sound came out of it. Maurice’s eyes blinked open, confused by her sudden retreat.

He glimpsed the look of horror on her face and his mind was set alight. A truth he’d dared not consider revealed itself at last. No. Louise had never killed Vera, nor Aaron. She might have wished to avenge her beloved Calista, but someone else had got to Vera first. He thought back to the strange moist film Dr Hart had found on Vera’s body. Somebody else… *Something else that lived in water. Ovee.*

There was a violent tug and he realised something was pulling at Louise. She fell forward, dropping her axe. Flat on the ground, she was dragged away from him, her high-pitched screams resonating in the chamber.

Maurice rose. He stared in disbelief. Something he’d never seen, something he could not name wrestled with Louise March in the dim light, right there, before the operating table.

By the glow of the candlestick, he saw limbs that were at once unfurling and snakelike but also steady and strong. An undefined form, viscous, and glistening wet, heaved itself, its limbs deployed to frightening length. It fought off Louise’s flailing arms, coiling itself around her wrists and then her neck.

Gripped by sheer terror, the housekeeper cried out in breathless moans. The creature thrust a limb down her throat, blocking her screams. Maurice could not take his eyes from the devilish sight. Louise's white gown turned a darker colour as urine trickled between her legs.

Maurice could still not identify what had taken her but he knew it was not Medusa. Nor was it a vengeful spirit. This was a living creature. Whatever its nature, its body now slid atop Louise's chest, then inched towards the housekeeper's throat until it had covered her entire face with its still mass.

Maurice held his breath. He knew now what had happened to Vera. Louise would die in the same way, gasping for air.

Louise kicked. Her entire body convulsed. An agonising scream rose from deep in her throat, echoing through the underground as though all the souls of the animals that had died here were screaming to be heard. It was a sound so monstrous, Maurice would have rushed to her aid but what he witnessed was so astonishing, he remained transfixed, unable to react. Like taut leather, the creature's limbs tightened around Louise's neck. Then it went completely still.

Minutes passed and the screams ceased. The housekeeper's limbs fell inert to the ground.

Only then did the creature writhe anew, pulsating with frightening motions. Its aspect had altered and where previously, as it fought its victim, it had adopted a virulent black colour, now it slowly took on a whitish hue.

"Ovee…" whispered Maurice. His lips trembled as he spoke its name.

Now the creature slid off Louise's inanimate corpse, and its swollen form glistened with a curious moisture.

Silence filled the chamber.

The candlestick light flickered over Ovee's shimmering body. It stared at Maurice who could barely blink. Then it began to retreat. It moved slowly as if weakened. It crawled towards the Power cage and by its limbs, which clung to the glass, it climbed to the edge of the Power cage. Ovee slid into the water. Maurice seized the candlestick. He ran to the Power cage and shone the light onto Ovee.

Stirred by the creature, the cage's waters turned murky. Disturbed particles swirled round a large grey form huddled in the far corner, directly beneath the steel pipes. Ovee had gently curled within itself– and it was strange – but to Maurice, it now resembled a rock, as though it had forever been here, inside this cage, unseen and still. The limbs that had seemed Medusa-like, and elicited such horror, were tucked away, rendered almost invisible, while their owner appeared to have shrivelled. With its lidless blue and black eyes, it was staring straight back at him.

Maurice pressed his hands against the glass, captivated by the creature's eyes. A jolt passed through him as he recognised the gaze he had seen through the keyhole many nights ago. Where those eyes had appeared fierce, now they seemed almost gentle and weary.

"You are ill," said Maurice. And then he recalled what he had read in Aaron's journal, how it was doomed to not live long at all. Ovee was dying.

It dawned on him why Aaron had suddenly changed his will. If no one entered the cellar for a period of six months, Ovee would have died and could do no harm. Yet Aaron had never realised that Ovee, undaunted, could roam the house at it wished. His precautions had been in vain.

Maurice frowned. Something eluded him. Why would Aaron suddenly feel threatened by Ovee so as to change his will and prevent anyone from entering the cellar until his subject had died? Aaron could not have suspected that this creature could kill. Unless...

Maurice wondered again how Aaron had died. He brushed away an idea, in disbelief.

In his mind, Ovee had only killed twice.

The first time, had been to avenge Calista's death. Somehow, it must have been inside Calista's room when she was murdered. It had witnessed everything. Later, it haunted Vera, changing its shape and form so she would not see it, but watching her every move. It could recognise her face. It knew her for what she was. It had waited patiently to take her life one night. A few spoons was all it had taken to make her trip. Then it smothered Vera's breath in the same manner in which she had murdered Calista. It had left a thin film of moisture on her face and inside her nose.

And now it had killed to protect Maurice...

Maurice remained in awe. The secret of Alexandra Hall had been unveiled at last. "I don't believe there was ever a ghost," he whispered through the glass. "It was you. You crept out of the

Power cage. Like Willy, you discovered the hidden opening linking the house to the cellar. You moved through the house. Everywhere you went, you left a trail of moisture. It was you who rattled my door at night. It was your eyes that stared back at me through the keyhole. You came into my room. You coiled yourself round my arms as I slept… Unbelievable… Of course! You crept inside Calista's locked room by the dumbwaiter shaft. Once inside her closet, you shoved at the doors. It was always you…I know it. When I was down here the first time, you were outside the Power cage. You wished to frighten me so you could return to the water. So you rattled those crates and threw those objects at me…"

He smiled. "There was never a ghost. It was you who ransacked Gerard's kitchen. You took those spoons and used them to entrap Vera. And when you had no need for them, you… Of course. Is that why you left those spoons on the operating table, near Aaron's murderous instruments? You were trying to tell me you no longer wished to kill."

Maurice's breath came fast on the glass. He pushed his hands against the cage's walls. "Ovee… if then, it is true that you can hold spoons… then you can hold a pen…"

But as he recalled the writing in his journal, he was uncertain. "But how could you write your own name?" he asked. For no creature he knew could recognise symbols, let alone reproduce them.

And at this moment, a wave of childlike wonder washed over Maurice and it seemed to him that Ovee might be more extraordinary than any spirit who might restlessly roam the house.

For hours, Ovee remained still, while the waters gently lapped at its dying body. And as Maurice stared at it, oblivious to time, he knew that he beheld a creature of immense intelligence.

Months earlier, Aaron Nightingale had also discovered this. Aaron, man of learning, man of order, calculating being who planned for years, who exerted such masterful control on others, and on how those others saw him – Aaron did not like being humbled. He did not like losing. He must have been furious. He rotated Aristotle's bust, for he could no longer face the Greek philosopher. Aristotle had been wrong all along. Wrong beyond imagining. Oh, the trick played upon him! For Ovee was a clever creature. More so than the Greek philosopher could have guessed.

For hours, Maurice stared through the glass, holding Ovee's gaze, never averting his eyes. And in that time, which felt to Maurice like he had been reborn, the life drifted out of Ovee.

There was a flurry of sounds from above. Then excited murmurs reached the chamber through the opened cellar door. Rapid footsteps began their frantic descent. Animated voices, those belonging to Madeleine, Alfred and Gerard, filled the staircase. Then at last, a blinding light was shone into the underground, laying bare all its terrible secrets.

Chapter 15

Aaron's Plan

August 1848

"πάντα χωρεῖ καὶ οὐδὲν μένει" – Ἡράκλειτος

"Everything flows, and nothing abides." – Heraclitus

WITH his back facing the Power cage, Aaron could sense its vindictive gaze behind him, the lidless eyes drilling into him.

Shortly after Calista's death, he had lost all desire to carry out further experiments. Even if she still lived, it would have been too dangerous – what with Ovee having shown yet more signs of aggression. He was resigned to the idea of abandoning the quest he had embarked on for so many years. He had no choice but to end it all.

He had prepared a poison. Enough to kill an animal the size of Ovee. The vial he'd filled weeks ago lay on the corner of his work table, taunting him daily. And though it occasionally caught his eye, he had not yet decided on the date. For to administer poison spelt failure, and it wounded Aaron to end it so abruptly.

So instead of reaching for the poison, he would spend idle hours in the underground, sitting silently at the large table, revisiting the journey of many years as recorded through his journals. At intervals he would pine for a substance to dull his mind, and he'd reach for a little glass vial which he'd filled with laudanum and whiskey, ever since she had died.

That loyal bottle was sensibly within reach and when he sipped at it, it brought a delicious foggy mist not devoid of pleasure. It always calmed him, even though it stirred another kind of monster. For Ovee seemed to know exactly when he had descended into his drugged state, and then it would watch him avidly, sensing that Aaron might be vulnerable.

No one else was with him in the cellar that afternoon, yet Aaron spoke out loud, irritated by the eyes that were forever watching him. He spoke to Ovee and by some profound mystery of nature, the creature seemed to understand all he had to say. As it often did, Ovee had left the Power cage and now it sat there, turned to a virulent reddish tone, and eyed Aaron from its sinister vantage point.

How it had grown. Ovee was now fully adult, not the tiny being found and packed by Greek divers and who'd eaten its siblings during the journey to England, surviving against all odds. Aaron knew it could rise and leap at him if it wished and he'd be no match for its strength and shapeshifting body. He'd had his fair share of surprises in the past when he'd cut off one of Ovee's limbs only to see it regrow. But that was in the early days before the rage had settled in. Now the threat was real. There was enough hate in it to murder the entire house if it wished. It would want to start with Aaron, no doubt. If that were the case, then Aaron would only have to reach into his top drawer and find the revolver and while he might be under the effect of laudanum, he would surely not miss.

Those were the thoughts coursing in Aaron's mind daily. But after two hours of seething tension between them, Aaron could no longer stand it. His voice rose in the underground chamber.

"You do not know the half of it, so don't judge me," he barked. "I've seen your kind before. You think I'll let you live? That I'll not deal with you the way I did the others?"

He turned his head, slowly, to confront the creature behind him. Beside the Power Cage, Ovee was resplendent. It looked almost regal, while the rageful colour on its body only gave it a more threatening appearance. In contrast, Aaron's haggard chin lay buried in an unkempt grey beard that had reached his chest since his wife's passing. Deep furrows lined his eyes and forehead, laying bare the twisted preoccupations of a lifetime.

"Years of planning, and it has come to this," he muttered. "Don't you look at me!" he thundered at the creature. Undeterred, the black and blue eyes followed his every move; attentive, predatory...knowing.

Aaron flinched. He grew attuned to a burning ache in his insides and as he stood to face Ovee, the pain intensified. He gripped the back of his chair and took a deep breath, passing a hand over his stomach.

"Damn."

He reached for the familiar vial of laudanum and gulped the last of it, determined to drown whatever ailed him. Ovee still watched. It was almost fascinating to observe this creature's will. Aaron was amused, but as he emptied the small bottle, he was instantly aware of an uncanny movement in Ovee. And in that black and blue gaze which never left him for a single second, Aaron saw what he would have never imagined in any animal, let alone a marine creature. For Ovee seemed to recoil slightly, its limbs appeared to relax, almost as if it were relieved, as though for the last hour, all it had done was not watch, but rather, *wait.*

Wait for that moment…

Aaron still held the laudanum bottle in his hand and his eyes now drifted to it and back at Ovee, then from Ovee and onto the bottle. An impossible thought crept into his mind and he stared, dumbfounded at the remaining vials assembled on the far end of the table, his eyes suddenly bulged.

A crippling spasm caught Aaron unaware. Buckled by pain, he brought the vial to the lamp on his desk. Squinting in vain to read the blurred label, he examined the colour of its contents. His jaw dropped. A bone chilling fear ran through him. Overcome by nausea, Aaron scrabbled across the desk for the poison he'd intended for Ovee. The label did not lie. It was the laudanum. "How!" he roared. How had he mistook the two? But he had not.

The two vials had been swapped. Aaron doubled over in pain. He reached for the revolver, aimed it towards the Power cage, then spun round, still aiming. But the astute Ovee had slid away unheard. It was already gone, hiding in the cellar, out of sight. It knew how to disappear.

"To the devil with you!"

Aaron looked around in desperation. There was little time. The poison had yet to invade his bloodstream. He had an hour at most. He was much larger than Ovee and perhaps he would find a way to delay the poison with a little milk. Then he would lock this place forever.

He fumbled to his journal, found the last page and tore it. Then, casting one last sorrowful look at the underground chamber that had failed to fulfil his dreams, he clambered up the staircase.

Days later when Mrs. Cleary, having wondered at length where he was, forced open his bedroom door, she discovered Aaron's corpse on his bed, his altered will upon his lap. Upon fishing the document from a pool of vomit, she glimpsed the words, "Be wise and do not enter the cellar until the spring", scribbled in frantic ink at the foot of the page.

She never looked beyond the bed, into the chimney ashes. And it did not matter, because the private letter Aaron had torn from his journal, in shame, was no longer there. The page had long been devoured by the flames, taking its secrets with it:

"It knows. It knows she is gone, never to return. It smells her death on me.

A quiet malice has possessed it since Calista has gone, and it grows more violent every day.

Last month, as I wrote in my journal, I felt it emerge from the Power cage. It was the first time I had witnessed this behaviour. Calista suspected it for weeks prior to her death, but I could not fathom it and so I did not believe her.

Now my fears have been made real, for the beast not only left its rightful place, but it seemed quite content to exist outside the water for almost an hour. And during that time, I felt it advance stealthily towards me.

For a few moments I dared not turn my head but I could feel its presence behind me. It has no voice, but the curling limbs possess in them an essence that screams of evil. I am to blame as the creator of its wrath.

In an instant, and shaking violently, I had seized the revolver in my drawer, loaded it, and aimed my weapon at this creature who had come to a halt near me. It stared back at me with such malevolence I might have thought it had in it some wickedness that resembled revenge.

I don't know what came over me, but as I studied its eyes, I was overcome by a frightful notion. I could not move. I believed it to be her, my wife, and I could not pull the trigger.

In the meantime, it had somehow understood I meant to kill it, and it promptly returned to the water, still staring at me with its blue and black eyes.

I have asked myself for the last months – why would I believe that Calista continues to live through Ovee? There is no answer. In my delusion, I have come to wonder whether the two of them might not remain bound by her magnetic energy, which has not only eluded death, but flowed elsewhere.

Have I erred?

For every time in the past years when I foolishly believed Calista dissipated the anger and the pain in each of these creatures, was she instead absorbing their rage inside of her?

And is she now returned, bound to this creature, animating it with the rage she carries within her?

If not, where has this rage gone to? It cannot be gone. For how can I explain the new dark patterns which the creature has exhibited before me ever since Calista's death?

I have pondered now for months.

And each day, not a moment goes by when its bestial eyes are not upon me, following my every gesture. What can it see? What can it understand?

Does it suspect I intend to take its life? That soon, I will pour the poisonous liquid into its watery cage while it rests, and I will put an end to its wickedness.

Chapter 16

How to disappear

London, May 1853

WHITSUNDAY brought a throng of visitors to Regent's Park. A great part of the thousands were regulars, taking advantage of this rare glorious day for an outing in London's beautiful park. On this occasion, they were joined by the curious who had been lured upon hearing of the talk of town.

The Zoological Society had newly erected a building in the Zoological Gardens, and it was said that the structure was the first of its kind in the entire world.

Those who reached this building were astounded to discover that the ocean kingdom along the country's southern coast, could be brought right here, in the middle of London, for their enjoyment.

"Ah, you've come to visit the aquatic vivarium," said a well-to-do lady whom Maurice had approached for directions.

He'd not returned to London for almost five years. He'd arrived last week to attend a magical theatre piece where Madeleine featured as lead for the first time. Having a little spare time, he'd read about the new attraction at Regent's Park and wandered off to this green oasis in the middle of London.

Maurice was surprised. The *aquatic vivarium*. Is that what it was called these days?

"Yes, where might I find it?" he asked.

The lady gave him instructions on how to reach the new building before enthusing, “It’s exceptional. You’ll love it. Are you fond of sea creatures?”

“I am,” replied Maurice.

He had strolled through the park, lost in thought, feeling the anticipation rise within him, until he finally reached the new glass and iron building.

He was surprised to discover a tug at his heart as he entered. Then a rush of emotions overcame him. The time had come to finally reunite with an old friend. A friend he had known for only a week.

A smile drew itself on his lips as he discovered the interior of this ‘Fish House’. Laid out on each side of the building, were Power cages. There were thirteen of them in total and each measured about six feet in length. Maurice drew near, his throat tight with emotion.

They were now called ponds or vivariums, and each of them were set in glass, with a sandy bottom littered with shells where seaweed grew in abundance and marine life thrived. The thirteen glass arrangements offered an exceptional show of colours and natural beauty that captivated visitors.

Maurice lingered near one of these ponds. Upon his face, was mirrored the wonder of children who peered intensely at the glass surface, enthralled by the rare glimpse into the treasures of the sea.

Behind him, Maurice could hear murmurs among the crowd.

“Never seen so many people,” observed a gentleman.

“It’s busier than last year,” agreed a lady.

“They didn’t have this last year, it only opened this month,” replied another.

“Yes, it is unique in the entire world,” assured the first man.

Maurice eavesdropped happily, taking in the whispers around him, feeling strangely at peace, almost invisible among the crowd. About him, children ran, calling out to each other, excitedly pointing at the different ponds to attract attention to each new sighting. Here a star fish, there a Crustacea, over there an odd-looking fish and look – there, a shell-fish, just behind that sea anemone – and oh, that name upon everyone’s lips: the aquatic vivarium. What a marvel!

After a long visit, Maurice had to resign himself: Ovee was not present.

He knew what animal to look for. But it seemed the Zoological Society had not judged it proper, as far as he could tell, to feature this creature in its aquatic vivarium.

Maurice had known the name of the creature for five years now. However, it wasn't until he'd left Alexandra Hall and returned to his hometown in Normandy that it had struck him. It came to him in the form of a memory, words upon a page, Latin words buried among a scientific passage which he'd overlooked while searching through a book in Aaron Nightingale's study; a book by a certain, Cuvier.

Aaron had been fond of initials. After all it was his own and Calista's which graced the front doors of Alexandra Hall. He had also devised a means of naming his experimental subjects by employing the initials of their animal name.

The origin of the name, Ovee, had to be a set of initials. Aaron had written, Ovee where he could have easily scribed the letters, O and V.

The creature Cuvier had described in his volume was the same as the one Aristotle had observed centuries ago. It lived a mere year, perhaps a little longer.

"Excuse me, sir," said Maurice to a tall attendant in charge of supervising the crowds.

"How may I help you, sir?" asked the gentleman.

"If you permit me asking, would I, by any chance, be likely to find the *octopus vulgaris* in the aquatic vivarium, today?"

The man smiled with indulgence and shook his head.

"Not today, I'm afraid. It might be some time until the vivarium comes to house such a creature. But visit again, perhaps next year, and you might be lucky."

Maurice thanked him.

He left the building shortly after. He remembered a time, a long time ago, when he had been afraid of Ovee's touch.

He thought of the night when this *octopus vulgaris* had held fast to his arms as he slept. How he'd awoken with red welts. He remembered the fear he'd felt as he discovered he was bruised from its tight embrace.

Why had it saved me?

He'd asked himself this question for years.

What secrets had it read within me?

Had it sensed we were alike?

Spring filled Regent's Park with its blooms and Maurice stared in wonder at the gentle colours.

Like him, Ovee had been a vulnerable child once. It had learnt what it was like to be fed and housed by one's torturer and to have no means to escape. It had known the soul-breaking dilemma of holding on to a home that was both a source of survival and pain. For while Calista gave Ovee her endless magical love and bonded with it like no one could, there also, in Alexandra Hall, lay Aaron's cruelty and perversions. Like Maurice, Ovee had learnt to survive by keeping watch of every detail in its home. It had found ways to remain everywhere but unseen.

Maurice, too had known such a home, a home where the hand that fed him was the one that also hurt him. He had lived it. And then, there were countless others. Others for whom no one ever spoke.

Like Mary, who, while plucked from an orphanage and given a dignified profession, was brutalised by her mother. Unknown to Mary, her real mother was a certain Louise March, a 'fallen woman', who'd once tried to murder the bastard child in her womb before she was prevented. Her infant had been taken away to an orphanage. With the help of influential friends, Louise had changed her name to Mrs. Jane Cleary and managed to evade being sent to a penal colony. She found and adopted Mary whom she beat mercilessly whenever fear and tension within her rose to unbearable levels.

Maurice walked to the edge of Regent's Park, where he hoped to meet Madeleine. He had now become a lone figure in the blooming expanse. His thoughts so absorbed him that he became oblivious to the crowds. And it was strange, for in his mind, he had completely disappeared and nothing could touch him.

All the trauma Aaron had inflicted upon Ovee had gifted it with a sense for recognising this same pain in others. *Yes*, thought Maurice, *we were the same. I don't know how, but it knew this.*

Ovee was caged in a torturous existence, yet it had survived, feeding on Calista's love until her murder.

Upon avenging Calista, it could have left itself to die. Yet it grew restless in its last days. It went hunting, perhaps for more rats. It ransacked the kitchen, the many rooms of Alexandra Hall… it shape-shifted, like a colourful illusion. In despair, it returned to Calista's bedroom, absorbing the last of her love…the last of her energy. Ellen had even seen it pressed against Calista's window and believed it was a face…

The days passed, and Ovee weakened.

Yet something kept it alive in that last week, aroused its curiosity, sustained it, and awakened in it something new.

That something was Maurice.

The day had come when, nearing death, it had employed the last of its strength to overpower Louise March and save Maurice's life.

Maurice smiled. *Ovee wished to save me.*

He felt a warm comfort as he recalled what had taken place five years ago in Alexandra Hall's cellar. The violence no longer haunted him. In its stead was a nurturing caress, a gentle reminder that he was far from alone; for Ovee had seen through him; it had recognised the wounds in him and understood everything he had once lived.

And whereas there were many who saw and did nothing, Ovee had used its dying breath to save his life.

Maurice believed this with all his heart, and he repeated it to himself now, as he would, for many years to come. It was a simple thought, but to him, it meant everything.

Author's Note

It is my sincere hope that you may only discover this Author's Note upon having fully read the mystery. Why spoil a surprise?

This story takes place in a sort of dark age, for it precedes three core events of the last centuries.

The first event arises soon after London revealed the world's first aquatic vivarium in 1853. It is the normalisation of the word, *aquarium*, and this pond's growing use in scientific research. Thanks to the ingenuity of Mrs. Jeannette Power, who it must be said, never met an Aaron Nightingale during her 1837 visit to England, and to her creation of the Power cage, observation of ocean life has greatly evolved, even if so much remains unknown.

The second notable event was the advent of publications which depicted this secret abyss – this ocean underworld that so captivates the human mind – and the literature's intense focus on a certain creature: Victor Hugo's *Toilers of the Sea* (1866), Jules Verne's *20000 Leagues under the Sea* (1870), H.G. Wells' *The Sea Raiders* (1896), and H.P. Lovecraft's *The Call of the Cthulhu* (1928).

These tales were published when the ocean world was a daunting, less understood realm; its creatures, even lesser known. We were long past the idea hatched by Aristotle that the creature I named Ovee, in this story, was stupid. But we were terrified of it, and of its related species. It was a period when literature fired the imagination wherever science had not yet offered facts.

My novel exists in that mental space, a time when an Ovee is a horrifying prospect.

As for Aaron Nightingale, he is an imagined scientific pioneer dabbling in Power cages. As the story would have it, he is also cruel and his methods are far-fetched. He represents curiosity gone wrong, but what I admired about him is that his work on cephalopods pre-dates the fantastique literature we know. Like his counterparts of the early 19th century, he is oblivious to our future conception of an Ovee. He is inspired by marine biologists of his time, including Forbes and Cuvier. He looks up to Aristotle, takes advice from Jeannette Power and on the esoteric front, he is a believer in Franz Anton Mesmer's animal magnetism.

And what of the third, more recent event? It is the 21st century surge in discoveries concerning that creature, Ovee. With it, comes our growing humility in the face of a being we've only begun to fathom and from which we yet have much to learn. And so a blend of love and awe for this creature sparked the idea for the book in your hands.

Even after years of fascination for it, there was so much I did not know. For what do we really know, even today? For my conception of Ovee's intelligence throughout the story, I was informed by latest scientific research on its senescence, its ability to live outside water for limited periods depending on air moisture, to change form and color as part of its camouflage, its remarkable aptitude for learning and recognising symbols, its ability to recognise human faces, to solve a cognitive test designed for young children, to make use of tools, to devise tricks that will lure a prey, and last, its unique ability to modify its RNA – its DNA template – in its own lifetime, to reflect the demands of its environment.

There might be more to come, but this is the Ovee we know today. To introduce it in a 19th century English mansion gave me a thrill. How would occupants of this house react to its intelligence? Would they project a ghost onto it, perhaps? At the start, I had not set out to create a ghost story but a spirit became the only plausible notion in the mind of my characters.

ABOUT THE AUTHOR

Laura Rahme is a French-Australian historical novelist of Lebanese, French and Vietnamese descent. She grew up in Senegal, France and Australia. A lover of mathematics and physics, she never imagined she would one day write novels. While living in Brisbane, she gained an Honours bachelor degree in Aerospace Avionics from the Queensland University of Technology then later, an Honours degree with a double major in Psychology and a single major in Media Studies from the University of Queensland. With a twenty-year career in information technology, she earned a living as a software engineer, and digital business analyst.

Her first historical novel, THE MING STORYTELLERS (2012) is set during China's Early Ming dynasty. Her second novel, THE MASCHERARI: A NOVEL OF VENICE (2014) is an epistolary occult mystery set in 15th century Venice. This was followed by the gothic thriller, JULIEN'S TERROR (2017) which spans the French Revolution and Napoleonic periods.

CALISTA is her fourth novel.

Laura lives with her husband in Brittany, France.